Murder Through the English Post

Books by Jessica Ellicott

MURDER IN AN ENGLISH VILLAGE

MURDER FLIES THE COOP

MURDER CUTS THE MUSTARD

MURDER COMES TO CALL

MURDER IN AN ENGLISH GLADE

MURDER THROUGH THE ENGLISH POST

Published by Kensington Publishing Corp.

Murder
Through the
English Post

Jessica Ellicott

KENSINGTON
PUBLISHING CORP.
www.kensingtonbooks.com

KENSINGTON BOOKS are published by

Kensington Publishing Corp.
119 West 40th Street
New York, NY 10018

All Kensington titles, imprints, and distributed lines are available at special quantity discounts for bulk purchases for sales promotion, premiums, fund-raising, educational, or institutional use. Special book excerpts or customized printings can also be created to fit specific needs. For details, write or phone the office of the Kensington Special Sales Manager: Attn. Special Sales Department. Kensington Publishing Corp, 119 West 40th Street, New York, NY 10018. Phone: 1-800-221-2647.

Library of Congress Card Catalogue Number: 2022934731

ISBN-13: 978-1-4967-2486-1
First Kensington Hardcover Edition: August 2022

ISBN-13: 978-1-4967-2492-2 (ebook)

10 9 8 7 6 5 4 3 2 1

Printed in the United States of America

Chapter 1

Beryl Helliwell found herself in a most unenviable position. Never one to stay in one place for long, Beryl had rarely felt the curious discomfort she was currently experiencing. In fact, it took her some time to put her finger upon what it might exactly be. She was familiar with restlessness, exhaustion, and even fear, but this was something both more subtle and far more distressing. It wasn't until she found herself in the library at the Beeches, actually considering reading a book, that she was able to decipher what she was feeling. Beryl realized with an alarming jolt that she was bored.

This was simply not the sort of thing that happened to her. As a confirmed adventuress she was far more likely to experience feeling slightly overwhelmed, which stemmed from an excess of stimulation and new experiences. But the sad fact of the matter was, she felt as though she was the one person in the household with very little to do.

Her dear friend Edwina had set off that morning for her very first session as the new local magistrate. Beryl had offered to accompany her and act as a cheering section from the gallery, but Edwina had declined. She had said she was feeling ever so slightly nervous and the notion that Beryl would be there to witness any false steps she might make only increased her sense of trepidation. So, Beryl had waved to her as Edwina set off for the village on her trusty bicycle, her second-best hat pinned firmly to her head.

Beddoes, the excellent domestic servant recently employed to assist them with the housekeeping, had continued to decline any offers of assistance with such cold ferocity that Beryl had finally given up suggesting them. There had been a real danger only recently of Beddoes actually leaving their employ. Beryl had made the egregious false step of offering to assist with a general bottoming out of the house. Beddoes had taken it to mean there was some concern about her competence for the task. Beryl did not wish to consider what might have happened if she and Edwina had not removed themselves from the property for several days.

After all, Edwina's sudden ability to spread her wings and take on new challenges, such as becoming the local magistrate, was, in large part, due to the assistance Beddoes provided. No one in the household wished to do anything to offend their newly acquired paragon of domesticity. So, despite the fact that Beryl was always eager to learn new skills, such as blacking the stove or polishing pairs of silver candlesticks until they gleamed, she cast her enthusiasm aside for the greater good.

Which left the sole member of the household, Simpkins, as a possible source of entertainment. Of course, she could have considered spending time with Edwina's terrier Crumpet, but the little dog was nowhere in sight. He tended to make himself scarce when Edwina set off without him. Every now and again Beryl would come across him perched on his hind legs in front of a window where he had the best view of whichever direction his mistress had headed off in. But, generally speaking, he found somewhere to curl up and sleep as if to put his consciousness on pause until Edwina's return. No, an interaction with Simpkins was the only way to avoid something as tedious as reading.

She cocked her head and tried to make out where in the house she might hear the elderly gardener and his hobnail boots. The floors had taken rather a beating since he had moved into the Beeches permanently, but by and large, it had been a beneficial arrangement for everyone. What were a few scuff marks and scratches on the floor when one considered how generously Simpkins had contributed to the overall financial picture in the household?

A few months earlier Simpkins had unexpectedly come into the majority ownership of the nation's most successful condiment company, and he had taken his responsibilities and privileges to heart. One of the first things he had decided to do with his newfound wealth was to invest in Beryl and Edwina's fledgling private enquiry business, thus making it a going concern despite their modest number of clients. Not only that, Simpkins had thrown himself headlong into the product development side of his business. With the sort of enthusiasm that the company had not seen in a generation, he had undertaken a number of trips to London in order to meet with the product development staff and to taste-test some of the offerings under consideration. He had even taken over responsibility for much of the cooking at the Beeches, supplying it with vast quantities of sauces, chutneys, and pickles to perk up the ordinary poultry and roasts that Edwina dutifully churned out.

While she certainly would not wish for Edwina to feel insulted, and under no circumstances would she consider taking over the culinary responsibilities herself, Beryl had to admit that she preferred the sorts of things that Simpkins came up with compared with most of the other meals she had eaten since arriving back in England some months earlier. She would never consider herself a gourmand, but she did prefer foods to be spiced with a heavier hand than Edwina generally felt a chop and mushy peas would require.

It was with these thoughts in mind she made her way towards the small sunroom at the back of the house, which Simpkins had converted to an office to fit his modest needs. She found him seated at a small gate-legged table that he used as a writing desk, drumming his gnarled fingers upon its surface. He looked up at her and gave one of his snaggledtoothed smiles as she entered the room.

"I thought you'd be off to the village with Miss Edwina this morning, considering it's her big day," he said.

"She said she'd be too nervous if I were there to observe, so she went off on her own," Beryl said.

"So what are you up to this morning instead?" Simpkins asked.

Beryl wasn't entirely sure she wanted to answer that question. Although she was not occupied, she had a feeling he had something particular in mind, and knowing Simpkins it could be unexpected and not necessarily in a way she would find pleasant. While she did not consider herself above physical labor, she might actually prefer to read a novel than to spread manure over one of the garden beds he lackadaisically tended. However, confident in the knowledge that she could turn down a request without feeling any guilt whatsoever, she decided to answer honestly.

"I am free of obligations and entertaining opportunities."

"I don't suppose you would care to join me at the farm for a spot of fruit picking, would you?" Simpkins asked. "Norman Davies was supposed to help out, but he's had to cancel at the last minute without so much as an excuse."

"Perhaps. What sort of fruit?" Beryl asked.

"Greengages," Simpkins said.

"What in the world is a greengage?" Beryl asked.

"It's a variety of plum. I don't believe they are as popular in the United States as they are here. They ripen about this time every year and I thought they might make an interesting new addition to the Colonel Kimberly's condiment line, so I've asked Mrs. Prentice if she wished to help me come up with some recipes," Simpkins said.

Simpkins had inherited his wife's family farm after the death of her younger brother. As he had moved into the Beeches with Beryl and Edwina and no longer had need of the cottage at the farm himself, he had generously offered to allow the Prentice family to live there rent free in exchange for keeping an eye on the place. The Prentice family was one of the many in the village who had seen hard times of late. Not only had they experienced the same dire impact of the economic downturn the entire country was enduring, but they also had to contend with the fallout of Mr. Prentice's shell shock from the Great War. He had developed a close relationship with the bottom of whiskey bottles since returning from the front and had had trouble holding down a job. He had actually worked at Simpkins's farm in the past but had been a casual laborer rather than someone who lived on the premises.

While Beryl did not particularly interest herself with children, she had a very soft spot for Jack Prentice, the oldest child in the family, and a rather bright lad who took on more responsibility than a boy his age should have to expect to do, selling newspapers on the corner and collecting his father at the pub most nights of the week long after he should have himself been abed. Beryl was always happy to see Jack, and the idea of taking her motorcar out into the countryside on a run set her heart aloft.

"Sounds like fun. I'll drive," she said.

Edwina looked down from her spot behind the bench at the assembled townspeople before her. She forced her eyes to remain on them rather than allowing them to turn towards her dear friend Charles Jarvis, who had promised to guide her through whatever might be needed of her. It was Charles who had first suggested she take on the responsibility of local magistrate after the recent death of Gordon Faraday. Women had only recently begun to serve as magistrates, and while Edwina was flattered that Charles had thought her capable of the job, she was not quite sure she shared his confidence in her.

The room was decidedly stuffy, and matters were not helped by the great number of people who had assembled. Unable to reconcile the vast number of people in the gallery with the short number of cases to be brought before her, she turned to Charles with a question. She dropped her voice low enough that she hoped no one besides him would be able to hear her. He leaned in close as if he understood she wished discretion. Or, as Beryl might likely point out, Edwina thought to herself, perhaps he simply wanted a chance to draw near to her person. Whatever the reason, she was grateful that she did not need to explain herself. It seemed that everyone was watching her every move, and she had no desire to add to their interest.

"Is it always this crowded?" Edwina asked.

"Not generally. There are always those who like to come to the court to gawk at their neighbors and to collect any juicy bits of gossip that might unfold, but this is an unusually large crowd."

"So they don't all have business before the bench?" Edwina asked, feeling a sense of relief wash over her.

"Certainly not. I would guess that they are here to get their eyes on you. It's not every day we have a new magistrate in Walmsley Parva and certainly this is the first time the magistrate has been a woman," Charles said.

Edwina was not sure how to take that. She already felt a great deal of pressure to perform in a new role. She did not relish the idea of being some sort of oddity to be stared at. However, she had become more and more adept at shaking off the rules of convention and all of the curiosity that went with such decisions. After all, when she and Beryl had decided some months earlier to open a private enquiry agency, a great deal of notice had been taken at the time. The novelty of it had still not worn off for most of her fellow villagers.

Thinking back to the successes they had achieved in that sphere, Edwina felt her spine stiffen and she lifted her chin slightly as she looked out over the assembled crowd. Here and there she spotted people she would consider friends, like Alma Poole, the hairdresser who flashed her a smile and an enthusiastic waved from a seat near the back. Nora Blackburn was there, too, but she looked more worried than pleased to see Edwina sitting on the bench. Edwina had to wonder why, considering Nora was a woman employed in a nontraditional profession herself as a co-owner of the local garage along with her brother Michael.

Before she could give it a great deal more thought Charles cleared his throat and shuffled some papers on the desk in front of him. Edwina took that to be a hint she ought to call court into session. She reached for her gavel in the way that she had been schooled by Charles at a practice session in the living room at the Beeches the day before. All talking in the room ceased and every eye turned towards her at the same time. She felt a bead of sweat rolling down the back of her neck and under her collar and could not attribute it entirely to the warmth of the room.

But despite her concerns, the first few cases passed before her with relative ease. She stumbled a few times with procedure and relied upon Charles a great deal to assist her in her protocol, but as time went by, she felt her confidence grow. Charles had encouraged her to accept the position based on her civic mindedness as well as her ability to listen impartially to different perspectives on any given occasion. In his opinion she would make the perfect magistrate for a small village that required an intimate understanding of how trivial matters took on great importance in such a tightly knit community.

It wasn't until they had been at it for about an hour that she understood why Nora had looked so uncomfortable. There in front of her in black and white was a summons for brawling in the street, handed out by local constable Doris Gibbs. The altercation had taken place on the high street between Nora's brother Michael Blackburn and another young man from the village, Norman Davies. Edwina was quite surprised to see that something so unpleasant had erupted between that particular pair of young men. Both of them had generally genial dispositions and had been known to be on friendly terms.

When she called them both to stand before her, she could feel anger pulsing from Michael in a palpable wave. Norman, on the other hand, simply seemed baffled by his presence in the courtroom and also by Michael's attitude. She looked out across the room and saw that Constable Doris Gibbs was seated near the front of the room. She was wearing her police uniform and looked every bit a capable official. She returned Edwina's questioning glance with a curt nod as if to encourage her to simply get on with the proceedings.

"Now, what seems to have brought the pair of you in front of the bench?" Edwina asked.

Both young men gave each other a poisonous look and then began speaking at once, raising their voices to be heard over the other. Edwina held up a small, sturdy hand to silence them, to no avail. The two young men had begun shouting and stepping closer towards each other. Edwina wondered if her first day on the job would end in bloodshed. She looked towards Charles for guidance, but he shrugged subtly as if to say he had no idea what could possibly be going on. With a growing sense of annoyance, she rigorously employed her gavel to attract their attention.

"I'd like to call Constable Doris Gibbs before the bench," she said.

Constable Gibbs got to her feet and came forward, positioning herself between the two young men like a human buffer. It was a testament to her ability to manage mischief in the village. Both of the young men took a step away from her. They fell silent and both looked sheepishly down at their shoes.

"Constable Gibbs, would you please describe for the court the circumstances around the summons of these two men," Edwina asked.

Constable Gibbs pulled a notebook from her uniform jacket pocket and flipped it open to a carefully marked page. No one could say that Constable Gibbs was not prepared to defend her position.

"On Thursday, August fifteenth, at approximately two o'clock in the afternoon, I was making my rounds through the village when I spotted Michael Blackburn and Norman Davies locked in a physical altercation. There was a great deal of shouting and shoving and, unfortunately, it actually came to blows. Before I could convince them to separate, Michael Blackburn landed a few of them on Norman and a final one on my own person," Constable Gibbs said.

She turned her face towards Edwina, exposing her left cheekbone, which allowed Edwina to make out traces of a fading bruise.

Edwina was aghast. While drunken brawling was not something unheard of in Walmsley Parva, she had never before heard of an assault upon Constable Gibbs. She turned towards Michael Blackburn and reminded herself to breathe in slowly through her nose.

"You must have had a great deal of provocation to have lost your temper so thoroughly. Would you care to share with the court why I should take that into consideration before I sentence you to either an uncomfortably large fine or time in the local jail?" Edwina asked.

"I was grievously provoked," Michael said. He stepped towards the bench; his face suffused with color. "It's one thing to make up lies about a man. It's another to deny it to his face when he calls you out on it."

"Are you suggesting that Norman Davies was making up stories about you in some way?" Edwina asked.

Michael nodded and shot a glance over at Norman. "He called my honor into question, and when I taxed him with it, he denied knowing anything about it. I completely lost my rag, and any man here would have done the same," he said, turning towards the gallery behind him and including them all with a large sweeping motion of his hand.

"I still don't know what you're on about," Norman shouted. He turned towards Edwina as she banged her gavel on the bench. "Miss Davenport, the whole thing is just beyond me. I have no idea what set him off."

Edwina looked over at Nora Blackburn, Michael's sister, for any sign she had a notion of what was involved. All color had drained from Nora's face and Edwina suddenly had a sickening suspicion. Could Michael be taking one of his turns again? She looked over at Charles, whose eyes had widened ever so slightly. She could tell from the stricken look on his face that this was not the sort of matter that generally came before the court. She wondered if he was thinking the same thing about Michael's mental stability. It wasn't exactly a secret in the village that he had had a very bad war experience and had not been entirely the same since he had returned from the front.

"Michael, I'm afraid you're going to have to share with us what exactly it is that you think Norman was saying about you. You need to give him a chance to dispute it and to put your mind at ease," she said.

"He's been spreading lies about how I got my injury," Michael said, pointing to his damaged arm with his good hand. "And that from a man who didn't serve at all."

"I have never said any such thing," Norman said. "And I'll have you know I did my best to serve here on the home front.

If I'd been allowed to enlist like you, I would have done so in a heartbeat. Do you think I wanted to be left at home planting potatoes and harvesting peas?"

Norman's shoulders sagged with discontent. Edwina remembered the way so many young men who had been part of reserved occupations had been treated during the Great War. Norman had borne up remarkably well in the face of that difficulty, and she had always admired the fact that he never seemed to try to bring down those men who had served. The two of them had often been seen together fishing at the river or entering or leaving the Dove and Duck, the local pub together. None of it seemed to make sense.

"Do you have any proof of your claim that Norman was speaking ill of you?" Edwina asked, not sure if such a question would help matters.

"I thought you'd ask, so I brought this with me." Michael dug inside the pocket of his trousers and fished out a folded envelope. He stepped forward and placed it on the bench in front of Edwina.

The envelope seemed to be a perfectly ordinary sort. In fact, there was nothing about it that called any notice. It certainly did not seem the sort of thing to provoke offense. In fact, the handwriting was extremely tidy and legible. It was addressed to Michael Blackburn at the garage and had been neatly slit open with a letter opener. There was no return address and it had been postmarked for the previous week. Edwina slipped her hand inside and extracted a sheet of paper. She unfolded it and to her surprise saw before her a document comprised of letters and words cut from newspapers and magazines. She quickly read through the information it contained and then looked back at Michael.

"I can see why it is that you would be infuriated by receiving this." She turned towards Norman. "Norman, did you tell customers at Mr. Scott's shop that Michael had not in fact received his injury by fighting the enemy but rather had been shot while trying to desert his unit?" Edwina asked, tapping her finger against the offensive document.

She kept her eyes trained carefully on Norman Davies's face. She considered herself to be quite a good judge of dishonesty and all she saw flickering across his face was complete and total bafflement. He shook his head slowly as if stunned by what he was hearing.

"I would never say a thing like that. I would never even think of things like that. Michael and I have been friends since we were boys and I know exactly what kind of man he is. Who would say such a hateful thing about him or about me?" Norman said, turning back towards the assembled crowd in the gallery.

Who indeed? Edwina wondered. She looked out across the assembled crowd as well and a cold, sick feeling filled her stomach. The letter unfolded before her was calculated to cause just the sort of painful disturbance it had done. Was it some sort of a distasteful joke? Was there someone in the village with a slightly unbalanced mind? Did someone simply have it out for either Michael or Norman? Whatever the reason, she couldn't shake a feeling of discomfort at the notion that someone had sent this to a neighbor in her own village. Still, she had formalities to honor.

"Are you denying that you made such a statement?" she asked.

"I am absolutely denying it." Norman looked over at Michael, and Edwina was relieved to see that something in his tone must have convinced the injured man that he was telling the truth. Michael's posture relaxed ever so slightly, and the high color began to fade from his face.

"Michael, have you considered that it's possible that someone simply wanted to drive a wedge between the two of you for reasons of their own and that perhaps Norman said no such thing?" Edwina asked.

"I suppose that makes as much sense as the idea that Norman would have taken it in his head to besmirch my character so badly. After all, I was really surprised to think he would say such things about me," Michael said, turning his body slightly towards his friend.

"It seems to me the person who has been most harmed in all of this, besides Norman, who has had his own character called into question, is Constable Gibbs." Edwina focused her attention on the police officer. "Constable Gibbs, would you like to press charges against Michael for assault? You would be well within your rights to do so."

Constable Gibbs folded her arms across her chest and looked Michael up and down. She turned towards Norman Davies and did the same. Edwina noted they both stood ramrod straight, as if at attention. Constable Gibbs was a force to be reckoned with. In the same way that Edwina was an unusual woman in her time, both as a magistrate and a private enquiry agent, Constable Gibbs was her own manner of female trailblazer. She had taken on the job as constable during the Great War, which had been surprising enough despite the rarity of men available to do the job. It was a testament to her capability and iron resolve that she had managed to keep it after the men had returned from the war, especially with so many of them looking for employment.

But the fact of the matter remained that nobody had ever done as thorough a job of policing the community in a way that was both firm and fair as Constable Gibbs. Edwina and Beryl had not always seen eye to eye with the constable, but over the last few months they had developed a working relationship that seemed to suit them all. Edwina wished to make sure that Constable Gibbs felt supported in her role and that her voice was heard. While Edwina was all for equal rights for women, she had no intention of allowing a robust young man like Michael to be allowed to assault any woman in the village without being called on it. Even if it was a mistake.

"Sometimes these things happen in the heat of the moment. I

know that there was no intention to involve me in their altercation and that it was simply a matter of things getting out of hand. I believe I was just in the wrong place at the wrong time. If Michael is willing to patch things up with Norman, I don't think there's any call to make more of this than has already been made." With that, she took a step backward, leaving the two young men without a buffer between them.

"Then it is up to the two of you. Are you willing to let bygones be bygones? If Constable Gibbs can put this behind her, surely you can make up as well, can't you?" Edwina asked.

"I can if he can," Michael said, taking a step towards his friend.

He extended his good hand and Edwina was relieved to see that Norman enthusiastically reached out to grasp it. She banged her gavel down and dismissed them. Looking at her stack of papers, she realized that that was the last case for the morning and with relief dismissed the court. As people filed out of the courtroom whispering and gesturing enthusiastically, Edwina felt her discomfort return when she looked down at the letter on her desk. Who would have written such a thing? She couldn't seem to shake the uneasy feeling that there was still some sort of trouble that had taken root in Walmsley Parva.

Chapter 2

Simpkins clambered up into the passenger side of the motor-car. It was a beautiful day for a ramble out into the countryside and Beryl double-checked the latches securing the top into the open position. In no time at all they were tooling down the country lane leading away from the Beeches and out towards the open fields surrounding the village of Walmsley Parva. Despite the fact that she had been a resident of the village for many months, Beryl had not quite grown accustomed to how idyllic it all seemed. After years of jouncing about the planet, racing from one adventure to the next, she had not been in any one place long enough to develop a sense of the passage of seasons and what that meant to a single location.

It was with a vague sense of surprise that she felt as though she were a part of her environment in a way she never had experienced before. She noticed the way the color of the leaves on the shrubs in the hedgerow had changed subtly from a lush, vibrant, spring green to the full emerald tones of high summer. It wouldn't be many months before she had been there for an entire year. Perhaps that explained her earlier feelings of boredom and restlessness.

As much as she enjoyed living in Walmsley Parva, and how much she valued being part of a household where someone cared what happened to her on a daily basis, she had enormous amounts of energy, and in order to be happy required that something was always on the boil. It had not been that long since they had their last new client, but Beryl could feel herself itching to get involved with a new case once again. Surely that was why she had managed to be content for as long as she had in the sleepy little village. There was just something about setting herself up as a private enquiry agent, especially in partnership with her dear friend Edwina, that provided the sort of constant interest that she so craved.

Once they were well out of earshot of the house and some way off from the farm, Simpkins shifted in his seat to face her.

"I've been thinking about adding a new sort of product to the Colonel Kimberly's line and I wanted to get your opinion on my idea," Simpkins said.

Beryl was surprised to hear him ask for her opinion. She knew Simpkins to be intelligent and thoughtful in the things that concerned him, but she had not known him to be someone who solicited advice from others with any degree of frequency. She was intrigued by the idea that there was something pressing upon him enough that he would wish to pick her brain.

"I'm all ears. What is it you have in mind?" Beryl asked.

"What I am about to say needs to be held in secret, mind." He kept his eyes firmly fixed on her face awaiting her assent to keep quiet concerning whatever he was about to reveal. When she nodded, he continued. "After watching you and Miss Edwina working in your new business and listening to some of the talk from other women in the village, it occurs to me that there might be room for some sort of convenience products to be added to the line."

"What do you mean by convenience products?" Beryl said. "Aren't jam and chutney forms of convenience products already? It's not as though opening a jar requires too much inconvenience."

"Not our existing product line—something new entirely. But the mention of simply opening a jar is exactly what I had in mind." He nodded and gestured enthusiastically with his gnarled hands. "We already have the capacity for sterilizing the bottles and putting things up in jars and tins. All of the expensive infrastructure is in place for such a thing. I am considering something more like sauces and stews and all-in-one sorts of complete dishes that could simply be opened and heated above a gas ring for those types of career women who live in bedsits. Or they could even appeal to the sorts of women like yourself and Edwina, who would appreciate a decent, healthful meal that could be prepared with very little effort at the end of a long working day."

Beryl stole a quick glance at him with astonishment. It wasn't that she didn't think of Simpkins as someone who was capable of deep thoughts, but she had not considered that he was someone particularly attuned to the unique challenges the average woman in his life faced. Although, the more she thought of it, the more sheepish she felt. Hadn't Simpkins been the one who had bankrolled the hiring of Beddoes in the first place in order to give Edwina the chance to really dive into her role as a private enquiry agent? And come to think of it, hadn't Simpkins been the one to bring up the idea of starting their business in the first place?

Perhaps Simpkins was far more attuned to the trials and tribulations being a modern woman presented than she had given him credit for. In light of those thoughts, it seemed quite logical that he would be interested in adding a line of convenience food products to the Colonel Kimberly's offerings. And it also seemed quite logical that such a thing would prove to be as much of a success as had the hiring of Beddoes or the establishment of the private enquiry agency.

Beryl pulled the motorcar into a lay-by at the side of the lane and switched off the motor. She shifted on her own side of the seat to give him her complete attention. While she was an expert pilot of all manner of machinery designed for speed, the way she preferred to drive tended to demand her full attention in order to conduct the occupants of the vehicle to their destination in safety. Simpkins's suggestion demanded more focus than she could safely give it whilst careening down the road.

"I think it's an absolutely marvelous suggestion. Why someone hasn't thought of it sooner I can't imagine. What do you propose to begin with in terms of offerings?"

"I thought perhaps some types of curries. You and Miss Edwina both seem to enjoy eating them when I whip them up, and it has been my experience that they tend to taste better when reheated than they do the first day I've made them. It seems to me something that performs that way when cooked from scratch would make an ideal candidate as an item to be bottled and then heated up again in someone's own home."

Beryl felt her eyes grow even larger in her face. Simpkins had once again offered up a brilliant suggestion. The average home cook across the empire was not likely to be the most adept at churning out culinary extravagances from far-reaching points of the globe. In her experience, the average British cook was more likely to lean on tradition and easily sourced local ingredients regardless of how predictable or bland such creations might be. Beryl had been craving a wider variety of foodstuffs on many occasions, but as she was never inclined to be the one to do the cooking, had not felt it her place to complain about what was on offer. But the notion that one could simply open a tin or a jar and heat up one of Simpkins's delicious curries in a saucepan atop the cooker was a stroke of sheer genius. She could imagine women all across the nation doing just that thing.

"I think it's brilliant. Absolutely brilliant. Were there any other things you were considering adding to the list besides curries?" she asked.

"Well, I thought perhaps it would be wise to also add things that were far more familiar to the average consumer, like beef stew and other forms of soups. Maybe even some already prepared gravy wouldn't go amiss."

Beryl was delighted to see a hopeful and enthusiastic look on Simpkins's face. He had had several setbacks over the past couple of years between the loss of his beloved wife Bessie and the death of his brother-in-law. But with this new venture with Colonel Kimberly's, it was as if he was being fertilized and watered for the first time in ages. If she could do anything to encourage him, she would be pleased to help.

"I think whatever you come up with will be spot on. I think your instincts are very good and you should follow along with whatever interests you. You know I'm always happy to do some taste-testing in order to help out," she said with a smile.

"I'm glad that you said you would be happy to help because I have something else in mind that I would like for you to consider doing."

"Ask away," Beryl said with a breezy wave of her hand. "I'd be happy to help with whatever you need."

"It's not just you I'm thinking of."

"You need something from Edwina, too, don't you?" she asked.

"I think it would be best coming from the both of you."

"You'd best come out with it then," Beryl said.

"I thought something like this that's a bit revolutionary could really use the added boost that a spokeswoman would provide."

"Are you asking if I'd be willing to be a spokeswoman for your products?" Beryl asked. "You know I'm happy to do that sort of thing for any number of products, but I'm afraid my reputation as someone who is not much of a cook may be working against you in this case."

"That's what I suspected, which is why I need Miss Edwina. I thought if the two of you were recommending it, not as *Beryl*

Helliwell, adventuress, but as *Davenport and Helliwell, private enquiry agents,* it might just be the sort of kick-start such a thing could really use. With your name and Edwina's experience, the two of you could speak to either side of the issue and give it a bit of pizzazz."

Beryl leaned back against the seat and drummed her hands on the steering wheel in front of her. Simpkins had made an excellent point. She could see the advertising campaign building right in front of her very eyes. Print advertisements and radio announcements with voice-overs and quotes from Edwina and herself. She could see a photo shoot with the two of them wielding can openers and long wooden spoons or dashing back from a case holding a jar of Colonel Kimberly's Curry aloft as if it were the final clue in a difficult case.

But then she thought of Edwina's likely rejection of any sort of public role. Edwina was not one for shining a spotlight upon herself, and such a thing might be considered too forward in her opinion. Beryl could just hear her protesting that she wasn't enough of an authority on the working woman's plight to begin to consider being a spokesperson for such matters. She would likely point out that Beryl was not someone whose opinion on the subject of foodstuffs could be trusted in any way considering her idea of cooking involved eating directly from a tin of beans, quite possibly with a penknife.

No, this would take some sort of finessing in order to make it possible. Still, she could see how Simpkins was right to ask them to participate. Surely their recommendation would go some ways to launching the new product line successfully. One way or another she would help to convince Edwina to say yes. She felt that fluttering in her chest that signaled enthusiasm for a new adventure.

"One way or another we'll manage to get her on board. You just leave it to me." Beryl checked the rearview mirror and stomped down on the accelerator.

*   *   *

Edwina pushed her bicycle slowly up the high street feeling weighed down by worries. Not that she hadn't felt concerned on her way to the Magistrate's Court only a few hours earlier. But now she was concerned about her own ability to perform her duties as assigned. With each step her sense of unease about the letter Michael had entered into evidence grew. From the depths of her memory, Edwina recalled some incident involving a poisoned pen during her childhood.

She had never been made privy to the specifics of it all, as it would have been inappropriate to include a child in such goings on. But what she did remember distinctly was that it had been deeply unsettling and that her parents had been quite concerned. Her mother was always inclined to work herself up into a state over the smallest of matters because she enjoyed the drama of such things. But Edwina's father had been made of completely different sort of stuff and she distinctly remembered that he had been particularly worried about how such things might turn out.

There was nothing she could do about it by simply worrying, however. After all, her role as the magistrate was to make rulings on evidence and cases actually brought before her, not to speculate on what might come to be in the future. As she pushed her bicycle, she could not help but note that the day was warm and bright, and a pleasant breeze cooled her as she exerted herself. She decided to put such dark matters out of her mind and instead to mark the occasion of her first day as a magistrate by stopping in at the Woolery and selecting a skein or two of yarn to knit up some sort of project to commemorate the experience. She thought perhaps, given the time of year, something made of lightweight wool or even cotton would not go amiss. She had a sudden hankering to knit up a jaunty beret. There had been a pattern for one in a recent issue of her favorite lady's needlework magazine, a publication she barely had time

to read, let alone put into use of late with all of her other obligations and enthusiasms. But she was suddenly overwhelmed
with the desire to cast on a chic little hat with a slouchy crown
that would perch atop her head throughout the rest of the summer and into the crisp days of autumn.

With a lighter heart she pushed her bicycle along at a faster
clip. In only a few moments' time she found herself coming
alongside the Women's Institute building. Cornelia and Godfrey Burroughs were exiting the squat, stone structure just as
she drew alongside it. She raised her hand in greeting as soon
as she spotted them. For a moment she couldn't imagine what it
was the pair of them were doing at that time of day at the Women's
Institute. Then, with a jolt, she realized she had missed yet another meeting of the Walmsley Parva Garden Club.

She had always been a faithful member until recently and
suddenly wished she had traversed the route from the court a
little more sedately. Cornelia did not return her friendly greeting as she turned a large brass key in the lock upon the door. In
fact, Cornelia scowled at her, and unless Edwina was very
much mistaken, made a decided tut-tutting noise. Godfrey
looked at her apologetically but did not bring himself to appear
overtly friendly. Never one to go against his wife's wishes, he
trailed in Cornelia's wake carrying an armload of cartons to
the motorcar they had left pulled up against the curb in front of
the building. Cornelia clambered up into the vehicle and positioned herself behind the wheel. Edwina came alongside as
Godfrey carefully stowed the cartons in the boot. She slowed
her footsteps, despite Cornelia's forbidding looks, and peered
at the contents of the cartons.

Edwina felt a sudden surge of disappointment as she realized
that the cartons held a variety of cuttings from member gardens. She had somehow gone and missed the summer cuttings
swap. Never, in all the years of her adult life, had she been absent from a plant swap meeting. She had even managed to muster

the strength to attend on the occasion she had contracted food poisoning from a dodgy fish paste sandwich. What on earth had become of her well-ordered life that she would have neglected to make a note of such an important event? Not only had she missed out on the opportunity to add some fine new plant varieties to her own garden at the Beeches, but she had also not provided her fellow horticultural enthusiasts with the opportunity to obtain cuttings from her own collection.

Cornelia pulled away from the curb, pelting her with an admonishing spray of gravel. Edwina could hardly blame her. It would not be wrong to say Edwina's cuttings were one of the most prized features of the swap events. Only the plants from Dr. Wilcox's garden were more eagerly sought after. In fact, much of the continuing, keen interest of the club could be attributed to the anticipation of access to their offerings. Her absence would have been noted and far from appreciated. Cornelia, as chairwoman of the club, would have expected some sort of notice if Edwina had not planned to attend.

As she continued on her way towards the Woolery at the far end of the high street, she reflected on how many ways her life had changed over the last several months. She could barely recognize the person she had been before Beryl had unexpectedly turned up at the end of her driveway in search of a place to stay. Edwina's economic situation had improved, her loneliness had abated, and she had found she had quite a talent for getting to the bottom of local criminality. She had even gone ahead and acknowledged her lifelong dream of writing a novel. Quite a shift in only a few months' time. She wondered briefly what her mother would think of all of it since she was not one who approved of independent women or modern lifestyles.

But as she thought of her mother, and of the poisonous look Cornelia had flung in her direction, she was overcome with a feeling of rebelliousness. It was her life after all, and if she did not wish to place herself at the beck and call of those who wished to lay claim to her time, she need not do so. It was not as though she had shirked any official duties with the garden club. Moreover, she had spent her morning in service of her beloved village in a new way. With her head held high, Edwina quickened her pace once more and found herself eager to explore the latest in offerings the Woolery would be sure to provide.

Chapter 3

Beryl pulled to a stop in front of Simpkins's farm. During the weeks since the Prentice family had taken over the daily running of the place, it had slowly but surely come back to life. While Simpkins's brother-in-law, Hector, had allowed the fields to fall fallow and choke with weeds and even some of the venerable trees to become distressed during a recent one hundred days of drought, the Prentice family had thrown themselves headlong into the restoration of vitality to the property. Beryl wondered if perhaps Mrs. Prentice had been working herself too hard in an effort to remain on Simpkins's good side, but when she appeared in the dooryard, she had a healthy glow and a bit more meat on her bones than was the case when last Beryl had seen her.

Mrs. Prentice wiped her hands on a floral pinny and waved for them to follow her into the house. Beryl stiffened slightly as the Prentice children raced towards them from the fields beyond the cottage and swarmed around the motorcar. She was relieved when Simpkins proved the primary object of their interest, presenting him with the sticky contents of their pockets or jumbled stories of childish conquests.

Jack, the only Prentice child who truly interested Beryl, was conspicuously absent. She thought it likely he was somewhere in town hocking newspapers or finding some other way to earn a shilling or two. While he helped out as often as possible at the farm, there was no denying that the money he brought in as a newspaper boy was still of real use.

Beryl followed Simpkins and the gaggle of children into the tidy cottage kitchen. Mrs. Prentice had done wonders with the place. After Bessie had died the soul had gone out of the cottage and Hector and Simpkins had simply existed in an increasingly grubby shell of what had once been a happy family home. But in short order, Mrs. Prentice had revitalized the place.

Gleaming copper pots hung from a wrought iron rack above the cooker. A jelly jar filled with wildflower blossoms sat upon a freshly scrubbed worktable in the center of the room. The cooker appeared recently blacked, and baskets and crates heaped with newly plucked fruit sat higgity-piggity all about the room. A warm, sweet, and spicy scent filled the air.

Just below that aroma she thought she detected the yeasty scent of freshly baked bread. She inhaled deeply. Turning her head surreptitiously, she spotted what appeared to be two pillowy loaves cooling beneath a tea towel. But not surreptitiously enough from the way Mrs. Prentice's gaze followed her own.

"Are you hungry?" Mrs. Prentice asked.

"I could eat a bite of something," Simpkins said, having disengaged himself from the smallest child in the group. "It smells like you've been putting the greengage harvest to good use."

Mrs. Prentice nodded and pointed at a large pot on the stove. "I've been tinkering with the recipe just like you suggested, and I think we may have gotten close to what you are looking for. Would you like to give it a try?" she asked.

"As long as you've got something to spread it on, I do. Although this one is likely to be happy eating it right off a spoon." He jerked his thumb in Beryl's direction and shared a conspiratorial wink with Mrs. Prentice.

"I've made up a fresh batch of bread this morning knowing you prefer to sample it the way it will be eaten," she said, taking a step towards the tea towels and removing a loaf.

She sliced off two thick pieces and slathered them each with a heaping helping of what had been bubbling away on the stove. Simpkins kept his eyes riveted on Beryl's face as she bit down on her slice and chewed it slowly. Her eyes widened in surprise as she looked from Simpkins to Mrs. Prentice and nodded enthusiastically. What filled her mouth was an almost magical flavor. It was like liquid honey and plums and a hint of flowers all at the same time.

She'd never cared much for plums before that moment. She was willing to eat them, of course, but they just never seemed to pack the same burst of flavor as many other fruits, like peaches or citrus or even raspberries. But something about greengages was entirely different. She swallowed with some effort as she didn't really wish for the flavor to leave her mouth even long enough to take another bite.

"It's not like anything I've ever tasted before," Beryl said.

"I hope you mean that in a good way," Simpkins said.

"I do indeed. I would say this is an absolute winner." Beryl took another bite and Mrs. Prentice sliced off pieces of bread for her children, who stood jostling each other and fidgeting nearby. She slathered jam on each of their slices before handing them out. Simpkins kept his eyes trained on each of the children in turn as they took their first bite and nodded with pleasure at their reactions.

Before Beryl could embarrass herself by asking for another slice, Mrs. Prentice told the children to head back out into the field and that they would be following them directly. She gathered up a few empty baskets from beside the door and handed one to Beryl and another to Simpkins. "We'd best get the rest of the plums picked if we're going to make some more jars of this. If you think that this final version is the way we want to go, I can make enough sample jars for you to send out to all of the people on the list that you gave me."

"I'd say that it's a winner. How many trees are left needing to be picked?" Simpkins asked.

"Nearly three-quarters of them. Despite the early drought, the harvest has been a good one this year."

They joined the children in the rolling fields beyond the cottage. Row upon row of heavily ladened fruit trees stretched out before them. There were ladders propped up in two or three of the trees, but the children, by and large, simply clambered up trunks and branches as children do without the use of any such equipment. They carefully handed pieces of fruit down, hand to hand like members of a well-practiced fire brigade, and seemed quite adept at stripping the trees bare.

She wondered how much practice the Prentice children had had stripping fruit from trees they were not authorized to pick during those years when their parents had struggled so much with the family finances. She didn't think they had become quite so adept in only a few days of picking greengages. She looked over at Simpkins, who nodded appreciatively at their prowess but kindly held his tongue.

The sun was high, and the day had grown decidedly warm when Beryl noticed a figure making his way across the field. Norman Davies was dressed in clothing that seemed too formal for fruit picking. It also didn't look like the sort of thing he generally wore to make deliveries for Mr. Scott's greengrocery service, either. He quickly closed the distance between himself and the fruit pickers and offered an apology.

"I'm sorry not to have been here earlier. You'll never believe where I've been," he said.

"A wedding or a funeral based on those fancy togs you've got on," Simpkins said.

"I wish that was the case. I was called to the Magistrate's Court, and I thought I'd best clean up some before I appeared before Miss Davenport. She's a bit of a stickler, isn't she?" he said. "Although I have to say she was more than fair to Michael and me."

Beryl's ears perked up. What on earth had Norman Davies and Michael Blackburn done to be hauled up before the court? And how had Edwina performed? She was dying to know how it had all unfolded.

"What were you and Michael doing before the bench?" she asked.

"We had gotten into a scuffle in the street after Michael accused me of bad-mouthing him at the greengrocer's When I told him that I'd done no such thing he completely lost his rag and started to pummel me. Unfortunately, Constable Gibbs got in between us, and he landed a blow on the side of her head. That's what did it."

Beryl could well imagine that Constable Gibbs would not have appreciated any such goings on in the village—but certainly not something that would lead to her being on the receiving end of physical blows.

"You say Michael thought you were bad-mouthing him at the greengrocery?" Simpkins said. "You two fellers have been friends for years. What would have made him think you'd do a thing like that?"

"Michael received an anonymous letter accusing me of saying he was trying to desert his unit and that's how he came by his injury." Norman shook his head as though he still could not believe the words that were coming out of his mouth.

Beryl gasped. Who would have written such a cruel thing? Michael had completely lost the use of one of his arms during his time on the front. She had never heard the faintest whiff of scandal attaching itself to Michael's character even though he had been one of the many unfortunate men who had returned from the front with what was called a thousand-yard stare. He had spent considerable time in the hospital wing of a local

manor house recovering his senses. It had taken months before
he had been able to pull himself back from wherever his mind
had gone in order to recover from the atrocities he had witnessed.

Even though the residents of Walmsley Parva never mentioned it, all of them seemed to understand how much Michael
had gone through and were silently grateful to him for sacrific-
ing his own well-being for the good of the group. She certainly
couldn't imagine Norman, or anyone else in the village, saying
anything to the contrary.

"That's simply monstrous. What did Edwina have to say
about it?"

Norman let out a long sigh. "She accepted the letter into evidence and suggested that it was simply a cruel hoax and recommended we make up. Michael and I agreed, and I think
things are back to normal. I was quite relieved that the constable decided not to press charges. She can be at least as much of
a stickler as Miss Edwina."

Edwina propped her bicycle against the side of the Woolery's brick exterior wall and mounted the shallow set of steps to
the door. As she pushed it open and stepped inside, she felt the
strains of the day fall away from her slim shoulders. Just surrounding herself with the baskets and bins filled to the scup-
pers with colorful, squishy skeins of wool lowered her heart
rate and demanded her undivided attention.

A deep aubergine, heathered hank of yarn attracted her attention. She reached out and plucked it from a basket filled
with a variety of skeins she was quite certain were made of
Scottish Highland wool. She had been considering creating a
beret with a knit and purl pattern, but as her gaze roved over
the wide variety of colors available, she suddenly felt a hankering to try her hand at a tam created in the Fair Isle manner. She
could just picture it flying off her needles and perching gently

on her head as she took her bicycle out for a jaunt into the countryside surrounding the village. Or perhaps, it might even serve as a sort of driving cap for those occasions she forced herself behind the wheel of Beryl's motorcar.

She selected several skeins from the basket, and as she spread them out on a table in the center of the shop, she began to consider how she might combine them to create the most pleasing effect. As she sifted, shifted, and sorted the colors into order, a sniffling sound reached her ears. She paused in her musings and cocked her head to one side, straining her head towards the back room. She had been so absorbed in her pleasant task it had not occurred to her that Mrs. Dunstable, the Woolery's capable proprietress, had not come out to greet her. It was unlike Mrs. Dunstable not to make herself available to customers from the moment they stepped through the door. Perhaps she was busy unpacking some fresh stock in the back room. But no, there was the noise again.

Edwina left the skeins of yarn on the table and took a few steps towards the threshold of the back room. She felt unsure of her welcome. If the noise she heard was what she suspected, it might be perhaps Mrs. Dunstable would prefer not to be disturbed. She raised her small hand and knocked upon the door jamb.

"I'll be right there," Mrs. Dunstable called out.

After a moment's pause, she appeared in the main room of the shop with red-rimmed eyes and a crumpled handkerchief held to her nose. Edwina would not say that she and Mrs. Dunstable were the closest of friends, but they had a warm and long-term acquaintance that was only strengthened by their shared love of knitting. Edwina's heart went out to the other woman as it became clear that Mrs. Dunstable was having a great deal of trouble keeping her emotions in check even in the face of her professional duties. It was no time to stand on ceremony.

"Mrs. Dunstable, whatever is the matter?" Edwina said, taking the unprecedented step to reach out and place her hand upon Mrs. Dunstable's arm and give it a tentative pat. Her unexpected attention provoked exactly the opposite effect than what she had hoped. Mrs. Dunstable burst into a noisy spate of tears.

Edwina guided the sobbing woman to one of the chairs ringing the table at the center of the room and encouraged her to sit down in it. She locked the door of the shop and flipped the sign hanging upon it to the closed position. Then she bustled into the back room and looked about for a tap and some sort of drinking vessel. Finding a small area set aside for the making of tea, she busied herself with the kettle and the gas ring.

As she stood there waiting for it to come to a boil her gaze roamed about the small room. Her breath caught in her chest as she spotted on the shelf in front of her an envelope that, at a glance, looked astonishingly similar to the one Michael Blackburn had presented in evidence at the court. The envelope appeared to be of the same sort, and the block printing with Mrs. Dunstable's address at the Woolery upon it looked similar as well. Although Edwina was not a betting woman like Beryl, she would have laid odds on the sender being one and the same.

Simply noticing the letter existed, she told herself, was not the same thing as snooping. She refrained from extracting the contents of the envelope and returned her attention to the gas ring. The kettle let out a shrill shriek and she added a generous scoop of tea leaves to the Brown Betty teapot she found nearby. Within a moment's time she had returned to the shop with the pot of tea and two cups neatly assembled on a tray. In her absence Mrs. Dunstable had managed to stop sobbing and sat slumped in her chair looking sheepish.

"You looked like you could do with a cup of tea. I hope you don't mind that I took over your kitchenette to make it," Edwina said.

"That was very kind of you. I don't know what's come over me," Mrs. Dunstable said.

Edwina drew out another of the chairs placed around the table and sat. She gazed steadily at Mrs. Dunstable as she poured the shopkeeper a cup of tea. She waited until she had poured one for herself to call Mrs. Dunstable's statement into question. It couldn't be considered prying, could it, if she was concerned about the impact on the village in her role as the local magistrate?

"It seems to me that you have perhaps received some disturbing news. It happens to us all from time to time. Don't you think you would feel better if you told someone about it?" Edwina said before taking a sip of her tea.

She glanced over the rim of her cup, giving Mrs. Dunstable time to consider whether or not she wished to answer.

"I wouldn't say I've had bad news exactly. Can something be considered news if it's not the truth?" Mrs. Dunstable asked.

"I suppose the fact that someone might be in receipt of information that could be called an untruth is newsworthy. Have you found yourself to be in such a position?" Edwina asked.

Mrs. Dunstable took a sip of her tea and then replaced the cup noisily in the saucer. She looked Edwina over as if to evaluate whether or not she wished to share a confidence. Edwina prided herself on her reputation as someone who knew how to keep those things quiet that ought to be held in secret. And she also felt that she had a well-deserved reputation for putting the right word in the right ear to do the most good. Such a reputation had come in remarkably handy in the private enquiry business.

"I've received the most disturbing letter. It was quite cruel and completely unexpected," Mrs. Dunstable said.

"How unpleasant for you. Did this just happen?" Edwina asked.

Mrs. Dunstable nodded. "It was sitting on the mat with the

rest of the morning's post. It must have come whilst I was attending the garden club meeting. I can't imagine what would have provoked such a thing."

"Did the sender disclose his or her identity?" Edwina asked, quite certain that no such thing had occurred.

"No. The sender was completely anonymous. Someone without the courtesy to even identify themselves has felt moved to announce that Nurse Crenshaw was heard spouting lies about me in the post office," Mrs. Dunstable said. "And to think I've always thought of her as such a pleasant woman whenever she would come into the shop or when I had need to visit Dr. Nelson's surgery."

"Gossiping at the post office doesn't sound much like Nurse Crenshaw to me, either. Are you quite certain that the sender is relaying the truth?"

"The things the letter reports her as saying about me were certainly not true," Mrs. Dunstable said. She looked at Edwina again, her eyes shimmering with tears. "The writer says that Nurse Crenshaw was telling everyone within earshot that I acquired the money to open the Woolery by blackmailing my fellow villagers."

"Preposterous," Edwina said.

"I am glad to hear you say as much. I'll have you know I inherited a small lump sum upon the death of my aunt. She was an avid knitter and had taught me to be the same and it seemed a fitting tribute to her memory to open the shop. The idea that someone would claim I had the wherewithal to do so based on illegal and immoral pursuits instead of the generosity of a beloved aunt is deeply troubling."

"I am sure no one would believe a rumor such as that. But why would the sender think you would believe that Nurse Crenshaw would say such things about you?" Edwina asked.

Mrs. Dunstable leaned back in her chair, her mouth opening in a perfect O of surprise. She snapped it shut and glanced up at the ceiling as if scrolling through her memory bank. She looked back down at Edwina and shook her head slowly.

"You're right of course. I've never had any cause to believe Nurse Crenshaw would go about saying such things. In fact, her position as the village nurse depends upon her being the sort of person who would be more discreet than that. But why would someone send me a letter claiming that she was disparaging my character in public?" Mrs. Dunstable said. "What could someone possibly have gained from such a thing?"

What indeed, Edwina had to wonder. That uneasy feeling she had first felt at the court had returned.

Chapter 4

Beryl felt pleasantly tired and as though she had done a good morning's work as she pulled the motorcar to a stop in front of the Beeches once more. Although she thought of Simpkins as rather vigorous and possessing of more than his fair share of physical strength, her heartstrings plucked slightly as she noticed the older man easing himself out of the vehicle with decided stiffness. Perhaps Colonel Kimberly's ought to be adding a line of arthritis ointments and rubs to its offerings in addition to convenience foodstuffs for working women.

She thought it likely he was interested in some other sort of pain-relieving lubricant as he made a slow but determined beeline for the potting shed round the back of the house rather than entering the building through the front door. Simpkins had long claimed the potting shed as his personal domain even before he had managed to become ensconced in a back bedroom on the second floor rather than merely visiting three times each week as a jobbing gardener. Still, some habits die hard, and Beryl had often joined him in his lair amongst the bags of potash and limestone, cones of jute twine and packets of seeds for a surreptitious afternoon tippling session, particularly when Edwina seemed keen to spend the afternoon banging away on the Remington portable typewriter churning out page after page of her novel.

Beryl entered through the front door and listened for any sign of Beddoes racing round with the carpet sweeper or Crumpet capering towards her looking for his mistress to turn up. But all that she found was a rather untidy pile of post left uncharacteristically on the hall table. Generally, as soon as the flap of the mail slot clicked open, Beddoes appeared to scoop the envelopes from the floor as if the very sight of them was an affront to her housekeeping standards. She would hastily and efficiently sort them and stack them according to recipient.

Although Edwina thought Beddoes's routine performance of small services like that a testament to her superiority as a domestic servant, Beryl suspected it was a way to stay informed about the household occupants and their private business. Beryl never did manage to say or do the right thing when it came to well-trained, old-fashioned sorts of servants, and although she would not want to do anything to cause Beddoes to give notice, in the privacy of her own mind she was willing to admit that, in some ways, she preferred life at the Beeches before Simpkins had gone to the trouble and expense of hiring household help.

As she looked at the mail left on the table, Beryl wondered fleetingly if Beddoes had taken ill. For the briefest of moments, she allowed herself to entertain the idea of a few days of Beddoes tucked away in her rooms on the third floor, feeling ever so slightly feverish and keeping her self-satisfied scowls to herself. But as she was never a mean-spirited sort, she bid the notion good-bye and set about making herself useful by sorting and stacking the post herself.

There were a few pieces of correspondence addressed to Simpkins including one or two using his title as president of

Colonel Kimberly's Condiment Company. Along with her usual thick stack of personal correspondence, Edwina had received catalogues offering seeds, the latest in millinery, and exotic plants for discerning gardeners. Beryl had no idea how her friend managed to keep up with such a lively correspondence considering her other duties. But day after day letters streamed in and letters streamed out, and Beryl could not help but admire how industriously her friend spent her time. If she was not knitting or entertaining guests for bridge parties or investigating cases or serving on a committee, she was answering letters. And since Edwina had taken on the bookkeeping duties for their fledgling business, any correspondence that was addressed to Davenport and Helliwell, Private Enquiry Agency landed in her stack, too.

Beryl had a robust correspondence of her own. There were always solicitations from various charities or companies that wanted her to provide them with either a donation or an endorsement. She was pleased to think she now had a valid claim on her time as a spokesperson for Colonel Kimberly's and could turn those jobs down without any ping of conscience. At least she could if Edwina agreed to participate. She was not surprised to see a postcard from her Australian reporter friend Archie Harrison, who was forever sending her such missives displaying interesting locales around London in a futile attempt to entice her to pay him a visit.

While she enjoyed Archie's company thoroughly and enthusiastically from time to time, she had no intention of being at his beck and call. It was nothing personal towards Archie. She had no intention of being at the summons of anyone, least of all a man. As she finished the sorting, a final envelope addressed to her caught her attention.

It was of the unremarkable sort to which one paid no particular mind. The quality of the paper was neither cheap and tawdry, nor was it the sort that put one in mind of mahogany-paneled studies in ancient manor houses or newly moneyed persons bent on impressing the recipient with their taste and resources.

No, it was the handwriting that caught her attention. It was notable in that it was almost devoid of any sort of personality. Written entirely in capital letters in a precise block printed style, it was completely legible, and she felt certain she did not recognize it. Beryl wondered if the sender had been subject to criticism from Prudence Rathbone, the local postmistress, for hastily and illegibly addressing envelopes in the past. Intrigued, she extracted a bobby pin from her hair and slit open the envelope.

Her eyes widened as she unfolded the letter. While the outside of the envelope had been so carefully printed, the inside held no handwriting whatsoever. All of the words on the page had been cut from newspapers or magazines or possibly even old books and then were neatly pasted to a sheet of stationery. But it wasn't just the unorthodox construction of the message that grabbed her attention, it was the contents.

According to the anonymous sender, Vicar Lowethorpe had been heard on more than one occasion to decry the living arrangements she, Simpkins, and Edwina so shamelessly engaged in. The sender disclosed that the good vicar had been overheard to say how much he regretted the sullying of Edwina's good reputation and the further proof that Beryl was the sort of woman who provided an extraordinarily corrupting influence upon those with whom she came in close contact. It went on to hint that the vicar was not entirely sure that poor Simpkins had not become ensnared in some sort of unmentionable triangle with the two hussies at the Beeches.

Beryl burst into laughter. She had, by nature of her unconventional lifestyle, received many letters over her long career in the public spotlight that criticized her choices. While she had been lucky enough that overwhelmingly her interactions with the public were positive, she had learned to take those that weren't in stride. But this letter was different. Never before had she received something so ridiculous and yet so imaginative. The claim of sordid and indecorous behavior on the part of Edwina struck her as uproariously funny.

She could not begin to imagine what her friend would make of the implication that there was something carnal going on between themselves and Simpkins. What sort of fevered imagination could have considered that the two of them would be vying for his affection in any sort of a way? It was preposterous and just the sort of thing that made village life so intriguing. She could hardly wait to find Edwina to show it to her.

Even the sight of Crumpet racing out to greet her from wherever he had been hiding did little to raise Edwina's spirits. Her encounter with Mrs. Dunstable had left her feeling even more concerned than she had been before. Obviously, the person sending such missives was bent on causing disruption in the village. Edwina wondered who possibly could be the sort to have done such a thing. It wasn't as though she had heard any rumors about Mrs. Dunstable that would suggest she was the sort of person who would be the target of such maliciousness.

As so often was the case, Edwina decided to distract herself from the worries at hand by putting in an hour or so on her novel. With Crumpet capering at her heels, she made for the morning room, which she had taken over as a sort of office for their business as well as the place she spent time working on the adventures of Bart Dalton, cowboy-gunslinger. She sat at the desk and looked out over the gardens at the Beeches. Simpkins had hired a younger man to assist with the gardening earlier in the season, and between that extra pair of hands and the influx of funds Simpkins had provided for the renovations, the gardens were slowly but surely returning to their former glory. As she slid a piece of typing paper under the roller bar of the Remington portable, she felt a surge of pride in her home.

When her parents had been alive and she was still quite a young girl, the gardens of the Beeches had been amongst the most attractive in the village and indeed the district. Simpkins had worked there as a young boy, growing up alongside Edwina's mother and learning the craft of botanical husbandry from his own father, who was the head gardener. But over the years, the estate taxes and overall circumstances had taken their toll. Not only had Edwina had no money left to pay for full-time garden help, but there was also no help to be had. So many young men had been lost to the war that able-bodied men in search of that sort of employment were far and few between and certainly unwilling to work for the wages she could have possibly wrung from the food budget.

But Simpkins had proven remarkably adept at remembering how things had been in the past while making suggestions for the future. And his vision had started to take hold. Edwina had created a koi pond and had surrounded it with plants that preferred moist conditions during the final months of her mother's life. It was now a well-established and central part of the garden and one Simpkins had set off to great effect by the new installations he cultivated around it. It suddenly struck her as she sat there that Simpkins just might have planned the new arrangements to provide the best view from the very chair where she spent so much time.

As she launched herself into her work, tapping away on the keys, she found herself introducing a character with a snaggle-toothed grin and oversized ears who happened to have a soft spot for greenery. Just as she was beginning to warm to that character and provide him with a moment of heroism, a discreet knock landed on the morning room door and Beddoes popped her head around the threshold.

Edwina glanced up from the typewriter, surprised to see the housekeeper looking far less imperious than was her habit. In fact, if Edwina had to make a guess, she would say that Beddoes was well and truly rattled. Not only that, one of the things she had appreciated about the housekeeper was that she made a habit, unlike some other people in the household, of never interrupting when the sound of the typewriter could be heard. Edwina removed her hands from the keys and gave Beddoes her full attention.

"Was there something you needed?" Edwina asked. Beddoes hesitated in the doorway and then squared her shoulders as if she had resolved herself upon a course of action. Edwina's stomach gathered into a queasy knot. It was not the sort of look one ever wished to see upon the face of an employee considered an asset.

"As much as I loathe to disoblige you, I'm afraid I must offer my notice," Beddoes said.

Edwina had worried something like this could be in the offing. While Beryl had done a valiant job of trying to rein herself in, there was no denying the fact that Beddoes found her to be a sore trial. As an American, Beryl had not become entirely accustomed to the concept of the finer points of class in society and had made a nuisance of herself by her unwavering insistence on crossing those invisible lines, which were so obvious to the English.

Beddoes had been routinely insulted by Beryl's enthusiastic offers to assist her with any manner of tasks. In fact, only recently, they had resorted to removing Beryl from the building entirely for some time in order to allow Beddoes to bottom out the house in a way she saw fit without the interference of one of her betters. It had all proven to be quite extraordinarily exhausting and Edwina had spent not inconsiderable time and energy soothing Beddoes's ruffled feathers and attempting once again to explain the nuances of class structure to Beryl whilst generally fretting over the entire mess.

Matters had not been helped by Edwina's new duties at the Magistrate's Court. More and more of the responsibilities for the household were falling on Beddoes's capable shoulders, and

Edwina, in the privacy of her own mind, had to admit she was quite enjoying the opportunity to rely upon someone whose professionalism in such things was so trustworthy. While Edwina was a more than capable housekeeper and household manager, the fact of the matter was, it was not where her heart lay. She found that she enjoyed her work as a private enquiry agent, a novelist, and now a magistrate, far more than she had ever enjoyed her role as mistress of the Beeches. At least not mistress of the Beeches who also did all of the heavy cleaning and running of the day-to-day tasks such a property required.

An icy finger ran up her spine as she considered what she would do without Beddoes's assistance. She was afraid that she was going to have to give up one of her new roles, and truth be told, she had very little clarity about which she would most prefer to release. They all were so interesting, and each had something of value to offer.

She certainly couldn't leave Beryl in the lurch by pulling the plug on her part in the private enquiry agency, nor would she wish to do so. And she had taken on a public responsibility by agreeing to serve as the magistrate, at least for the time being. With a sigh Edwina looked down at the typewriter keys once more and realized that her book would be the thing that would have to be abandoned. As her gaze glanced over a bit of dialogue on the part of her snaggle-toothed character, she felt a lump making its way into her throat. But perhaps, she might be able to work Beddoes round. She looked up and felt the lump lodge more firmly as she noted the expression of steely resolve in Beddoes's face.

"Have I done something to upset you?" Edwina asked.

Beddoes shook her head violently. "No, miss. I should never wish for you to think that. I have no grievance with you in the least."

So, Edwina thought, *it is Beryl.* "Has someone else at the Beeches done something to upset you? You have only but to mention it and I will be happy to speak on your behalf," Edwina said.

Beddoes's chin wobbled ever so slightly. "It's not that either, miss. But I am afraid that I am resolved to quit your employ by the end of the week at latest."

"Will you not at least provide me with some sort of explanation?" Edwina asked. "If you are not unhappy here, what could be the possible reason for you to leave? Has something happened with your family?"

Beddoes shook her head again, this time with even more force. "It's nothing like that, but I'm afraid I find it impossible to disclose my reasons. You have my notice."

Beddoes wheeled round and fled out through the open doorway, failing even to close it behind her. Edwina drummed her slim fingers on the desk in front of her. While she was definitely a proud sort of servant, Beddoes was also one who viewed the role in a traditional way. If she had a grievance, she would have said so and expected that Edwina would put it right. If Beryl or Simpkins had been at fault, surely Beddoes would have made that clear. What could possibly have happened to trouble her?

Edwina looked down at her typewriter and felt the joy she generally would have experienced at the sight of a freshly created page of her novel evaporate. Her novel held no pleasure for her now as she considered how bleak the future looked without Beddoes's expert assistance. Even if they could find a new servant to replace her, there would be the inevitable trials and tribulations of breaking in a new member of the household as well as developing a dynamic between such a person and the rest of them.

It was not every domestic servant who would tolerate the sort of arrangement that existed at the Beeches. With two working women to contend with, as well as one jobbing gardener installed in a back bedroom, it was unconventional in the extreme. The sort of servant who would uphold the kind of standards that Edwina admired was unlikely to be as willing as Beddoes had been to accept such a position. Servants had their pride and their reputations to think of, and unfortunately the goings on at the Beeches were unlikely to prove attractive to most. Whatever was she going to do?

Chapter 5

Beryl carried her letter to the parlor and settled herself into her favorite chair. She wasn't as young as she used to be, and a morning spent climbing up and down ladders and reaching overhead to pluck orbs of ripe fruit had tired her out more than she would have expected. Off and on during her time in Walmsley Parva it had occurred to her that her level of fitness had begun to decline quite shockingly.

Even though she undertook health regimes with some frequency, it could not be claimed that she was an enthusiast. She had never needed to think particularly of such things when they were a natural by-product of her lifestyle. Treks into jungles or up over mountains as part of other sorts of adventures managed to keep her in trim without needing to set out deliberately to do so.

But life in a sleepy village like Walmsley Parva provided no such adventures. If she were to maintain any semblance of an active body, she was going to need to put in more effort. As she was considering how best to go about such a thing, whether to take up golf or perhaps even to purchase a bicycle of her own in order to accompany Edwina on some of her jaunts out into the countryside, Simpkins appeared in the door of the parlor.

Beryl thought he looked less focused than he had when they arrived back at the Beeches, confirming her suspicion that he had visited the potting shed to do a spot of afternoon imbibing. But he seemed cheerful enough and the two of them were soon engrossed in a lively debate as to which horse might win at an upcoming race. They were just deciding whether or not to lay bets on their favorites with Chester White down at the Dove and Duck that evening when Edwina burst into the room. Edwina was not given to bursting, and even the slightly stupefied Simpkins appeared startled by the energetic rate with which she began to pace the floor in front of them.

"Which one of you did it?" Edwina asked, pausing in her steady trudge back and forth across the well-worn carpet.

"I'm afraid you'll have to be more specific. I am sure that between the two of us we have managed to do quite a lot of things since we last saw you," Beryl said.

"Which one of you has committed an offense so grievous that Beddoes feels forced to tender her resignation?" Edwina said, shaking a finger at each of them in turn.

"Beddoes has given her notice?" Beryl asked.

This was in no way good news. As much as Beryl did not particularly enjoy their new domestic servant's presence in the house, she prized the freedoms it provided to Edwina.

Beryl racked her brain for any minor insult she could have inadvertently given. Ever since their removal to a nearby manor house in the course of an investigation, Beryl had thought that the two of them were on slightly more solid ground. She had come to realize that it was unlikely Beddoes would ever warm to her, but she did not feel as though she remained a constant thorn in the housekeeper's side. As a matter of fact, after Beddoes had given the Beeches a total bottoming out, she seemed in a far better mood than she had been ever since her arrival. It was almost as though the condition of the house reflected so poorly on her abilities that she couldn't find any sort of peace or comfort until she could look about her with satisfaction.

No, Beryl could think of no occasion she had given offense that would explain Beddoes's desire to tender her resignation. She was willing to take responsibility for all those things she felt that she should accept, but this was not amongst them unless Beddoes were to give her side of the argument and reveal something Beryl had not considered.

"She has indeed," Edwina said, her voice rising in both volume and octave.

"Did she give a reason?" Simpkins asked.

He seemed as agitated as Edwina. He shifted from one buttock to the other on the sofa as though he was forcing himself to remain there rather than jumping to his feet and hurrying off to confront the housekeeper with her impending disruption to the household arrangements.

"I asked her, but she categorically refused to provide one. She simply said that she would be leaving by the end of the week and that was the last she would say on the matter." Edwina's small fists crept to the sides of her hips leaving her looking like some sort of furious fairy.

"Well, I certainly didn't do anything to give the lass reason to leave us," Simpkins said.

He and Edwina turned their gazes on Beryl as if one body. Most of the time Beryl found that she and Simpkins had more in common than he ever did with Edwina. But on occasion, the two of them seemed to have some sort of tacit understanding of life in the village that she felt she would never quite comprehend. This was just one more of those occasions.

Despite the difference in their own class upbringing, they seemed to be of one mind when it came to how one engaged with domestic staff. Even with Simpkins's outrageous behavior in moving into the Beeches as a permanent resident or his unorthodox backchat when speaking with Edwina, he still understood that he was an outlier and did not represent the way one should interact with the average member of staff.

"Unless she says otherwise, I cannot think of a thing I've done to cause this to happen. I've been on my very best behavior ever since we returned from Maitland Hall. I wasn't even here this morning to do anything to rile her up, now was I?" Beryl said, turning to Simpkins with her palms upright in supplication.

Simpkins shifted and faced Edwina. "That's true. She went with me to the farm to help with the greengage harvest since Norman Davies called to cancel," Simpkins said.

"Then I simply cannot imagine what has happened."

"Perhaps she's been offered a better position elsewhere," Beryl said.

"I suppose that's possible," Edwina said, exchanging a cryptic look with Simpkins.

Beryl wondered if she was implying that a better position could be had anywhere that Beryl was not in residence. She was beginning to feel slightly defensive about the atmosphere in the room. It wasn't as though she gave extra trouble to the servants. While she wasn't the tidiest of persons, she didn't strew her possessions about the house, nor did she ask for any sorts of extra accommodations in any way. She had never ordered Beddoes to lug hot jugs of water to her room or whip up confections that only she enjoyed. She had never ordered her to do anything at all. No, this was not her fault, and if Beddoes had taken offense to something she couldn't even remember doing, then perhaps it would be best for her to leave.

"Well, as the age of serfdom is over, at least in England, I suppose there's nothing to be done if she's determined to leave. Dwelling on it will only make you more miserable. We shall simply have to advertise for a new member of staff and see who turns up. I'm sure we'll manage somehow even with your new responsibilities as the magistrate. Speaking of that, how did it go on your first day?" Beryl asked.

Edwina crossed the room and dropped into her own usual chair. She leaned forward and propped her elbows on her knees, cupping her chin in her hands.

"Things went along quite swimmingly at first despite my trepidation at fulfilling my duties. Charles was as sturdy and capable as always and I felt as though with his help I managed to navigate the first cases with little difficulty," Edwina said.

"It sounds as though something knocked things off course though," Beryl said.

"I'm afraid so. The reason Norman Davies wasn't able to join you in the greengage harvest was he was appearing before the bench," Edwina said.

"He told us about that when he finally got to the farm," Simpkins said. "Something about an anonymous letter."

"That reminds me. I should have thought of it at once," Beryl said. She reached into her pocket and pulled out the letter she had found in amongst the post. "I received something similar myself and found it rather amusing." She held it out to Edwina, who turned pale as soon as she saw the envelope.

"This came to the Beeches today?" Edwina asked.

"It must have done. It was piled up with the rest of the mail," Beryl said. "Take a look for yourself."

Edwina extracted the letter from within the envelope after carefully looking over the handwriting neatly printed on the outside. Beryl kept her eyes fixed on Edwina's face as she watched her friend read through the contents. A furious blush rose to Edwina's cheeks.

"This is preposterous and exactly the sort of troublesome thing that brought Norman Davies and Michael Blackburn before the bench. Not only that, but someone else has sent an anonymous letter espousing equally cruel things to Mrs. Dunstable at the Woolery. I must admit, I am alarmed by it all," Edwina said.

"Come now, you don't think anyone will credit this sort of nonsense as true, do you?" Beryl said.

"What's it say?" Simpkins asked.

Edwina pulled back as though she were not going to allow him to read it. Then with a flicker of determination crossing her face, she thrust the letter at him. Beryl had expected him to find it as amusing as she had. After all, Simpkins was always one for a joke and certainly not opposed to the notion that any ladies might fancy him. He seemed to think such things rather flattering. But rather than breaking out into an enormous grin or chortling delightedly, he simply shook his head solemnly.

"I don't like the sounds of this at all," he said. "It seems much like the one Norman received and as clearly bent on stirring up trouble."

"That was my thought exactly," Edwina said. "There doesn't seem to be any personal gain to be had by what was said, but only the satisfaction that causing trouble amongst one's neighbors might provide."

"But surely no one will take this seriously. It's so patently ridiculous that any thinking person would simply dismiss it out of hand without question," Beryl said.

Once again Edwina and Simpkins exchanged a significant look. A creeping feeling ran up the back of Beryl's neck. The pair of them looked deeply troubled.

"Things in a small village like Walmsley Parva are not the same as larger, more anonymous places. The type of rents in the social fabric that this sort of insinuation creates could prove permanently damaging. I am quite concerned about the consequences that may come of this," Edwina said.

"I'd have to agree," Simpkins said. "And bear in mind, not everyone who receives a letter like this would be willing to speak about it freely. In fact, I'm betting most people would keep it to themselves and suffer in silence. But the damage to the relationships they have with their neighbors would be done regardless of whether or not they speak out."

Edwina nodded. "This sort of thing could do untold damage to the community. I am really very worried about it. Unless I miss my guess, this is just the beginning."

There was no doubt about it, it had been the most trying morning Edwina had experienced in ages. In truth, she could not remember a day where so many disturbing things had happened in such rapid succession. It was one thing to have witnessed from the relative distance of the magistrate's bench the destructive force of a letter like the one Michael had received. It was quite another for such a missive to be slipped through the letterbox of one's own front door. And then to have Beddoes offer her resignation on top of it all was simply too much to be borne without the fortifying effects provided by a strong cup of tea, heavily sweetened.

Beryl could say what she liked about the stiffening power of a strongly alcoholic cocktail in the American fashion, but when push came to shove, as it certainly had that day, Edwina would always plump for a cup of hot sweet tea. Her teeth almost ached at the thought of it as she hurried down the hall towards the scullery.

Crumpet followed along behind her at a much more sedate pace than was his habit. He seemed to always know when she was feeling up for a spot of ball or would rather simply have his quiet companionship and soothing presence somewhere nearby. She resolved to carry her cup to the back garden and to sit upon a bench in the summerhouse where Crumpet could curl up next to her. She was not sure why his wiry fur was so soothing when she stroked his scruffy head, but that was simply how love worked, wasn't it? Inexplicable and utterly comforting.

Edwina was never one to create a great deal of noise as she passed by. Her mother would not have tolerated such behavior from a daughter and thus Edwina learned from an early age to carry her slight frame even more lightly than she might have done had she been raised by a woman not so attuned to appearances. As it happened, she was remarkably well prepared for life as a private enquiry agent, at least in terms of sneaking up on unsuspecting people caught in the act of villainy. And so it was she happened upon Beddoes so silently that the maid did not notice her as she stepped across the threshold of the scullery and spotted her housekeeper about to stuff a sheet of paper into the firebox of the cooker.

"Beddoes, stop that this instant," Edwina said, her voice unexpectedly sharp.

She took a step forward and snatched the piece of paper from her startled employee's hand. Beddoes straightened and a bright red flush covered her face. Edwina kept her eyes firmly averted from what she held. But as she stroked her thumb back and forth across the surface of the paper, she could feel the edges of words cut from newspapers grazing her skin.

"Please, miss, that's my property," Beddoes said, recovering her voice.

"Beddoes, I am not going to do you the disrespect of reading your private correspondence without your permission," Edwina said. "I would, however, like to know if what is contained within this letter is your reason for tendering your resignation."

Beddoes gasped. "How did you know about that, miss?" she asked, staggering backwards.

"I'm sorry to say there has been someone making a great deal of mischief here in the village by sending out the most distressing anonymous letters. The first I knew of it was when a case caused by one came before the bench this morning. Mrs. Dunstable at the Woolery has received another. And come to find out, Beryl has received a third. Without requiring a look at what is written upon the one you received, I can assure you that there is absolutely nothing in it that you should believe. I am quite certain it is reporting lies about you and lies about the fact that someone else was spreading them," Edwina said.

Beddoes's shoulders sagged, but Edwina could not tell if it was from distress or relief. Whatever had caused it, the fight had drained from her imperious housekeeper. Edwina risked the possibility of offending her and took her by the arm and guided her to the kitchen table. She gestured towards the chair and made sure Beddoes sat in it before she laid the letter face-down upon the table surface.

She turned her attention towards the teakettle, filling it with cool, fresh water and placing it upon the hob. It looked as though she was not the only one who would be benefiting from the healing properties of a strong cup of tea. She kept her back turned towards Beddoes, providing the other woman with the privacy she might need to collect herself. Edwina busied herself pulling china teacups and saucers, a pair of spoons, and the sugar bowl from the cupboard. She spooned loose tea leaves into a Brown Betty teapot, much like the one at the Woolery, and as soon as the kettle threatened to boil, pulled it off the cooker and doused the leaves with hot water. She snuck a peek at Beddoes, who had inched her fingers towards the offending letter and dragged it towards herself. Edwina carried the tea things to the table and then settled herself in the chair across from her employee.

"Don't you think you would feel much better if you told me what this was about?" she asked.

Beddoes glanced up at her, and for the first time since Edwina had met her some weeks before, she felt as though she were seeing the private woman behind the professional housekeeper. Edwina had respected the fact that Beddoes was a servant of the old-fashioned variety who maintained strict boundaries between herself and her employer and expected others to do the same. There was no informal nonsense about her interactions with the mistress of the house as there always had been with Simpkins.

However, that did not negate the fact that Beddoes was a living, breathing human being with a personal life and preferences, vulnerabilities, and a variety of foibles. As much as Edwina had appreciated the professional side of Beddoes, she was surprised she found this personal side of her much more intriguing.

"You're right about the letter. I should have told you about it rather than simply giving my notice, but it was so upsetting, you see, and I would not have wanted you to think poorly of me," she said.

"I can't imagine how I could possibly think poorly of you, Beddoes," Edwina said. "You are every inch the epitome of domestic perfection. I still have difficulty believing Simpkins managed to magic you here in the first place. I have no idea what I could possibly have done to deserve your assistance here at the Beeches. Short of you losing your mind and murdering us all in our beds, I can't think of anything you would do or that would be said about you to change my mind about you in the least," Edwina said.

Beddoes's eyes widened slightly as she took in Edwina's words. Perhaps she had not been in the habit of hearing many complimentary things said about her character or capabilities. Or perhaps Edwina had simply not been forthcoming enough about how much she valued what Beddoes had to provide. Whatever the reason, a crack had appeared in her impervious veneer.

"That's very good of you to say, miss," Beddoes said. "But you see, I wasn't quite sure how you would have felt about reading the contents of this letter. I couldn't have stood for you to think poorly of me. It's been such a privilege to work in a household where the mistress understands how things ought to be run and doesn't take any guff, if you know what I mean."

Edwina felt startled once more. She always thought of Beryl as the one who took no guff. Sometimes she felt as though all she did was find ways to circumvent the fuss and bother expected of women of good breeding. The fact that Beddoes had been able to articulate what she most hoped would be true of her, that she had found a way to walk the line between honoring the past and forging a new future, was not something she would have expected, and it touched her more deeply than she would have thought possible.

She cleared her throat and poured out two cups of tea, then slid the sugar bowl and a cup closer to Beddoes. The maid had come to a decision. She flipped the letter right side up and slid it across the table to Edwina.

"Are you sure about this?" Edwina asked.

Beddoes nodded without a word. Edwina reached for the letter and quickly read through the hateful message pasted upon the page. There in black and white someone had thought it his or her place to alert Beddoes to the information that Prudence Rathbone had been overheard stating in the post office that Beddoes had been forced to seek employment in a new town because she had been accused of theft at her previous employer's home.

No wonder Beddoes had not wanted to share the contents of the letter with Edwina. It was absolutely a devastating blow. Even in an age where it was almost impossible to acquire any sort of household help, let alone someone as skilled as Beddoes, such claims could destroy a career. Most would argue it would be vastly preferable to have no help at all than to allow thieves inside one's own home.

Not to mention, a reputation was all that a servant really had to stand on. If the accusation was made, most people would simply accept that it must be the truth. It was not the sort of thing to be bandied about lightly as everyone understood the consequences. It was simply not the done thing to falsely report something so damaging. How Beddoes must have suffered in the time between opening that particular letter and hearing Edwina's declaration that she was not alone in her torture.

"Do you see why I wouldn't have wanted you to read it?" Beddoes said, looking down into her teacup.

Edwina reached out a hand and tapped her fingers on Beddoes's wrist. The housekeeper looked up.

"I have no reason to believe anything written here. Even if others had not received such letters, I wouldn't have given it credit. However, I can see why you would have been terribly distressed to receive this. It is exceedingly malicious, and I assure you it will not go without consequences."

"What sort of consequences?" Beddoes asked, her voice trembling.

"Not consequences for you, but rather for the sender. While I know that you and Beryl have not always seen eye to eye on the way a household should be run, I can assure you that there is nothing she likes more than to put malicious gossip spreaders in their place. If you will consent to remain with us rather than giving your notice, I assure you that Beryl and I will do our utmost to get to the bottom of this."

"I wouldn't want you to go to any trouble," Beddoes said.

"It won't be any trouble at all. In fact, as far as Beryl would be concerned, I'm sure she will view it as a pleasure," Edwina said. "When she first came to Walmsley Parva, I was in the uncomfortable position of being the subject of some rather nasty gossip myself. And Prudence Rathbone had been the one spreading it, as you might well imagine from her reputation as the most confirmed gossip in the village."

Beddoes's eyes opened even wider. "I can't believe it, miss," she said.

"Well, it is the truth. And frankly the gossip that was being spread was unfortunately true. People of the serving class and working classes are not the only folks whose economic situations became quite strained over the past few years, and the sad fact of the matter is I had run up some overdue accounts with local merchants. Prudence made sure that no one forgot," Edwina said.

"But I thought that you were only putting that out as a rumor in order to get a message to Miss Beryl," Beddoes said.

So, Edwina thought, the gossip about her involvement as a secret agent of the Crown had made its way persistently through all members of the community, even those most recently arrived. She supposed she'd also have Prudence to thank for that.

"I'm sorry to say that Beryl not only has an informal relationship with domestic servants, but also with the truth. However, she oftentimes uses her unorthodox behavior to assist others, as she did in that case. I'm trusting you with this secret in hopes that you will have confidence in Beryl's interest in helping others who have found themselves the victim of such unpleasantness. I do hope you will keep it to yourself, however. I shouldn't wish for people to once again remark upon my previous financial situation," Edwina said.

"Your secret's safe with me, miss. But what do you think can be done about any of this?" Beddoes said.

"That's what we shall have to put our heads together and discover. But just leave it with me and with Beryl. Don't give it another thought," Edwina said, reaching for her teacup.

Beddoes released a deep sigh of relief and got to her feet. She allowed the barest flicker of a smile to pass across her features, and when she turned her back to begin washing up some crockery in the sink, Edwina was quite sure she heard her utterly professional servant begin to whistle under her breath. Edwina could only envy her. She had no idea how they would get to the bottom of any of it. But she was quite certain that something had to be done before matters got even further out of hand.

Chapter 6

Despite the fact that he was not previously engaged with an appearance before the Magistrate's Court, Norman Davies was once again unavailable to assist with the harvest. He was behind with his own small market garden as well as deliveries that he made for Mr. Scott, the local greengrocer. So, when Simpkins asked Beryl if she would accompany him once more to the farm to finish up the harvest, she readily agreed.

While she was feeling the effects of clambering up and down a ladder and hauling heavy bushels laden with fruit back to the cottage for processing, she could not deny the sense of satisfaction she had earned from doing a bit of physical labor. Besides, she clearly could use the exercise. And if she were to admit it, she would also say she had rather enjoyed the company of the Prentice family despite the fact that there were so many children underfoot.

And so, shortly after breakfast, she found herself pulling into the dooryard of Simpkins's farm once more. The children all piled out of the house as eager to greet them as they had been the previous day, and in no time at all they had each taken up positions scattered amongst the trees like so many monkeys swinging and hollering and diligently grasping ripe fruit. Everything had gone along quite swimmingly until suddenly Beryl heard one of the children cry out from two rows over.

Out of the corner of her eye she glimpsed the sudden movement of a figure heading precipitously downward. Before she realized what she was doing she found herself racing down her ladder and kneeling over one of the youngest Prentice children's crumpled forms. At first, she thought the child had been grievously injured. His eyes stared at her large and pleading, and no sound came from his lips, although he seemed to be straining for breath. With a start she realized he had knocked the wind out of himself, and she found her inclination was to offer him words of steady comfort. How unlike herself, she thought as she drew him to his feet and patted him gently on the back, all the while assuring him that the situation would resolve itself shortly.

No sooner had he taken a deep, shuddering breath than a steady trickle of blood flowed over his pale forehead and cascaded down past one of his sandy eyebrows. Fortunately, Beryl knew how to kit herself out for any sort of expedition, whether it be trekking across a vast desert or clamoring up a tree to pick fruit. She reached into her pocket and withdrew a cambric square, very like the ones she had carried with her on an untold number of adventures. Before Mrs. Prentice arrived at her son's side Beryl had folded it neatly and pressed it against the wound on his head. With remarkable speed, the makeshift bandage was soaked with the child's blood.

"I think you'd better call for a doctor," Beryl said.

Mrs. Prentice took one look at her son and dropped to her knees. Simpkins hurried to join them, and Beryl repeated her opinion about the need for the village doctor. Simpkins nodded and took off for the cottage far faster than Beryl would have expected possible considering the pace with which he usually moved through life.

"I don't think it's too serious, but I expect that it would be best for the doctor to take a look. I think he may suggest stitches," Beryl said quietly to Mrs. Prentice.

The boy clutched at her hand and squeezed it hard as her words reached his ears. Mrs. Prentice withdrew the bloody bandage and replaced it with a pocket handkerchief of her own. That too was soaked through in no time flat, and it was with some relief that in a quarter of an hour's time Beryl heard the sound of an approaching motorcar.

Beryl had expected Dr. Nelson, the village physician, to be the one who would appear to attend the child. But striding across the hillocky field was another person altogether. Simpkins loped along beside him, the pair of them an aged duo of urgency. Coming alongside Beryl, Dr. Wilcox placed his bag on the grass, lowering himself to his knees slowly and deliberately.

"I see you've lost an argument with a plum tree," the doctor said, having removed Mrs. Prentice's blood-soaked handkerchief and peering at a gash on the child's scalp. "You were right to call me. This is going to need some stitches to help it to heal properly. Let's get you inside, boy. I'm too old to work as a field surgeon."

With that he picked up his bag and got to his feet. Mrs. Prentice carried the boy back to the cottage and Beryl held back as the rest of the children gathered round their mother in a clamoring gang of excitement. Simpkins matched her pace, and she took the opportunity to ask about the newcomer.

"I would have thought that Dr. Nelson would have been the one to attend," Beryl said.

"Generally, he would be. I'm not sure why Dr. Wilcox is the one who showed up. Nurse Crenshaw said nothing about it when I telephoned Dr. Nelson's surgery," Simpkins said.

They caught up with the family and in no time the doctor had finished repairing the damage to the child. He scampered off to join his siblings for a game of tag in the field beyond the cottage.

"Oh, to be so young once more and so filled with energy and the blissful ability to forget," Dr. Wilcox said as he smiled at the child's retreating back.

"I thought that you were retired," Beryl said. "What happened to Dr. Nelson?"

"He has been unexpectedly called to take care of a personal matter. I said I would be happy to fill in for any emergencies that cropped up. This certainly qualified as one," the doctor said. "I may be old but I'm still capable of stitching up a few scalps over the course of a day."

"You seem to have made quick work of it," Beryl said. "And it was good of you to come."

"It makes for change now and again. Although I do see a few patients still from the old days. It's nice to keep my hand in. Speaking of former patients, how is Edwina keeping?" he asked.

"Edwina is in fine fettle. You must have heard she's serving as the magistrate," Beryl said.

"I had heard something to that effect. It made quite a bit of gossip and comment at the gardening club meeting the other day when she once again was not in attendance."

"Edwina has not had the same amount of time for any of her former activities lately. Between her work with the private enquiry agency and her volunteer position as the magistrate, she has been pressed for time," Beryl said.

"Very worthy, I'm sure. Still, she missed a good meeting, I can tell you that much. People brought in a quantity of plant cuttings to swap, and I had brought in some blossoms from my nerium that has finally come into bloom. I had been particularly hoping she would have made it because I know she was eager to see how it turned out."

"I'm sorry she missed it," Simpkins said. "I'm sure it was a beauty."

"I'll tell you what, why don't you let Edwina know that she's welcome to stop by anytime to see it in the garden. I know that she would find it just delightful," the doctor said, snapping his case shut and grasping it by the handles. He swung it off the table and then with a cheery wave headed for the door.

Edwina had decided to spend a few hours at the desk working on her novel as a balm for the previous day's distresses. She had just rolled a third crisp, white sheet of typewriting paper underneath the roller bar of her Remington portable when she heard Beddoes's discreet knock at the door. Her heart seized and she gave a thought to the possibility that once again her domestic servant was about to offer her notice. Edwina pushed the thought from her mind and bid her enter.

Beddoes gave no sign of abandoning her post as she popped her head round the corner of the door and announced that Constable Gibbs was requesting a visit. Edwina waved to signal she should escort the officer into the morning room, then set aside her thoughts of Bart Dalton's further adventures, at least for the time being.

Constable Gibbs appeared in the doorway a moment later. If Edwina had not known her for ages, she would have had difficulty discerning the look of unease stamped across her countenance. But as Edwina had spent time in Doris Gibbs's company under any number of circumstances, and in an ever-increasing collaborative professional relationship, she could see that something was troubling her.

The constable did not bluster and fuss as was her usual habit. Instead, she plopped herself down without invitation into the desk chair opposite Edwina and leaned across the desk.

"You look as though something is weighing on your mind, Doris," Edwina said encouragingly.

Constable Gibbs nodded. "Some very disturbing news has reached my ears, but it's of an extremely delicate nature. I trust that I can count on your discretion if I ask for your opinion," Constable Gibbs said.

Edwina thought back to the beginning of her private enquiry venture with Beryl some months earlier. How much had changed since then, not the least of which was her relationship with Constable Doris Gibbs. Where once the officer had done anything within her power to hold the private investigators at arm's length or to outright forbid them from pursuing lines of enquiry into any local wrongdoings, now she was eagerly soliciting collaboration.

Edwina thought it was a mark of growth on both their parts that Constable Gibbs would seek her out in this way. She felt a warm glow of pride in both of them and nodded enthusiastically despite the fact that she had no desire to hear any more upsetting news.

"Of course, you can count on my discretion. What is it that I can help you with?"

"I've just been speaking with Dr. Nelson on a grievous matter. Of course, you will remember the letter Michael Blackburn received that caused so much of a dustup with Norman Davies," Constable Gibbs said.

"Naturally. Have the pair of them gotten into more trouble? I thought it looked as though they had resolved their differences when they left the court yesterday," Edwina said.

"No, the trouble is not with Michael and Norman. But it is related to their difficulty. The letter writer who started the trouble in the first place seems to have been at it again," Constable Gibbs said.

Edwina leaned backwards in her chair, hoping that the constable had not heard anything about Beddoes's note. She was not sure that her employee would believe her if she said that she had not shared that information outside the four walls of the Beeches.

"Someone else has received a similar letter?" Edwina said,

unsure that she had any right to share Mrs. Dunstable's worries, either. If Mrs. Dunstable did not wish to share them with Constable Gibbs, she was not sure that it was her place to do so on her behalf.

"I've just come from the Nelson residence. Dr. Nelson called me in because his wife received a similar letter. This is the part that you mustn't mention to anyone besides Beryl," Constable Gibbs said. Edwina nodded encouragingly. The constable continued. "Mrs. Nelson's letter said that she was being accused by Nurse Crenshaw of being the one responsible for the death of her son Alan."

Edwina gasped. What a terribly cruel thing to say to a grieving mother. "But he died of influenza," she said.

"The letter acknowledged that, but the anonymous sender said that people were saying that if she had not been so neglectful, he would have survived his bout with the flu," Constable Gibbs said.

"What a monstrous thing to have done," Edwina said. "It has come to my attention that there's been quite a rash of these letters running through the village. I am afraid that it would be breaking a confidence to tell you the names of all of the people who have received them, but I can tell you that Beryl has been a recipient. One arrived here at the Beeches only yesterday."

"I'm afraid it's a little more complicated than simply the fact that she received the letter," Constable Gibbs said.

"More complicated?" Edwina asked.

"While I promised Dr. Nelson that I would make no official investigation into what occurred, the fact of the matter is Mrs. Nelson attempted to take her own life after she received it. It was a wonder she didn't succeed, according to her husband," Constable Gibbs said.

Edwina's heart sank. Margery Nelson had been a charming woman in the years prior to her son's death. She had been one of those sweet and unassuming types who was a pleasant hostess and willing participant on any volunteer committees in which she took part. She was a pretty woman who took care with her own appearance and had taken great delight in the way she cared for her son. Alan Nelson had been not quite two years old when the influenza epidemic that swept through the nation had laid him in his grave.

Margery had never fully recovered from the loss and had in fact blamed herself. She had gone through repeated bouts of despondency ever since his death and it could easily be argued that anyone remotely familiar with her circumstance would have been well aware of how much damage such a letter could do. The fact that the writer of the letters blamed Nurse Crenshaw was even crueler somehow.

Nurse Crenshaw was exactly the sort of practical and efficient kind of woman that Margery was not. In many ways Nurse Crenshaw had taken over the sorts of roles that doctor's wives often shouldered for their husbands. She kept the doctor's diary in order, was a sounding board for his concerns about his patients, and even had been known to perform small tasks like shopping for gifts for family members when Margery could not find it in herself to do so. Such a terrible accusation combined with a sense of betrayal by one close to the family would have been doubly harmful.

"How is it that you think I can help?" Edwina asked.

"I promised Dr. Nelson that I would not make an official enquiry into his wife's suicide attempt. As such a thing is illegal it would just make matters far worse, and I don't see how that's in anyone's best interest. But I do think that it would be best for the village overall for a stop to be put to this sort of nonsense. I don't like this malicious behavior going on in the village, not on my watch. But I don't know that I can officially investigate without causing a stir. Which is where you come in," Constable Gibbs said.

"I'd be happy to do anything I can to help. Since this situation had already come to my attention outside the Magistrate's Court, Beryl and I already have a client for whom we are working. We could certainly pursue this along with that investigation without raising any eyebrows," Edwina said.

"Would you like to share who your client is?"

"You do understand that the nature of the accusations are entirely false and simply meant to do harm, correct?" Edwina said in a hushed tone. While she did feel that she owed Beddoes the benefit of privacy, she did not think that there was anything to be gained by keeping Constable Gibbs completely in the dark. In fact, the constable had resources she herself did not have and the two of them worked well when they collaborated.

"After what Dr. Nelson showed me, I would be inclined to dismiss any rumors lodged in these letters. You can feel confident that I will not hold what's contained in one against whoever received it," Constable Gibbs said.

"Privately, we will be pursuing an investigation to get to the bottom of a very injurious letter received by my housekeeper, Beddoes. But publicly, in order to keep her name out of things and to keep her reputation from being sullied, we will be pursuing it on behalf of Beryl and myself."

Constable Gibbs allowed herself a ghost of a smile.

"I imagine there are plenty of things anyone bent on mischief might have to say about Beryl. And honestly, your unconventional living arrangements with Simpkins," Constable Gibbs said.

"Are you sure you're not the one who wrote the letter yourself?" Edwina asked.

"I wouldn't have had to have written it to imagine what could be low hanging fruit on the vine of village gossip. You may have managed to ignore it, but there have certainly been plenty of things said about Simpkins moving into your back bedroom. While most people pay it no mind, it certainly has made for some lively conversations across bridge tables, at the

Women's Institute meetings, and certainly at the Dove and Duck."

Edwina leaned back and tented her fingers. She felt as if she were floating above herself and looking down at the exchange with the constable. Only months earlier, when the economic situation she had described to Beddoes had been raging, Edwina had been so humiliated by the rumors being spread about her that she hadn't been able to bring herself to go into town for any purpose whatsoever. She had become no more than a hermit, keeping to the property boundaries of the Beeches, or occasionally taking Crumpet for long rambles in the woods where she would be unlikely to encounter any of her fellow villagers.

But since Beryl's arrival, she had felt the imaginary shackles that were made of concern for the opinions of others falling away link by link. It amazed her how little effect this news had upon her sense of well-being. People could say whatever they wanted, and it really made no difference as to who she actually was inside or how she chose to comport herself. It was entirely liberating, and she wished that more people might feel the same way. People like Mrs. Dunstable and Beddoes. Certainly, people like Margery Nelson.

"It wouldn't take a particularly creative person to come up with regurgitating rumors that are already in existence.," Edwina said.

"I really hadn't thought of that. You don't suppose Nurse Crenshaw actually had been spreading that kind of gossip about Mrs. Nelson, do you?" Constable Gibbs asked.

"If so, it's particularly hateful," Edwina said. "And why would she do such a thing?"

"Sometimes, for a private investigator, I think you're a bit sheltered for your own good. There have been plenty of instances of women falling in love with their employers. If

Dr. Nelson suddenly became a grieving widower, Nurse Crenshaw might not continue to be unmarried for long."

The notion was shocking, and one Edwina did not much care to entertain. She had no real fondness for Nurse Crenshaw, but she didn't like to imagine something so cold-blooded from her. The very idea left her feeling deeply unsettled long after Constable Gibbs had taken her leave.

Chapter 7

Constable Gibbs was trundling along the hallway towards the front door as Beryl entered. The constable greeted her but hurried on her way. That suited Beryl just fine. After the events of the morning, she was eager to have a decent lunch and to sit back with her feet up, preferably for a bit of an afternoon nap in the summerhouse in the garden. There was nothing quite so restorative in her considered opinion, besides a dry martini, as half an hour's rest in the fresh air and the shade.

But first she had a message to deliver from Dr. Wilcox as well a project to undertake on Simpkins's behalf. She found Edwina right where she expected to, in the morning room seated at the desk. Nothing sent her friend for the comfort of imaginary worlds of her novel like a stressful few hours on the domestic front. But when she arrived in the morning room, she found Edwina not bent over the typewriter as she had expected but pacing the rug that ran the length of the room. Clearly the constable had shared something that had added even more concern to her already burdened shoulders.

"I just saw Constable Gibbs leaving the house. Had she come about something important?" Beryl asked.

Edwina halted her pacing and nodded.

"I am sorry to say that the poisoned pen has struck again, only this time the consequences have been far more serious than someone tendering their resignation. Dr. Nelson's wife, Margery, received one accusing her of being responsible for her son's death through her negligence. She just tried to kill herself," Edwina said.

Beryl was not easily shocked. She had known many people throughout the war years to be driven to the brink of despondency. She had sometimes felt she could almost understand their feelings. But in the end, no matter how difficult things became, she had so much enthusiasm for each day as it came, no matter how bleak it might be, that she could not imagine herself putting an end to things, at least not deliberately.

She had often been accused of neglecting to value her personal safety to the point of being careless of her own life. But it had not ever occurred to her to follow through with anything directly self-destructive. She had more of a devil-may-care attitude towards such matters, trusting in the belief that if it was her time to go, go she would. If it wasn't, she wouldn't attempt to hasten things along. That did however explain why Dr. Wilcox was the one to attend to the Prentice child that morning. Dr. Nelson would have obviously needed to make his wife and her care a priority.

"How absolutely ghastly. But what was it that the constable wanted besides to inform you of what had happened? Did she think we ought to pay a call on Dr. Nelson or on Margery?"

Edwina shook her head. "No, she wanted us to investigate. Since suicide is a crime, bringing any official attention to what happened would simply add cruelty upon cruelty. But getting to the bottom of this troublemaking is in the best interest of the entire village."

"I expect you're right. Considering the venom of the letters, who knows where else it might lead."

"I anticipated that you would agree, so I told her we'd be

happy to help out. I suggested that we use the letter you received as the reason we are investigating. I was quite sure you wouldn't mind, considering it amused you so much yesterday when you received it," Edwina said.

Beryl was surprised and not just a little pleased. The Edwina she had encountered months earlier would never have considered suggesting airing dirty laundry in front of the village no matter the circumstances. She would have been far too concerned with what others thought to put herself in such a position. Beryl thought her influence upon her friend was a part of the reason for her change of attitude, but she expected that the successes Edwina had enjoyed in the cases they had solved might have played a part in her transformation as well. Beryl had always found that nothing built confidence like trying something difficult and succeeding, especially if that something was a task or role for which one felt entirely unprepared.

"So, we have a new case to work on then," Beryl said.

"I suppose we do. Although this one is not going to provide us with any form of monetary compensation, I shouldn't think."

"Perhaps we should consider that some of our cases are really more about the public good," Beryl said.

"I should like to think that all of our cases boiled down to being for the common good," Edwina said. "But I would prefer that we were doing our part to make a go of it financially with the business. I don't like to feel as though we are simply being subsidized by Simpkins's generosity rather than earning our own way," Edwina said.

"It's funny you should mention that. I have a way that we can repay his generosity if you're willing to try something a bit out of the ordinary," Beryl said.

Edwina was not always the most interested in trying something new. Beryl had to give her credit for all the ways in which she had adapted to the way the world had shifted beneath her feet and even had taken on new rules of late. But despite her recent successes in the growth department, her first reaction to such opportunities was never one of enthusiasm. Generally speaking, she needed to be worked around and maneuvered in order to say yes to such things.

"What is it you have in mind?" Edwina asked, a shadow flickering across her face.

"Simpkins has told me of an idea he's had for a new line of convenience food products to be added to Colonel Kimberly's offerings," Beryl said.

"What in the world is a convenience food?" Edwina asked, a furrow developing between her two dark eyebrows.

"It's a sort of prepared food item that makes it easier for the cook. Apparently, such things are starting to gain a little bit of market share and he wants to be a part of it," Beryl said.

"Like what sorts of prepared foods?" Edwina asked.

"He mentioned things like soups and stews and even some of his curry concoctions that he's forever whipping up here in the kitchen of the Beeches. He thought that by offering them in tins and jars for people to simply open and heat, he might create an entirely new revenue stream for the company," Beryl said.

"I suppose there are people who might find that useful," Edwina said in a tone that sounded less than convinced.

"That's just what he was hoping you would say," Beryl said.

"Why? Does he wish for me to taste-test some of what he develops?" Edwina said. "You know I don't care particularly for all his curries."

Sadly, that had proven to be the case. Beryl was more than enthusiastic about foods with a bit more spice, but Edwina seemed content with tried-and-true experiences, at least in the culinary space. Why she exhibited so much curiosity towards other areas of life and so little towards branching out into using seasonings beyond salt and herbs she could grow in pots in her own garden Beryl would never know. Black pepper seemed to be about as much spice as Edwina wished to allow near her fork.

"No, not as a taste-tester. He had something rather more interesting in mind for the pair of us," Beryl said. "Do you know whom he is imagining as the most enthusiastic adopters of this line of convenience foods?"

"I should think it would be anyone who was responsible for doing the cooking. So, women I suppose," Edwina said.

Beryl nodded. "Exactly. But he hopes to appeal to a very specific sector of that market. He's interested in attracting the attention and the pounds and pence of working women. Women rather like us," Beryl said.

The furrow in between Edwina's eyebrows deepened. "I suppose we are working women now, aren't we?"

"We most assuredly are. And you haven't had a great deal of time to spend in the kitchen of late, have you?"

"No, I suppose I haven't. Between my magisterial duties, the enquiry agency, and writing my novel, I expect we would be surviving on beans on toast if it weren't for the help Simpkins has been providing."

"Which is exactly the sort of thing Simpkins is hoping that you would be willing to be quoted as saying. He'd like to use our images and our words in print advertising for the company."

"Simpkins wants us to appear in magazines or newspapers supporting his new line of food products?" Edwina asked.

"Precisely. Who better than a local magistrate or a pair of females in a private enquiry agency to be the very model of modern womanhood when setting new standards for how to feed one's family?"

"Do you really think we qualify as modern women?" Edwina asked, her eyes wide with astonishment.

"I most certainly think that we do. I've always considered myself at the forefront of such things and you have come up to speed with remarkable swiftness. I think that the fact that you have lived as a much more traditional woman for most of your life adds extra weight to your words. The times are changing, and you know how to change with them. You would serve as an incredibly inspiring spokesperson for any product you set your mind to, but certainly something like this," Beryl said, hoping she hadn't laid it on a little too thick.

Edwina was as likely to glow under the spotlight of some well-earned praise as the next woman, but she had an innate sense of modesty that would not allow her to accept compliments she felt she had not earned or ones that were exaggerated.

"I suppose if it would be of service to him, especially considering this case isn't likely to pay dividends, the least we could do is acquiesce," Edwina said. "You say there will be photographs?"

"Putting a face to the words is important if it is to be convincing. But you needn't worry about that part of things. I told Simpkins I would take care of arranging the photo session myself."

"I suppose, in that case, I should consider purchasing a new hat," Edwina said, allowing her gaze to drift to the ceiling with dreamy rapture.

Beryl knew that settled it. If there was one thing that could convince Edwina to take on a task she was not terribly inclined to tackle, it was the promise of a new hat.

Despite the intriguing distraction Simpkins's request provided, Edwina's thoughts kept returning again and again to Margery Nelson and to whoever could have been hateful enough to send her such a malicious letter. As much as it would have been comforting to imagine that there was no one in her beloved village who would go to such injurious lengths, she was not fool enough to believe it.

Evil-mindedness lurked in the most charming of places and to pretend it did not would do her no credit, especially as a private enquiry agent and modern sort of woman. Besides, the content of the letters was too knowledgeable to be attributed to an outsider. The sender had to know the members of the community well enough to be so well-equipped to harm them. The contents of the letters were outrageous or easily disproved, but the effect on the recipients was calculated to inflict damage in such a way that indicated an intimacy with the local residents.

While she had no interest in upsetting either Margery or Dr. Nelson, there was no way she could get to the bottom of who was writing the letters without paying a call to the Nelson residence. She powdered her nose and selected her second-best hat, a modest and somewhat somber piece of millinery from the hall tree. Pulling on a dark pair of net gloves and ascertaining that she had plenty of pages still left in her tiny notebook, she set off on foot for the Nelsons' home.

The day was a warm one and she made sure to take her time in order to not arrive looking disheveled. The Nelsons lived near the center of the village and in a quarter of an hour's time Edwina found herself standing before their tidy house with its attached surgery. Grebe Cottage had not always been a doctor's surgery. Dr. Wilcox had kept the home he had used for his own surgery when he retired and turned the practice over to Dr. Nelson only a few years earlier. Dr. Wilcox had put in considerable time and energy in developing his garden and wished to spend even more time on it once the daily responsibility for a medical practice was no longer his.

Not that Edwina was surprised. His gardens were an inspiration, and she always enjoyed the opportunity to pay a call to him there several times a year in order to see them. In fact, she had been absolutely delighted when Beryl had delivered a message from Dr. Wilcox informing her that his nerium was in bloom, and he wished for her to stop by to see it. She had regretted missing the chance to chat with him about his newest acquisitions and goings on when she missed the garden club meeting. She looked forward to their chats and made a mental note to send him a card asking when would be best to stop by.

The Nelsons, on the other hand, were no gardeners. While they could not be criticized for having an untidy patch of ground surrounding their home, it could not be said that it was in the least bit artistic or charming. The lawn surrounding the stone building was green and well-tended, but no other ornaments beyond a pair of yews flanking either side of the front door were to be seen. No window boxes graced the front of the stone cottage, nor did any garden beds filled with cheerful blooms dot the flat ground. Not even an urn overflowing with some sort of annual plant sat on the wide stone step leading to the front door. No, it would have been a terrible shame if Dr. Nelson and his wife had taken over Dr. Wilcox's property upon his retirement.

Edwina raised her small, gloved hand and firmly grasped the polished brass knocker shaped like a lion head. No one came to the door and after a few moments' pause she rapped upon it again, a bit more rigorously. She leaned her head close to the door and heard the sound of approaching footfalls. She reached up and straightened her hat just before the door creaked open. Dr. Nelson stood before her looking far less cocky than was his habit.

Charcoal-colored smudges sagged beneath his eyes, and he appeared to have aged by a decade. His hair looked as though he had not run a comb through it in days and his shirt had likely been worn the day before if the wrinkles and splotches it sported were any indication. On his feet he wore a pair of carpet slippers and Edwina found herself feeling rather startled by the pathetic and most unwelcome intimacy provided by a bit of his bare feet showing beneath his trouser cuffs. Somehow it seemed unseemly to be so starkly confronted with his grief.

"Miss Davenport, if you are unwell, I'm afraid I shall have to direct you to Dr. Wilcox. I am unable to attend to patients at present. The surgery is closed for the time being due to a family emergency," he said, making to close the door in her face.

"Dr. Nelson, I'm not here about myself. I'm here about Margery," Edwina said.

"Margery is not accepting any callers right now, either," he said.

"I am well aware of that. Constable Gibbs paid a call upon me today and asked that I speak with you discreetly. Perhaps that would be best done outside the view of interested passersby," Edwina said.

The doctor peered over her shoulder and nodded. It was never an easy thing to keep gossips at bay in such a small village. The longer Edwina stood standing and chatting with him in view of any pedestrians or motorists, the more likely it was that there would be speculation. Just the fact that she called upon him at all would be certain to arouse notice. Edwina was famous for her robust good health, and the idea that she would be attending the doctor's surgery would certainly provoke comment. He stepped back and drew the door open wide to allow her to pass into the hallway before firmly shutting it behind her. He led her down the short passageway and turned left into the wing of the house that had been converted into the doctor's surgery.

"I'm not sure what good Constable Gibbs thought it would do to involve you, Miss Davenport. I think of this as a matter that is no one's concern outside my own and my wife's," he said.

He lowered himself gingerly into the chair behind his large wooden desk like a man stricken with a terrible bout of arthritis. Edwina perched at the edge of the chair reserved for patients. She couldn't shake the sense that she might contract some sort of terrible disease simply by being in the same space as those persons who were ill. Perhaps it was the influenza epidemic that had left its mark upon her, but such worries, no matter how unfounded, were hard to dismiss.

Adding to her unease was the fact that Edwina had never been impressed by Dr. Nelson. Her dealings with him in the past had proven that his character was not of the caliber she would have expected to see in a medical professional. She felt doctors, who were in possession of sensitive information, ought to be held to a higher standard than the average person. She thought of them much as she did her dear friend and solicitor Charles—that they were bound to behave ethically in a way that other people might not be required to.

But in her opinion, Dr. Nelson had missed the mark somewhat. Not only had his previous behavior led her to be somewhat distrustful of him, she had not found him to be someone to whom she warmed based on his brusque personality. He had behaved patronizingly towards her and had acted as though any problems she might be facing were a result of her advancing age and lamentable spinsterhood. In fact, she had experienced him as the sort of man who dismissed women out of hand, and she found him more than a little repellent as a result of it. Even though she rarely needed the services of a doctor for herself, she had vastly preferred those of Dr. Wilcox before his retirement.

However, the man sitting before her was a pathetic specimen indeed. The worries about his wife seemed to have taken a terrible toll upon him. Edwina did not wish to make him suffer any further discomfort by prying into his private affairs, but unfortunately since what had happened to Margery was likely part of a larger problem, it couldn't be helped.

"The constable asked me to speak with you not as a matter of salacious gossip or to trouble you at what is already a difficult time, but rather in a preventative way," Edwina said.

"Preventative? The damage is already done. Not to put too

fine a point on it—my wife is lucky to be alive," Dr. Nelson said.

"But that's just it, you see. Your wife is not the only one to suffer," Edwina said.

"The letter said nothing about anyone else. I can't see how it has anything to do with others," Dr. Nelson said.

"Do you happen to still have the letter? It would be very helpful if I could see it," Edwina said.

"I destroyed it immediately, of course. After the effect it had on Margery, I could not permit her to encounter it accidentally for a second time," he said. "And frankly I am surprised at you. I can't understand your ghoulish interest in someone else's hate mail. This isn't any business of yours."

"It is not a matter of sordid curiosity, I assure you. I'm sorry to say that Margery is not the only person to have received a deeply disturbing letter from an anonymous sender recently," Edwina said. "You may have heard that I have begun to serve as the magistrate for the village."

"I had heard something to that effect," Dr. Nelson said, with a look passing across his face that expressed disapproval. "What does that have to do with my wife? I was assured by the constable that no charges would be pressed, so I cannot see how this matter has anything to do with the court."

"I assure you I meant nothing like that. It's just that a case came before the bench this week that involved a similarly distressing letter. Other people, including Beryl, have received them as well. Could you describe the letter to me?"

"I'm sure the constable informed you as to its contents. I can't see how going over it all again will be of use."

"I didn't mean the contents of the letter but rather the physical nature of the letter. Was there anything memorable about the way it was written, the sort of stationery used, or the handwriting?" Edwina asked.

The doctor leaned back in his chair and gazed at her steadily. He allowed a long moment before he spoke.

"I see. The letter Margery received had a very carefully printed address on the envelope. The letter itself was constructed of words cut from magazines and newspapers and then pasted down on a very ordinary sheet of writing paper. There was nothing to indicate the identity of the sender in what I saw."

"That sounds exactly like all of the other letters."

"That may well be, but I hope that you will keep what I've shared with you to yourself. Neither of us wants to be responsible for the consequences if Margery is distressed any further, I'm sure," he said, pushing back his chair and getting to his feet.

"Margery's name will not be connected to my investigation in any quarter that would be damaging to her, I promise you," Edwina said. "She has been through far too much already."

"We both have," the doctor said.

Edwina supposed that was true. Not only had the doctor also lost his child, but his wife was no longer capable of being the sort of helpful companion he had first married. Instead, she was a shell of her former self and someone who struggled much of the time to perform ordinary tasks or to be engaged in any of the sorts of enthusiasms she could well imagine a man like Dr. Nelson would wish to participate in.

A chilling thought struck Edwina as the doctor showed her to the door. She had never been particularly impressed by his character and in fact had not thought of him as a particularly good husband in many ways. But she supposed it could be argued that Margery had not ended up being the sort of wife he might like to live out his days alongside. Who better than Dr. Nelson to know exactly what sort of disturbance might push his wife over the edge? Was it possible that he himself had been the one who wanted to drive her to such a length as might rid him of her in the end? Could he have sent the letter to her himself?

Chapter 8

After receiving consent from Edwina that she would participate in the advertising campaign, Beryl eagerly set to work to make it happen. She felt a lightness and a zest in her heart that had been missing over the last few days. Every now and again she missed being off on a wild adventure, and if truth were told, the spotlight of being a celebrated adventuress had suited her remarkably well. She wasn't a publicity hound exactly, but her lifestyle had garnered widespread attention and she had never sought to shirk it.

It was good business, after all, to be the darling of the press and she knew exactly how to play to an audience. It seemed like ages since she had been the focus of any kind of attention from a camera and so it was with a great deal of enthusiasm that she pushed open the plate glass door of the local photography studio and stepped inside.

Beryl had yet to have any interactions with Bernard Stevens, but she had seen him from a distance around the village traipsing about with his camera equipment. He seemed to have an inexplicable passion for photographing the ducks who spent their days at the pond in the village green. If she were to be honest, she had rather avoided him on previous occasions as she was not holding out a great deal of hope that a man who found ducks to be such a worthy subject for photographs would be likely to be a scintillating conversationalist.

Still, he was the only photographer in Walmsley Parva and had a decent reputation as a man who knew his business. Certainly, he would be capable of creating photographs sufficient for the sort of print advertising Simpkins seemed to have in mind. If they had required someone with a moving picture camera, she would have looked further afield to be sure. But for something that would be printed in black and white in a grainy newspaper edition she was sure his services would suffice.

She entered the shop and looked around but found herself quite alone. She stood in front of the counter where an array of photographs used as examples of his work were spread out. Perhaps he was busy with something in his darkroom. She looked up and down the counter and spotted a bell. She leaned over and gave it three quick thumps, sending a loud peal through the shop. After a moment she heard a shuffling sound coming from the back room and in the doorway Bernard himself appeared.

Her first impression was that he looked nothing like the man she had seen blissfully snapping photographs of local waterfowl. In fact, if she had to guess, she would say she was in the presence of a man practically choking on rage. His face was the color of a dusky plum and his breath came in shallow pants. Clutched in his hand was a sheet of paper that sent a shiver of recognition up her spine.

"Mr. Stevens, if I had to guess I would say that you have received a rather nasty letter," Beryl said, leaning across the counter and batting her long eyelashes at him.

She had found that sometimes such behavior by an attractive woman drove murderous thoughts from men's heads. And

Bernard Stevens looked as though murder was on his mind. He opened his mouth widely and then snapped it shut again. He lifted his hand and rattled the paper in her direction.

"How did you guess that?" he said.

"Because I've received one myself. I expect that it says that one of your neighbors or friends is making nasty comments about you in a public place. Am I right?" Beryl asked.

"That's exactly what it says and there's not a word of truth in it," he shouted.

"I'm sure there is not anything in it worth believing. The same could be said for my letter and a few others that have been distributed about the village. I wouldn't let it trouble you. I'm not letting mine bother me in the least," she said.

"You're not?" he said, his eyes widening.

"Of course not. I wouldn't give the letter writer the pleasure of seeing it bother me. I would advise you not to either," Beryl said.

"But it could ruin my business. I've half a mind to hire you and Miss Davenport to get to the bottom of this. I simply can't let a thing like this stand." He thrust the letter towards her. "See for yourself."

Beryl read through the letter quickly, nodding at the appropriate spots. Truly he had good reason to feel as though he was being attacked. The letter writer indicated that Chester White, the village bookie, had accused him of snapping salacious photographs of local women either with or without their knowledge. It was decidedly grubby.

"This doesn't sound a bit like Chester. No bookie worth the name runs around gossiping like that. A bookmaker needs to remain discreet," she said.

"It says he's accusing me of being a Peeping Tom. And taking that sort of photograph, even with permission, could land me in hot water," he said. "I haven't given Chester reason to put a black mark against my name. I've never even been one of his customers."

"I'm sure that this is all just a bit of mischief, but if you would like to hire Edwina and me to look into it, I'm sure that we could find some time to fit you in."

"I would appreciate that. It would help me be able to get my mind back on my own business if I knew that someone was getting to the bottom of this."

"I'll see to it just as soon as I get back to the Beeches this afternoon. But I wasn't here to drum up business for myself. I stopped in because I would like to hire you," Beryl said.

"What did you have in mind?" Mr. Stevens asked, looking her up and down as if to assess whether or not she was particularly photogenic.

"I assume that you are capable of being discreet," Beryl said. "The matter I wish to discuss with you requires secrecy."

"I hope you are not implying that this letter means I'm open to snapping the types of photographs that should not be taken," he said, taking a step backward.

"No, nothing of the sort. It's simply a matter of business advantage. I wish to hire you to take some photographs for an advertising campaign, but it's important that competitors do not hear what's in the works before the campaign is launched," she said.

Mr. Stevens's shoulders lowered away from his overly large ears. Truly the concern about being seen as a risqué photographer had struck a nerve. She wondered if there really was something to the story. Did he have something to hide? She wondered what would happen when Edwina heard about the letter. She was not certain Edwina had become quite modern enough to have truck with someone tainted by that sort of a reputation.

"Now, that's something I'd be happy to do," he said. "What did you have in mind?"

"I need a photography session for myself and Edwina to promote some new products being offered through Colonel Kimberly's Condiment Company. I was thinking that something creative involving the kitchen at the Beeches might be arranged. Would that be of interest to you?"

Mr. Stephens drummed his fingers against the countertop.

"That sounds right up my alley. I will take a look at my diary and see when we could arrange a time that is suitable to all of us. Why don't you consult with Miss Davenport and then we will set something up? Here's my card. It has the telephone number for the studio printed upon it should you wish to save yourself the trip into the village. Perhaps we could work out an exchange of services rather than an exchange of money," he said. "I could do the photographs for you, and you could get to the bottom of this letter writing for me."

Beryl was always of a mind to accept bartering as a superior way of conducting business. She reached her hand across the counter, and they shook on it.

Edwina left Dr. Nelson's surgery feeling disconcerted. She liked to think of herself as someone who was able to seek the truth regardless of her personal opinions. After all, Charles would not have recommended her to serve as magistrate if she were someone inclined to be swayed by personal feeling alone. That said, she wondered if her concerns about Dr. Nelson stemmed more from her poor opinion of him than the likelihood of his culpability. She felt greatly in need of some perspective and from someone who would view the matter through the lens of a village insider.

While Beryl presented an invaluable balance to her own perspective on the world, sometimes the two of them looked at things from such opposite ends of the situation that it could be a rather circuitous route to arriving at a conclusion. She desired to speak with somebody who would be both discreet and who had a tacit understanding of the stakes involved. Beryl's wider view of the world outside village life was admirable and fascinating on most occasions. But it did sometimes render her less capable of seeing the way small incidents would accrue and turn into larger problems over time. Beryl had not had much experience of interacting again and again with the same few people and navigating the pitfalls that such a life can offer. As much as Edwina valued her dear friend's opinion on so many matters, this was perhaps not the sort of thing best discussed with her.

No, the person she wished to speak with was Mrs. Lowethorpe, the vicar's wife. Making her way down the street and leaving the surgery behind her, she turned down a narrow lane that led to the vicarage. Generally, Mrs. Lowethorpe could be found off doing good works of every sort. But it just so happened at this time of day she could always be counted upon to be at the vicarage listening to a radio drama that she had once, in an unguarded moment, confessed to Edwina she never missed. Edwina glanced up at the clock in the bell tower of the church and noted with relief that, if she dawdled, the radio program should be coming to a conclusion by the time she reached the vicarage. She slowed her pace just slightly in order to provide her friend with the time she would need to switch off the wireless and to appear as though she had been engaged in far more productive pursuits.

Edwina stepped up to the vicarage door and rapped upon it just two minutes past the time the radio program should have concluded. She could not see any particular reason to feel invested in the personal lives of characters featured on programs such as the one Mrs. Lowethorpe enjoyed, but she did know the pleasure that tuning into an entertaining program offered. She herself was devoted to a fictional detective program that aired on Saturday afternoons.

Mrs. Lowethorpe expressed pleasure in finding Edwina on

her step. She beckoned her inside and offered a refreshing cup of tea, which Edwina was glad to accept. She followed Mrs. Lowethorpe to the vicarage's cheerful kitchen with its freshly scrubbed floor and sparkling windows.

Mrs. Lowethorpe was the sort to find time to maintain a sparklingly clean home despite her constant commitments to good works around the village. She was a woman of boundless energy and Edwina admired her for it. Sometimes simply watching Mrs. Lowethorpe go about her day was enough to leave one a bit winded. Her hostess brought out a biscuit tin in addition to the pot of tea and the two women settled at the table for a chat.

"You're far too busy a woman these days, Edwina, to simply drop by unexpectedly because you had nothing better to do with your time," Mrs. Lowethorpe said, sliding the biscuit tin closer to Edwina. "And you have the distinct look of someone with something on her mind."

"I'm afraid you know me far too well for me to try and pretend I didn't come here with a purpose. Although it is always lovely to spend a bit of time with you under any circumstance. I felt quite troubled about something and wanted your perspective," she said, reaching into the biscuit tin and pulling out a ginger nut.

"That sounds serious."

"I'm afraid it just might be," Edwina said. "I'm here to ask your opinion of Dr. Nelson."

"Dr. Nelson? What about him?" Mrs. Lowethorpe said.

"What do you think of his competence as a doctor and of his character as a man, particularly as a husband?" Edwina said.

Mrs. Lowethorpe arched an eyebrow in surprise. She drew the biscuit tin back towards herself and took a moment choosing one as she considered Edwina's question.

"I think he's a very competent doctor. What did you have in mind exactly?"

"I wondered if you'd ever had reason to be distrustful of his services or dissatisfied with him in any way," Edwina said.

"I see. Well, when he started here in the village there were many people who were quite resistant to the idea of switching doctors. Dr. Wilcox had tended out on families in Walmsley Parva for decades and it was not surprising that it took people time to warm to the new doctor," Mrs. Lowethorpe said.

"Were you one of them?" Edwina asked.

"I wasn't. I felt it was my duty as the vicar's wife to set an example of how to treat adversity and change. I made a point to pay a call upon Dr. Nelson in a professional capacity soon after he took over the practice. And I made sure to let others know that I had been impressed by his youthful enthusiasm and his new ideas," Mrs. Lowethorpe said.

"So, you've never had any reason to be dissatisfied with him?" Edwina asked.

"I would say sometimes it takes a bit of getting used to to accept a more modern attitude towards patient care. Dr. Wilcox always had such a reassuring and calm demeanor about any sort of medical situation. I somehow always felt as though I were in good hands with him and that if something was actually very serious, he would let me know, but if it wasn't he wouldn't make more of it than was strictly necessary. Do you know what I mean?" Mrs. Lowethorpe said.

Edwina nodded and took a bite of her ginger nut. "You've put your finger on it exactly. Dr. Wilcox always left you feeling reassured that if something were really needing to be attended to, he would let you know, but other than that he took a very reserved attitude towards heroic interventions. No flashy medicines or newfangled instruments seemed to be part of his practice if it was at all avoidable."

"Exactly. Now not everyone feels that way, mind you," Mrs. Lowethorpe said. "There certainly were people in the village who just wouldn't make the switch without a great deal of grumbling. They simply did not wish to adapt to a new way of doing things or to a new doctor on principle. But a lot of other people in the village seemed to have been very happy with Dr. Nelson's modern outlook and in fact found him to be a refreshing change when it came to medical care."

"Do you know of any specific people who didn't wish to make a change?" Edwina said.

She hadn't realized that it was an option to simply refuse to accept that Dr. Wilcox had retired from practice. As much as she regretted the need to become a patient of the new doctor, she had not assumed she had the right to infringe upon Dr. Wilcox's newfound leisure time after he had decided to give up the practice. Although, if she had realized that she might do so, she perhaps would have strained the bounds of friendship in order to. Dr. Wilcox had never left her feeling like a shriveled up old biddy on the rare occasion she had needed to ring for his services.

"Mostly it was quite elderly people who felt that way. Some of them have passed on now. Since Dr. Nelson has been in practice for several years, the oldest patients perhaps are no longer a consideration. And then of course there were a number of people who did not survive the influenza epidemic," Mrs. Lowethorpe said.

Edwina needed no reminding of that fact. Her mother had succumbed to it and there had been absolutely nothing any doctor could have done. Edwina herself had not realized how unwell her mother had been at the time. Edwina's mother had been something of a hypochondriac throughout the years of her life and her widowhood had only increased the frequency of her complaints and her attention to her health. In fact, the week that she died Edwina had been far less solicitous of her mother's complaints than she generally had been in the past. She had come to the realization that ignoring half of what her mother had to say rather than encouraging her seemed to be the

fastest way to snap her out of her preoccupation with imaginary ailments.

So, it was with some surprise that Edwina had been confronted with the truth that her mother had in fact been actually deathly ill. Perhaps Dr. Nelson's reaction towards her mother's death was part of what she found so distasteful about the man. It wasn't just how he treated her. It was the fact that he had been the doctor who had officially pronounced her mother dead.

She felt a bit startled at herself as she considered that perhaps she was casting Dr. Nelson in a role he did not deserve. It was a good thing she had stopped by to discuss matters with Mrs. Lowethorpe. She knew she had been right to ask for a second opinion.

"We did lose quite a few members of the community to the influenza," Edwina said.

"I'm so sorry, Edwina. I should have been more sensitive. You know that better than anyone. If you want to speak with someone who is dissatisfied with Dr. Nelson's services I can make some discreet enquiries for you," Mrs. Lowethorpe said.

"I expect that won't be necessary. I find his manner to be a bit off-putting, but I suppose that he's altogether sound and that I shouldn't give the matter much thought as I am very rarely in poor health," Edwina said.

"I did wonder if perhaps something was ailing you since you asked," Mrs. Lowethorpe said in a voice that invited confidences.

"Oh, it's nothing like that. It's just that some information has reached me through sources I would prefer not to name, and I wanted an opinion I could trust as to Dr. Nelson's character and competence. I knew you would be able to help me sort out my own prejudices from the facts of the matter," Edwina said.

"That's what I am here for," Mrs. Lowethorpe said.

Edwina changed the topic and spent the next quarter of an

hour in pleasant conversation about the interesting things she had missed by being absent from the most recent garden club meeting. The conversation put Edwina in mind of the invitation offered by Dr. Wilcox to view his nerium. Noticing that Mrs. Lowethorpe was casting surreptitious glances at the clock mounted on the wall, Edwina thanked her for her time and her tea and headed out into the street once more.

Chapter 9

After having settled on an appointment time with the photographer, Beryl headed straight for the Dove and Duck. While she did not make a habit of tippling quite so early in the day, she felt no discomfort at entering the local pub or being seen to do so. She waved a greeting at the publican and, spotting her intended quarry, made her way to a table at the center of the large room filled with dappled sunlight.

Chester White sat in his customary space, a half-emptied glass of beer and a ledger book spread out before him. He looked up as she approached, and his face broke into a wide grin. Beryl flashed him one of her world-famous smiles and settled into the seat opposite him at the table.

"Are you here to place a bet?" Chester said.

"Is there anything I should be particularly interested in? Any hot tips that you've picked up in your wanderings?" Beryl asked.

"You know I never give tips," Chester said.

Beryl was well aware that Chester never offered opinions to his clientele on the chances of any particular game or race turning out in their favor. And he certainly didn't voice an opinion if he ever suspected something would not turn out in their favor, either. He simply took down the client's directions and collected their money. He was perhaps the most matter-of-fact bookie Beryl had ever encountered, and she had encountered her fair share. She just liked to see the look on his face when she needled him about it ever so slightly.

"Well, if you haven't any tips, then I haven't any intention of betting. I do have something I wanted to ask you about however," Beryl said.

"What is it then? I suppose you're here on some sort of a case."

"As a matter fact I am. I wanted to know if there is any truth to the rumor that you were overheard criticizing Bernard Stevens," Beryl said.

"Criticizing him how?" Chester said.

"You haven't been accusing him of taking naughty photographs, have you?" Beryl asked.

For a moment she thought that Chester was going to spew a mouthful of beer across his neatly filled-in ledger. But he managed to keep his lips together and swallow before letting out a loud guffaw.

"Naughty photographs, now that's a thought," Chester said. "I wonder what the odds would be on that being the truth."

Chester looked up at the ceiling as if doing calculations in his mind as to the odds and whether or not he might be able to start a pool on such a matter. If Beryl had been so inclined, she could have told him that the better bookie to have considered those kinds of odds was Alma Poole and the ladies of the village who liked to bet on matters much more like that than they did on jockeys and horses and football games. But being someone who knew how to be discreet when circumstances demanded, Beryl kept such knowledge to herself. The ladies of Walmsley Parva were doing a thriving business in pin money by carefully calculating the odds of the price of butter on a given day or the local death pool, which apparently she was favored to win by the vast majority of participants.

"Exactly. You look as though this is news to you," Beryl said.

"It certainly is. I think of him as a nervous sort of chap, very straitlaced. I wouldn't think that a man so obsessed with snapping pictures of the village duck population could be bothered to focus his camera on the local ladies," Chester said. "Why would you ask me such a thing?"

"I was just in to Bernard's studio and he has been the recipient of a thoroughly nasty letter informing him that you've been overheard saying that you know for a fact he was taking such photographs," Beryl said.

"I most certainly have not. I hardly know the man."

"It's rather worse than that, I'm afraid," Beryl said.

"How could it be worse?"

"The letter also suggested that you had accused him of also taking photographs without subjects' knowledge," Beryl said. "Not to put too fine a point on it, you have been accused of calling him a Peeping Tom."

This time Chester was unable to keep himself from spitting out some of his half-pint of bitter. He wiped the cover of his ledger with his sleeve.

"I definitely did not say anything like that. But you say he received a letter accusing me of gossiping about him? Who was it from?"

"Well, that's what Bernard wants to know. It was an anonymous letter, and the words were cut from newspapers and magazines, so the handwriting was not identifiable."

"That's what happened with Michael Blackburn and Norman Davies, wasn't it?" Chester said.

Beryl nodded. "Michael received a similarly hateful letter in his post as well. And honestly, so have I."

Chester leaned forward slightly. "I expect that your letter was quite a racy one, wasn't it?"

"I hate to disappoint you, but a lady doesn't tell. At least not to someone who refuses to divulge his own secrets in the form of tips," she said with a smile.

Chester nodded resignedly. "I'm sorry to hear that something like this has broken out in the village. It's a terrible thing when somebody is trying to sow dissent between neighbors."

"Any idea why someone would pick you as the person supposedly saying such things about Bernard? Is there any reason to suspect the two of you don't get on?" Beryl asked.

"I can't think of any grounds whatsoever. I've had no reason to be interested in having my photograph taken and he's not someone who ever places a bet with me," Chester said.

"Do you resent that fact?" Beryl asked.

"That I haven't had my picture taken?" Chester asked.

"No, that he doesn't place bets," Beryl said.

It was a valid question. Many, if not most, of the men in the village had been known to have a flutter from time to time with Chester White. If Bernard was not amongst them, he was a bit of an oddity and might have attracted notice.

"Of course not. I have plenty of business constantly streaming my way. I don't need to go out of my way to run down someone who doesn't wish to place a bet. Frankly, I think he's probably wise not to. The vast majority of people don't end up making out well in the end, now do they?" Chester said. "Present company excepted, of course."

"I do make a point of being exceptional. Thank you for your time," Beryl said, scraping back her chair and signaling to the bartender to bring a fresh drink to Chester for his trouble.

It was still quite early in the day when Edwina left the vicarage. Dr. Wilcox had said in his message delivered by Beryl that she should feel welcome to stop in anytime. There was no time like the present, so she took a chance that he might be in and started down a side street that led to the opposite end of the village from the new surgery.

Edwina deliberately allowed herself to slow down as she rounded the corner just as Dr. Wilcox's cottage came into sight. It was a beautiful example of its type, with its whitewashed walls, half-timbered beams, and thatched roof. The plants in the front garden were tucked in so closely that Edwina couldn't imagine weeds even being able to take root. Everywhere her gaze landed she was dazzled by a sort of higgity-piggity splendor.

At all times of the year Dr. Wilcox's garden was a thing of beauty. In the winter bright, twiggy stems of dogwood or lush carefully trimmed boxwood hedges and topiaries contrasted beautifully with the buildings and fences surrounding them. In spring carpets of bulbs burst up through the chilly earth and put on a riotous display of exuberant color. Great swathes of tulips and daffodils riotously greeted passersby for weeks on end. Dwarf apples and cherries showered fragrant petals down on the emerald-green lawn at the slightest breeze. Autumn gave way to ripe fruits and nuts of all sorts overhead and underfoot, twined round arbors and cascading over fencing. Brilliant glowing leaves covered the shrubberies, and annual displays of chrysanthemums and Michaelmas daisies greeted those lucky enough to be invited to his back garden.

But summer was the most glorious season of all in Dr. Wilcox's garden. From cheerful rudbeckia to serene Asiatic lilies, the good doctor's garden took Edwina's breath away. Bowers of roses hung low with fragrant blooms. Hibiscus syriacus hedges created a tapestry of exotic-looking blossoms in purples, periwinkles, pinks, and yellows. Nepeta sprawled over the edge of deep borders and tickled the edge of the lush, emerald lawn.

She was about to step up to the front door and knock when she heard the sound of whistling coming from the side of the cottage. She raised the latch on the gate and rounded the corner of the house instead. There, bent over a yew, stood Dr. Wilcox, a pair of hedge loppers clutched in his capable but gnarled hands. He must have caught some motion at the corner of his eye since he turned before she spoke and raised a hand in greeting.

"I see that you received my message," he said. "Come along and see what is showing off for us today," he said. Edwina hurried to his side and followed him deeper into the garden. Triumphantly, the doctor halted in front of a shrub that reached up to Edwina's knees.

"Would you take a look at that," he said, gesturing towards a variegated bush in front of them.

It was a thing of beauty with its glossy green and yellow leaves. The blossoms were a bright and cheerful pink ranked in a doubled formation. Edwina felt a twinge of envy as she thought of how much she would enjoy having such a plant in her own garden. But she had spent less and less time in the last few months attending to the grounds at the Beeches and in the years prior had not had the funds to acquire such an exotic specimen as this.

"It is absolutely spectacular. Wherever did you get it?"

"I had to send away for it from a plant catalog," the doctor said.

"I've just received a new one from Jenkins Tropicals myself that I'd be happy to lend to you once I've finished with it," Edwina said. "But perhaps you've received it already?"

"No, I haven't even heard of that one before. I shall eagerly await a perusal of it once you are through," he said.

"It tends to be filled with hothouse plants more than those destined for the open ground, but I'm sure you could find good use for it, anyway, couldn't you?" Edwina said, gesturing towards the hothouse at the end of the garden. The doctor had filled his garden with things he had started from seed himself. The nerium was a rarity in the fact that he had purchased it as a shrub rather than as a seed or even a cutting.

"Would you like a cutting from this beauty once I get around to it?" the doctor asked.

"Are you sure?" Edwina said. She understood how having an unusual plant specimen was something many gardeners enjoyed and she in no way wished to dilute his pleasure in his acquisition. She hoped that she had not admired it to the point that he felt he needed to offer even though he might not wish to do so.

"I would be delighted to make a gift of one to you. I can't think of anyone who would take better care of it or value it more than you, my dear," the doctor said. "Can I tempt you with a cup of tea in my garden?" he asked.

"I can think of nothing I'd like more," Edwina said, hoping she had room for yet another cup.

She could sip it slowly and she was in no way dissembling. She could think of nothing she would like more than to sit in a shady spot in Dr. Wilcox's garden inhaling the scents of the fragrant blossoms and watching lazily as the bees went droning from flower to flower all about them. In only a few minutes' time the doctor bustled back into the garden carrying a tea tray ladened with a plate of cake and a teapot. The doctor had never married and instead had devoted himself to his patients and to his garden. He certainly knew his way around the kitchen sufficiently to produce a decent pot of tea, Edwina knew from past experience.

They settled themselves into a pair of basket chairs and Edwina gratefully accepted a slice of cake. The ginger nut had been welcomed but she found she had grown rather peckish from all of her walking.

But there was more to her visit than simply admiring his beautiful garden. The news about Margery Nelson weighed heavily upon her. She did not think it would be considered gossip to mention it to Dr. Wilcox. After all, he was intimately involved with the Nelsons and likely would have known why it was that he was asked to fill in for Dr. Nelson.

"I hate to bring anything unpleasant into such a lovely afternoon, but I wondered if you were aware of the situation with Margery Nelson?" she asked.

"I know that Margery's taken ill quite suddenly and that her husband was very concerned about her. Beyond that I know nothing," he said.

"I understand that you are filling in for him while he is unable to attend to patients himself," she said.

"That's right. I was called to your Simpkins's farm to stitch up one of the Prentice children's heads. There were a couple of other emergency calls but nothing very serious. I have filled in for Dr. Nelson from time to time when he and Margery have gone on holiday. And on the rare occasion that the doctor himself has been ill. There was nothing unusual in that. Why do you ask?"

Edwina hesitated for a moment. If Dr. Nelson had not revealed his reasons for requesting help from Dr. Wilcox, she wondered if perhaps she was overstepping the boundaries of the investigation to do so. However, Dr. Wilcox had been a member of the community who had been taxed with its care for years upon years. She had never known him to be a gossip.

She also had an unworthy thought that if Dr. Nelson had been involved in some way with his wife's downturn of mood, Dr. Wilcox should be aware of it. After all, he had been Margery's physician when she was a child just as he had been Edwina's. Doctor Nelson was the newcomer to the village and had married a local girl. In fact, Dr. Wilcox had been instrumental in introducing the pair.

"I'm sure I can rely upon you not to say anything to anyone else, and I hope you will not consider me a gossip, but something very serious has happened," she said.

Doctor Wilcox sat up a little straighter and drew his gaze from a robin pecking away in the lawn and gave Edwina his undivided attention.

"What is it?"

"Margery received a vicious poisoned pen letter that accused her of being responsible for Alan's death by her negligence," she said.

Doctor Wilcox sharply drew in his breath. "But that's absurd," he said.

"We both know that, but unfortunately Margery took it to heart. Doctor Nelson needed you to fill in because she attempted to take her own life as a result of the letter," Edwina said.

Doctor Wilcox gasped again. "Of all the cruel things to do to someone, that must be amongst the worst. Do you know who sent the letter?" he asked, leaning towards her.

Edwina shook her head. "I have no idea, but Constable Gibbs has asked me if I would make some discreet enquiries. In your opinion is there anyone in the village you can think of who might be responsible for such a thing?"

"I can think of some folks who over the years have had strong grievances towards their neighbors and maybe even the bent of mind that would produce such a hateful action, but at present I can't think of anyone who would feel that way towards poor Margery. But I'm not in the same position to evaluate such things as I might have been in the past."

"There seems to be a rash of these letters going about the village. I know of several people who have received them, including Beryl," Edwina said.

"I've received one myself, but I thought nothing of it," he said.

"Was the letter in a fairly unobtrusive envelope with a block sort of handwriting creating the address?" Edwina said. Doctor Wilcox nodded. "And was the content of the letter made up of words cut from newspapers and magazines and pasted onto some stationery?"

"As a matter of fact, it was. The letter said that Constable

Gibbs was investigating Dr. Nelson for being drunk on the job and dangerously incompetent."

"Do you think that might have been the case? Has he ever showed any sign of such behavior?" she asked.

"Certainly not. He's a teetotaler. I gave it no further thought whatsoever, dismissed it as just a bit of garbage, and gave it no more consideration. If I had known it would lead to something as serious as what Margery has done, I most assuredly would have taken it to Constable Gibbs straightaway," Dr. Wilcox said.

"Did you think to ask Constable Gibbs if she had said anything to that effect?" Edwina asked.

"No, of course I didn't. There was nothing in it and I certainly wouldn't have wanted to start spreading any gossip by even asking the constable such a preposterous question. I am more than assured that Dr. Nelson is a competent physician who has the village's best interest in mind and is capable of doing his job."

"But not everyone feels that way, do they?" Edwina asked.

"Well, I daresay they probably don't. I seem to recall you making mention on occasion that he put your back up a bit with his brusque manner and insinuations that perhaps some of your maladies were all in your head," Dr. Wilcox said.

"I admit he's not my favorite doctor. But of course, that's you," Edwina said, reaching over and patting his liver-spotted hand.

"You just say such things so that I'll give you cuttings from my prized shrubberies."

"I say it because it's the truth."

As Edwina leaned back into her chair her mind turned again to Dr. Nelson. Perhaps he did have the village's best interest at heart. But did he have his wife's?

Chapter 10

After Edwina had returned to the Beeches, they discussed the lack of development in the case. Beryl suggested that it might be best to look a bit more closely into the gossip pointed at the Nelsons and proposed that the nurse should be questioned. Beryl offered to interview Nurse Crenshaw on her own. She had a sneaking suspicion that her friend was slightly phobic when it came to anything to do with doctors.

While she did not care to pry into those parts of the past that brought Edwina grief, Beryl suspected Edwina's reluctance stemmed from her mother's hypochondria. Edwina would go to great lengths to avoid the doctor herself even when it would have been wisest to avail herself of a physician's care. Fortunately, her stubborn little friend rarely was in anything but rude good health. Perhaps it was her insistence on walking or cycling here, there, and everywhere that kept her in such good trim.

Beryl had felt she had done enough walking of late by climbing up and down ladders in the orchard at Simpkins's farm and she allowed herself the luxury of driving her motorcar into the outskirts of the village to pay a call on Nurse Crenshaw. As she pulled her bright red beauty to a stop in front of the tiny cottage where the nurse lived, Beryl took a moment to assess the environment in which her quarry lay.

The nurse's cottage was serviceable but plain and rather cheerless. An attempt at cozying the space up had been made in the form of a wreath, left over from Christmas by all appearances, hung upon the front door. A bedraggled and faded bow clung valiantly to the even more disreputable looking greenery. Beryl wondered if the nurse simply had forgotten the thing, clinging forlornly like a ghost to her home, or if she was actually not a house-proud sort of a person.

One of the traits that Beryl had prided herself upon as she had ventured far and wide across the globe was her knack for absorbing information about the lifestyle of others without passing judgment upon it. From her point of view there was very little difference between a stone cottage roofed with thatch in the English countryside and a hut built from sticks lashed together by rope and topped off by bundles of long grass or leaves in Africa or South America. While she expected to find traditional Western style furniture inside the home, she would not have been ill at ease had she entered to discover nothing but cushions and rugs spread out across the floor upon which her hostess would bid her sit.

Beryl allowed herself a moment to cast her mind back to a particularly enjoyable stay she had had with the owner of one such sort of home. To her mind, the pleasures of a soft Western-style mattress were not equal to that of bedding spread across the floor of a hut with ample privacy. With some sense of regret, she roused herself from her memory and pushed open the door of the motorcar. She strode to the nurse's cottage and rapped up on the door.

The wreath looked even more unprepossessing upon closer inspection. The remains of a bird's nest sat nestled down deeply in the faded greenery. It occurred to Beryl as she stood up on the doorstep that perhaps this was not the entrance generally used by the mistress of the house. She took a step backwards and looked across the ground. A footpath of sorts had been trudged through the grass at the side of the house, and like the good tracker she was, she followed it.

A side door nestled against a deep bay window appeared before her. A large ginger cat sat in the window seat cleaning its fur and staring at her disdainfully. Beryl was just about to knock when Nurse Crenshaw's face appeared in the window. Beryl lifted a hand in what she hoped was a friendly wave. The nurse yanked open the door and eyed her with her usual efficient scowl.

"Good afternoon, Nurse Crenshaw. I wondered if I might speak with you for a moment," Beryl said.

"The surgery is closed. You shall have to make an appointment tomorrow at the earliest," Nurse Crenshaw said, attempting to close the door.

"I didn't want to see the doctor. It was you with whom I wish to speak. In fact, I think it would be best if the doctor were not to overhear us," Beryl said.

The nurse's eyes widened slightly, and her lips clamped tightly together. Beryl thought she was still going to turn her away, but then the nurse spoke.

"I suppose you had best come in," she said, pulling the door all the way open and stepping aside so Beryl could cross the threshold.

The cottage had appeared small from the outside, and a quick glance over its interior did little to change that first impression. The ceilings were so low that Beryl had to duck to avoid thunking her forehead against a dark wooden beam. Everything about the place felt close and small, but it was not without its charm. It was almost as if the nurse lived in a child's playhouse built upon a grander scale.

Nurse Crenshaw led her down a minuscule passageway so narrow that a sudden feeling of claustrophobia washed over Beryl. She fought down a rising sense of panic. Not all of her memories were as cheerful as the one involving remote huts and tanned limbs. Her heart thudded in her chest and the back of her neck felt clammy with that sudden flash of feeling one often had just before retching.

She staggered along behind the nurse forcing herself to refrain from reaching her hand out and steadying herself against the wall of the hallway. Her hostess led her into a sitting room at the end of the hallway, and to Beryl's enormous relief she found that the space was far more generously sized than the passageway had been. Certainly, it was by no means a large room, but the sense she was trapped in an underground tunnel evaporated in an instant. Light streamed through the small windows and beams of sunshine danced cheerfully on a row of silver picture frames neatly placed along the mantel above a surprisingly modern-looking gas fireplace. Nurse Crenshaw indicated she should take a seat in a nearby chair and settled herself in a matching seat opposite. The ginger cat appeared at Beryl's feet the moment she lowered herself into the chair and began rubbing its face against her leg.

"What is it that you wish to speak with me about, Miss Helliwell? I've had a difficult week and I would like to get back to my book," she said, gesturing towards a discarded volume lying open, its spine pointed towards the ceiling on the table next to her chair.

A teacup and a half-eaten biscuit sat beside it. Beryl wondered how many times she would interrupt someone's moments of repose with her prying questions. While she did realize that the investigations they undertook were for the greater good, she sometimes felt as though she and Edwina were more of a nuisance to the community than an assistance.

Fortunately for her, such things did not prick her conscience. What others thought about her and her behavior had never had very much influence on how she proceeded or indeed upon her self-image. She certainly was not about to allow someone who did not know how to treat a book with a leather spine to make her feel small. Or unwelcome for that matter. Beryl had always made an effort to assume she was welcomed wherever she chose to travel. The sitting room of a village nurse was not about to daunt her.

"I'll get straight to the point then, shall I?" Beryl said, nodding at the cup of tea.

"I wish you would," Nurse Crenshaw said.

"I'm here to ask you if you've had any reason to suspect that your employer is anything other than entirely competent at his job," Beryl said.

Nurse Crenshaw let out a small squeak of indignation. "Why on earth would you ask me any such thing?" she said.

"Because it's been suggested that there are those in the community who do not feel he is quite up to the task," Beryl said.

"I suppose that your friend Edwina has some sort of complaint that she did not feel equal to making on her own behalf and so she sent you," Nurse Crenshaw said, crossing her arms across her bust.

"Edwina is perfectly capable of voicing her own complaints about a doctor or anyone else, for that matter. No, I'd rather not name names, but it has come to my attention in the course of an investigation that your employer has been accused of incompetence due to drunkenness on the job," Beryl said.

She kept her gaze trained on the nurse's face despite the vigorous attention being paid to her by her hostess's cat.

"That's outrageous. The doctor is a consummate professional and a teetotaler at that," Nurse Crenshaw said. "This is just the sort of spiteful talk that makes being a doctor so difficult."

"I expect that gossip is part and parcel of life in a small village," Beryl said.

Not that she had all that much experience of it herself, having only been in residence for a few months' time, but even in such a brief stay in one place she had come to notice there was a tendency to make a great deal out of matters that would be considered too small to notice in communities where there was more hustle and bustle.

"Unfortunately, that is one epidemic we cannot seem to treat no matter how hard one tries," Nurse Crenshaw said. "It's just vile the things that people will say."

"I wonder why someone would make such an accusation about the doctor if it is so clearly untrue. Do you have any idea why he might be the target of such malicious gossip?"

"Dr. Nelson is the most decent and lovely man I think I have ever met. I have no notion as to why anyone who has ever encountered him would even think to attempt to besmirch his character," Nurse Crenshaw said. She patted her lap and the cat left off its attempt to leave most of its fur clinging to Beryl's stockings. The cat leapt up into his mistress's lap and commenced staring at Beryl as if she were a bird perched in a low branch of a nearby bush.

It seemed to Beryl that the tone of Nurse Crenshaw's voice had sweetened as she was describing her employer. Her face had softened from its customary scowl into a slightly wistful look. Unless Beryl missed her guess, Nurse Crenshaw was one of those poor, unfortunate women who had taken a shine to her married employer.

Beryl thought it rather telling that the gossip about the doctor had addressed his competency and personal habits towards tippling rather than taking the route of suggesting he was being unfaithful to his wife with the nurse. It seemed to Beryl that even someone as inclined towards gossip spreading as the poisoned pen appeared to be had not considered suggesting that he was carrying on a romantic liaison with his employee.

Beryl felt a wave of sadness for Nurse Crenshaw despite the fact that she found the other woman to be generally so unlikeable. Although she had never found herself to be in want of male attention, she had on occasion been taken with someone who was not available, and despite the fact that she had no concerns about breaking any marriage vows she herself had made when it was clear to her that such a union was not likely to last, she prided herself upon a stout refusal to insert herself into someone else's marriage.

"No one would blame the doctor if he had turned to strong drink as a way to alleviate his mind from his current troubles. Surely you must agree with me about that," Beryl said.

"The doctor is far too strong a character to lean on any such sort of crutch no matter how trying his circumstances or personal life might be," the nurse said, sitting up a little straighter and pursing her mouth once more.

"I had heard that his home life was not entirely free from strife," Beryl said. "But I'm sure you would know far more about that than the rest of the village."

The compliment seemed to soften Nurse Crenshaw once more. She leaned back against her chair and stroked the cat's back, sending waves of fur floating into the air.

"I suppose that's true. If I do say so myself, I believe that I offer a sympathetic ear to the doctor whenever he might need one. And I find he so often needs bolstering, the poor man. Who wouldn't with a wife like his?" she said.

"I understand that Mrs. Nelson has been troubled by ill health for some time," Beryl said. "That must be very difficult for a doctor to witness. If there was anyone he would want to be able to cure, I would imagine his wife would be the first."

A spot of bright color flushed into each of the nurse's pale cheeks. "Dr. Nelson is practically a saint with the way that he tries to tend out on that woman. The poor man is run off his feet attending to the needs of the village, and then when he comes home, instead of being able to relax and restore himself for another day of providing unflagging help to others, he is forced to cater to someone of such weak character as Margery Nelson."

Beryl watched as the cat writhed. The nurse's stroking along his spine grew more rapid and the puffs of fur floating up off his back reminded Beryl of messages sent in the form of smoke signals. One thing was for sure. Nurse Crenshaw was more than a little in love with her employer.

"It sounds as though you don't think she's actually unwell," Beryl said.

"Of course she's not unwell. She simply behaves that way to attract her husband's attention rather than focusing on her duty as a wife. In my opinion she has a selfish streak, and the doctor deserves someone far more helpful at his side."

"Did you have anyone in mind as her replacement?" Beryl asked.

Nurse Crenshaw urged the cat from her lap and stood.

"I believe I've heard enough questions. Should you wish to speak with me again please call in at the surgery rather than at my home. I'm sure you can find the door."

Beryl could feel the nurse glaring at her even as she turned and walked away. While Edwina had wondered if the poisoned pen that had sent Margery over the edge had been written by Dr. Nelson, Beryl felt far more convinced that the culprit was Nurse Crenshaw.

With Beryl off on her errand to question Nurse Crenshaw, Edwina turned her attention to her novel once more. But even though she had left off at a point where her hero, Bart Dalton, was about to force his nemesis into a confession about robbing the local bank, she found she could not concentrate on the blank page in front of her. She could not stop seeing Beddoes's face as she bent over the cooker about to thrust the poisoned pen letter into its fiery depths. Certainly, such agitation in the very fabric of the village made working upon something as frivolous as a novel set in the American Wild West irrelevant.

No matter how she tried to convince herself to imagine the canyons, caverns, and dusty plains with the big bright blue sky overhead, she could not remain focused upon a world of fiction when so much fiction was tearing apart her beloved Walmsley Parva. With a sigh she pushed back the chair of her writing desk and crossed the room to where her notes on cases at the Magistrate's Court lay neatly tucked inside an attaché case.

She popped open the latches and sorted through the papers until she found what she sought. Drawing the letter Michael Blackburn had presented at court out of its envelope, she carried it back to her desk and sat down to give it an even closer look.

Upon a second inspection it was even more clear that the envelope was a perfectly unremarkable sort. In fact, it looked quite like the ones Edwina used to send out invoices in connection with Davenport and Helliwell, Private Enquiry Agency. The stamp was like any other and the blockish printing with Michael's address gave little away about its creator. All the letters were capitals, and the pressure of the pen was moderate and even.

The postmark was for Walmsley Parva, so whoever had sent it had not taken the trouble to post it from outside the village. She wondered if there was any chance that Prudence Rathbone had paid attention to any of the letters as they had surely passed through her hands. Prudence was not known as someone cursed with a lack of curiosity. While Edwina hated to give Prudence the satisfaction of anything new to gossip about, Edwina thought it possible she might not be able to avoid questioning the postmistress.

She withdrew the letter from the envelope and unfolded it. Looking it over even more carefully than she had in the courtroom, she found it all the more chilling. Someone had taken a great deal of trouble in adhering each of the cut-out words to the page beneath. It was as if the sender wanted to be sure that the message was received exactly as intended.

Reading through the actual message once more, a new thought occurred to Edwina. Norman Davies had claimed he had not been gossiping at the greengrocery and she thought it likely there was one way to be sure. Carrying the letter into the front hallway, she lifted the receiver and held the instrument to her ear.

The switchboard operator connected her with Mr. Scott's greengrocery, and with a wince she yanked the instrument away from her ear as Mr. Scott's booming voice reached her. In short order she was able to confirm that Norman Davies had in fact not been in the greengrocery at the time the letter stated disparaging Michael Blackburn's character to all within earshot, but rather had been picking up a special order of broad beans in a neighboring village at Mr. Scott's request.

As she returned the receiver to the cradle, she wondered again at what the reason for sending such a letter could be. Was it just mischief making in general or was there some real purpose behind the sender's activities? Who was the target of the letters? Had the writer intended to deeply wound a particular individual, or had he or she intended to spread general chaos throughout the village? And if so, what could be the motivation for any of it? No matter which question she asked herself, Edwina could not shake the sense that something was very wrong in Walmsley Parva.

Beryl set off in her motorcar once more. On her way past the Blackburns' garage, she noticed Nora Blackburn standing outside it, her slight form clad in a greasy overall bent over the bonnet of the car. Struck by the sudden inspiration to speak with her, Beryl pulled up alongside the garage with a likely excuse.

Nora pulled her attention away from the engine in front of her and wiped her hands on a rag. She slipped a spanner into her pocket and lifted a hand in greeting at Beryl.

"Is there something wrong with your motorcar?" Nora said.

"I just wanted to be sure the tire pressure was correct. I felt a little tug to the right as I was coming along the high street and thought it best to have it checked before I ended up on the side of the road," Beryl said.

She was never one to feel that the truth was of great importance. In her opinion little white lies were the grease that made society's wheels go round and she had noticed that many people tended to be more comfortable discussing difficult subjects when their hands were busy with familiar tasks. She had often used exactly the same technique on Edwina when her friend clearly had something on her mind but had been reluctant to give it voice. Beryl would wait until Edwina had pulled one of her unending number of knitting projects from the basket next to her chair and started moving the wool across her needles before approaching whichever subject she thought was troubling her friend. It worked like a charm every time.

"Very sensible of you, I'm sure. Considering the rates of speed at which you drive, it wouldn't do to have a puncture," Nora said with a smile.

As Nora set about her task, Beryl broached the subject.

"I also wanted to ask you how Michael was faring. Rumor has it that he and Norman Davies had quite a row," Beryl said.

"Of course, you would have heard about that, with Edwina being the new magistrate," Nora said. She straightened up from the tire she was checking and gave Beryl her complete attention.

"I'm afraid that Edwina is not the only one who's been speaking about it," Beryl said. "In fact, I heard it from Norman Davies himself, who claimed to be completely shocked at the letter Michael received."

"I was shocked by it myself. Michael and Norman have always been quite friendly, and I would not have credited him with being so unkind. Norman has his faults, but I never think of him as malicious, which the letter certainly was," Nora said.

"I would have to agree. Has Michael gotten over it?" Beryl asked.

It wasn't just a routine question as part of the investigation. Beryl had quite a soft spot for both Michael and Nora Blackburn and hated to think of either of them as suffering needlessly. Not only were they excellent mechanics, but Michael happened to be a good card player despite having only one hand he could use to trounce opponents in any game. Well, trounce if the opponent didn't happen to be Beryl, that was.

And Nora was someone Beryl respected, not only as a mechanic but as a woman making her way in an unorthodox profession. The younger woman's attitude towards what was possible despite her gender warmed Beryl's heart and gave her hope for more equality for women in the future.

"I'll tell you the truth, Miss Helliwell, I'm worried about him." She lowered her voice and looked over her shoulder as if to verify that Michael was not within earshot. "He's been having bad dreams again and they started just after he received the letter."

Beryl was sorry to hear it. She had often had the odd nighttime wrestling session with wartime demons of her own. It was not the sort of experience she would wish on anyone else.

"Are you afraid he's going to have another episode?" Beryl asked.

Episode was a mild way of referring to the troubles that Michael had had when he first returned home from the front. He had been one of those unfortunate soldiers who returned to England with what was called the thousand-yard stare. In fact, it had taken the determined efforts of a clever hospital volunteer to bring him round in the end. The only thing he had responded to was the sound of someone reading one of his favorite books from childhood. Eventually, the exploits of Tarzan roused him from his stupor and returned him to the life he had known before the mud and the mire and the blood and the boom of guns. Beryl fervently hoped nothing would send him tumbling back into the abyss. A rolling boil of rage at whoever had taken it upon themselves to make such mischief rose in her chest.

Nora nodded. "I really don't know what might happen. He seems to have accepted that Norman did not make such accusations about him, but he can't shake the question of who it was that did. He's convinced that someone thinks that about him and was too cowardly to confront him with it on their own, blaming Norman instead and sitting back to watch the reaction. I'm afraid he's becoming paranoid, and I don't quite know what to make of it or what to do," Nora said, shrugging her slim shoulders.

"Michael's not the only one who has received a letter of this sort. If it helps, you could tell him I've received one as well, making some very foul accusations about my living arrangements and my moral character as well as Edwina's."

"You received a letter calling Miss Davenport's character into question?" Nora said, her eyes widening to round moons in her face.

Beryl couldn't help but notice that Nora's shock only extended to someone casting aspersions on Edwina's character. It seemed no one batted an eye at the sorts of impropriety she might be getting up to. However, she was pleased with Nora's reaction. Perhaps her outrage would be shared by Michael, who would take his own offense less seriously.

"Yes, it was quite foul, and we've undertaken an investigation into who might be behind the letters. Please reassure Michael that no one credits it in the least and that we will do our very best to discover who is causing such unrest."

A look of relief flooded Nora's face. "I'll be sure to let him know. I expect that notion that anyone would try to besmirch Miss Davenport will prove entirely reassuring."

"I'm sure that will provide Edwina with just as much relief as the news will give to Michael. She has been worried about him, too. But do feel free to ring the Beeches if you need any help with your brother." Beryl laid her hand on the younger woman's arm. "I've had quite a lot of experience with traumatized soldiers. Please do call if you need me."

Nora's eyes widened again, and she opened her mouth as if to ask a question, then seemed to think better of it and snapped it shut. She turned back towards the tires and then delivered the pronouncement Beryl was quite sure of before pulling into the garage.

"Everything seems fine with your motorcar. Thanks for stopping by."

Beryl looked in the rearview mirror as she pulled away from the garage. Michael appeared in the view and Beryl let up on the accelerator to watch as Nora took her brother by the arm and seemed to be telling him something. Still, despite the hopefulness of the scene, Beryl couldn't shake the sense that something was still simmering below the surface in Walmsley Parva.

As soon as Beryl returned to the Beeches, she and Edwina discussed what they had learned throughout their day. After mulling over the reaction Nurse Crenshaw had to the gossip about Dr. Nelson and the new information about the other victims of the poisoned pen, they decided that it would make sense to update Constable Gibbs. Within half an hour's time the constable was seated in the summerhouse in the garden of the Beeches, her uniform cap discarded on the seat beside her and a cup of tea in her hand.

Edwina felt a bit of the tension she had been experiencing ever since Michael Blackburn had presented his letter into evidence at the court seeping from her body. Even though it felt as though some things in village life had become uncomfortable and unpleasant with the advent of the letters, there were other things that were improvements. The fact that Constable Gibbs was willingly seated in her summerhouse for the express purpose of congenially discussing an active criminal investigation had to be chief amongst them.

Edwina's cheeks pinked with pleasure as she considered the fact that in only a few months' time the police officer had changed her opinion of the pair of them from meddling amateurs into useful and respected associates. Edwina had not expected life to take such a turn in any way, but she felt expansive and confident as she considered how eagerly the constable had sought their assistance in what she herself believed to be a very serious matter.

The change did not appear lost on Beryl, either. In a moment when the constable appeared absorbed in the act of spooning sugar into her cup of tea, Beryl winked at Edwina and inclined her head in the police officer's direction as if to say she could not believe it either. As much as Edwina was delighted in all the ways in which she had changed and grown and expanded her world of late, it had to be said the most marvelous part of it all was having a true companion with whom to share it.

The loneliness and feeling that her life had very little meaning beyond her volunteer work or the small pleasures she took in everyday life had been entirely replaced by a sense of connection and greater purpose. She hardly recognized herself as she thought about the woman who only months earlier had so dispiritedly placed an advertisement in the newspapers seeking a lodger. Her thoughts were brought back to the present troubles at hand as Constable Gibbs spoke.

"I assume that you must have some progress to share with me or you would not have requested a meeting. Please tell me you've made some progress on who may have done this," Constable Gibbs said.

"I wish that I were able to tell you that we knew who was at fault, but the sad fact of the matter is it seems that the problem is simply increasing and we're no more clear on who is culpable than we were when you first approached us," Edwina said.

"I have to agree with Edwina," Beryl said. "It seems as though you can't walk down the high street without encountering someone who has received one of the letters. But there doesn't seem to be a clear enough motivation to point out who might be the person writing them."

"You have no leads at all?" the constable asked.

"I wouldn't say we're not making any progress. As a matter of fact, I have followed up one of the outrageous claims, the one that started it all off for me, and have verified that the writer simply lied," Edwina said. Both Beryl and Constable Gibbs put down their teacups and gave her their undivided attention.

"How did you manage that?" Beryl asked.

"I took a second look at the letter Michael Blackburn received. It accused Norman Davies of besmirching Michael's character at the greengrocery on a particular morning. When I rang up Mr. Scott to ask if he remembered any such incident, he told me that Norman Davies could not have been gossiping at his shop that morning as he had sent him on a trip to Pershing Magna to pick up an order of broad beans for his store. Norman wasn't even in the village at the time he was accused of spreading malicious gossip," Edwina said.

"So, whoever is making such claims actually has no interest in letting out any real secrets?" Constable Gibbs said.

"It seems as though the point of the letters is to simply stir up trouble between villagers," Edwina said. "I also checked the postmark on the letter Michael received and verified that it had been sent right here in the village. The sender didn't bother to take it to an outlying post office in another village."

"That suggests something interesting, now, doesn't it?" Beryl said.

Constable Gibbs leaned forward. "And what's that?"

"Maybe this case is simply solved. Perhaps we've been making too much of the mystery of it and should have just gone with the easiest answer," Beryl said.

"And what would the easiest answer be?" Constable Gibbs asked.

"Why, that Prudence Rathbone is the poisoned pen, of course," Beryl said. She leaned back and a wide smile spread across her face.

Edwina knew that Beryl had no love for Prudence Rathbone, the local postmistress who also ran a sweet shop and stationer from the same tidy store in the center of the village. Prudence was the most notorious gossip in the village and, as she had confided in Beddoes, had made particular sport of Edwina during the course of her economic woes. In fact, Beryl had been the one who had put a stop to the constant stream of ugly, agitating gossip that Prudence had stirred up about Edwina, making her so miserable she had for the most part given up going out into the village at all.

Beryl had no patience with such petty-minded people or such deliberate bullying. Whatever one might say about Beryl, she was never unkind. Edwina's heart squeezed as she thought of how valiantly and flamboyantly Beryl had slayed the gossip dragon and made it possible for Edwina to hold her head high in the village once more. That said, she did not think that Prudence was a likely candidate as the poisoned pen. As much as she hated to contradict her friend or to burst her bubble, it would not be right to keep her thoughts to herself.

"I'm afraid I very much doubt that Prudence is the one who's been sending these letters," Edwina said.

"Why would that be?" Constable Gibbs asked. "I have to agree with Beryl that she seems the perfect candidate to me. As a matter of fact, I'm rather embarrassed I hadn't thought of it myself in the first place and spared the two of you the trouble of investigating."

Edwina shook her head. "I just don't think it's in Prudence's nature to go about things in that manner."

"What's not in her nature about it? She loves to gossip about her neighbors, and the more malicious the story is, the greater her interest in it seems to be," Beryl said.

"I would agree with you that she is the most determined gossip, but I can't see her writing poisoned pen letters. In my experience with Prudence the thrill she gets is from being the first with the story and the reaction that she gets to enjoy by telling someone something they did not yet know," Edwina said.

"But isn't that what the poisoned pen is doing?" Constable Gibbs asked. "Isn't this person shocking people with stories they had not before heard?"

"That may well be, but the poisoned pen writer is not able to have the pleasure of experiencing the reaction from the person firsthand. The letter writer is most likely forced to imagine what the recipient's reaction would be. That doesn't seem to be Prudence's style at all," Edwina said.

"Just because I like to have a slice of chocolate cake doesn't mean I don't also like a dill pickle," Beryl said. "Why should she be any different? Couldn't she be sampling the delights of both ways of being a mischief maker?"

"I have to agree with Beryl on this one," Constable Gibbs said. "The types of things being spread about sound very much like something Prudence would be overheard to say at the post office."

"Not to mention, who would be better than Prudence at sending out the letters undetected? She's the one who handles every bit of mail and is in the perfect position to pull off such a campaign without detection," Beryl said.

Edwina leaned back in her basket chair and considered what the other two had said. There was certainly logic in what Beryl said about not needing to adhere to just one sort of mischief. And there was also the fact that from a practical standpoint Prudence was in the perfect position to deliver the letters to the targets. Still, try as she might, she just couldn't seem to reconcile what she knew of Prudence's character with the sort of cold and calculating methodical behavior needed to create poisoned pen letters. She would have to have become a very different sort of person to carefully construct letters intent on ravaging the lives of others and to deny herself the pleasure of looking the victims in the face.

"I'm not saying she shouldn't remain on the list of suspects, but I am saying I wouldn't consider the case to be solved so easily as that. I just don't feel convinced that she would be satisfied with such an indirect manner of tormenting people. Besides, why would she have suddenly started sending them?" Edwina asked.

"That's a very good question, isn't it?" Constable Gibbs said. "Why would anyone have started sending these letters now?"

Edwina wondered too. Perhaps that was the whole key to the culprit. Who had had a change in their life or their circumstances? Who suddenly had a grievance, or a series of grievances bubble to the surface and the desire to spew them out in this particular way?

Chapter 11

Simpkins had left by the early train to London to present his idea for a line of convenience foods to the board at Colonel Kimberly's. Rather endearingly he had asked for Beryl to wish him luck in his meeting later that day. Beryl had assured him that his idea was a winner and that he needn't rely on luck. She thought it showed an enormous amount of growth on his part that not only was he thinking of innovative ways to grow his company, but that he was confident enough about his role to head to London on his own to advocate for his ideas.

When he had first been informed that he was the majority owner of the nation's largest condiment company he had been dazed and overwhelmed. Simpkins had never had more than a week's pay packet at a time in his pocket, and the idea that he not only had as much wealth as he could imagine at his disposal, but that he was responsible for the fortunes of his employees as well, had been quite a thing to wrap his head around. But Simpkins had proved resilient and flexible in ways that his appearance and upbringing might not have suggested would be the case and had taken on his role with energy and enthusiasm.

Beryl had offered to fill in for him at the farm in his absence and agreed to help Mrs. Prentice by taste-testing the different batches of greengage jam recipes they were trialing. As much as Beryl was no cook herself, she was always happy to sample the efforts of others. And so, it was with a light heart she set out in the motorcar once more for Simpkins's farm. As she pulled into the dooryard and the Prentice children flocked around her vehicle, she was surprised to notice she did not have the same feeling that she need brace herself for an onslaught that she generally did when encountering children. In fact, she was surprised to find she was rather looking forward to seeing them.

As she pushed open the door of the vehicle and felt a small hand tug at her sleeve she did not recoil with her instinctual reaction. Instead, she inexplicably placed her hand upon the child's blond head and scrutinized his face for signs of the stitches Dr. Wilcox had employed during her last visit. What on earth was the world coming to, she wondered? The day was made even brighter by the fact that her favorite Prentice child, Jack, was in attendance. He had grown by leaps and bounds over the last few months and Beryl wondered if perhaps all the children in the family were better fed now that they were living on the farm than previously had been the case.

"Mum's in the house and she said to wait outside for you to arrive," Jack said, lifting his hand in greeting. The other Prentice children scattered off towards the cottage, racing and tumbling and shouting as they went past. Beryl followed them into the small, tidy hallway thinking it a marvel that Mrs. Prentice managed to keep the place so clean with so many pairs of feet running about the place. As she followed them into the kitchen, she took one look at Mrs. Prentice's face and clapped her hands over her head. The children all turned and looked at her with surprise stamped on each of their freckled faces.

"I read in a magazine yesterday that a certain rare breed of toad has been spotted in sections of Kent. The toads are dark brown with orange splotches. Apparently, they are related to a tropical species whose skin exudes a sticky substance that hunters in the Amazon use to poison the tips of their arrows. I don't suppose you children have seen anything like that around here, have you?" she said, looking around at the small faces turned towards her. Each of the children shook their heads vigorously. "I'm sure that you would get your names in the papers if you were to discover them on this property."

Without a single question the children stampeded out of the kitchen, and before she could exhale Beryl heard the front door of the cottage slam behind them. She crossed the room and plucked a piece of paper from Mrs. Prentice's hand.

Mrs. Prentice's face was white with shock. The children had inherited their freckles from their mother; her cinnamon-colored splotches showed all the more clearly now that her face had entirely drained of any other color.

"Mrs. Prentice, take a seat before you fall over," Beryl said.

She fetched the teakettle from the hob and filled it under the pump. Replacing it on the cooker, she placed the piece of paper facedown on the table without glancing at it. She took a seat next to Mrs. Prentice and leaned back as if she were completely relaxed.

"Now let me guess. This piece of paper," Beryl said, tapping upon the upside-down letter, "says something absolutely untrue and horrifying and you are rattled to the core by it."

Mrs. Prentice looked up at her at least as shocked as she had been by whatever the letter had to say. She nodded wordlessly and her eyes filled with tears. Her thin shoulders started to shake, and great heaving sobs bubbled up in her throat.

Beryl was not adept at handling such displays of emotion. She enjoyed singing and dancing and whoops of delight. She enjoyed sweet nothings being whispered into her ear and rarely blushed at propositions that Edwina would have found distressing. But when it came to crying, Beryl found the whole thing caused her enormous discomfort. But she had been paying attention when Edwina navigated such situations and had picked up a few tips.

Tentatively she reached her hand out and patted Mrs. Prentice on the shoulder. It felt extremely awkward to do so, but surprisingly it had the desired effect. Mrs. Prentice dug into her pocket and retrieved an embroidered handkerchief. She dabbed her eyes with it and then blew her nose. When she had finally pulled herself together, she drew in a deep breath and found her power of speech.

"This came with the morning's post. I took a moment while the children were outside waiting for you to read what had come. And this hateful letter was in amongst it. I don't know what I'm going to do," she said.

"Do you mind if I take a look at what it has to say? I can assure you you are not the only one to have received a letter like this and none of the others have held a word of truth," Beryl said, hoping her voice sounded reassuring.

"So that's how you knew what this letter was about," Mrs. Prentice said.

"Exactly. I have received one myself, as a matter of fact," Beryl said.

"Go ahead and read it," Mrs. Prentice said. "But you must promise to say nothing to my husband."

If there was one thing Beryl knew it was how to be discreet with such matters. "I know all about keeping things from husbands. Don't worry yourself about that," she said as she pulled the piece of paper towards herself and flipped it faceup.

Although it was perhaps insensitive, she could not keep herself from chuckling. Mrs. Prentice stiffened slightly as Beryl's laughter bubbled up from within her.

"I can't see that there's anything funny about any of it," Mrs. Prentice said.

"I suppose you might if you had read my letter as well. It

seemed Simpkins is almost run off his feet with his amorous pursuits. The letter I received accused him of much the same sort of behavior," Beryl said.

Mrs. Prentice's eyes widened, and her lips parted into an O of surprise. "You don't say?"

"I do say. I see that you have been offered this cottage to live in in exchange for unspecified favors given to Simpkins. My letter suggested that Simpkins moved in at the Beeches in order to get up to all sorts of impropriety with both myself and Edwina. For a man of his age, he certainly does keep busy now, doesn't he?" Beryl said. She was pleased to see a smile ghost across Mrs. Prentice's face.

"That would be rather a lot of effort for just one elderly gentleman," she said. "Still, it is a very ugly suggestion, isn't it?"

"Quite. Do you have any idea who would have sent something like this to you?" Beryl asked.

"Not in the least. Do you know who sent yours?"

"No. Edwina and I have been attending to that very question for days. As I said, many people in the village have received such letters and they have created quite a lot of mischief. None of them have had a grain of truth to them, but they do seem to be specifically constructed to create a great deal of worry. I do hope you won't take it to heart," Beryl said.

"I think the thing that I'm most worried about is what will happen if this sort of tale gets carried to my husband. He's been doing so much better since we took up residence here at the farm and I would hate for anything to send him into a tailspin," she said.

Beryl could not help but agree. Mr. Prentice had been the subject of an investigation some weeks earlier and had been an easy target for suspicion based on his struggles with drink. As much as Michael Blackburn had had one sort of very bad war, Mr. Prentice had had another. While he was disinclined to discuss whatever memories were troubling him, he had been quick to try and block them out by getting to the bottom of any bottle of spirits he could get his hands on.

One of the things that had touched Beryl about Jack Prentice was the fact that she knew one of his responsibilities had been to lead his father home from the pub each night when he was too far in his cups to find his own way. Now that she came to think on it, perhaps part of why Jack had been growing by leaps and bounds was that the poor child was getting a full night's sleep for a change. Beryl most assuredly did not wish to see Mr. Prentice hitting rock bottom once more. The whole family stood to be the worse for it.

"I don't see any reason why anyone else should have to know about this—although I would like to share this letter with Edwina if you will give me permission to do so. As I said, we are looking into this in hopes that we can put a stop to it. It's just the sort of thing no village needs, but I assure you we will not be discussing it with your husband nor anyone else," Beryl said.

Even if they were to bring it up with Simpkins or Constable Gibbs, there was no way that either of those two would put Mrs. Prentice or her family in jeopardy. Constable Gibbs had been remarkably sympathetic to Mr. Prentice's troubles and Simpkins had a very soft spot for the entire family.

"I suppose that won't be a problem. After all, if it could help to expose who's responsible, you have my permission. But this isn't why you're here, is it?"

"No. Simpkins promised that I would be allowed to taste-test all of your hard work and offer an opinion on it," Beryl said, folding the letter up and tucking it into its envelope and slipping it into her pocket.

By the time she and Mrs. Prentice had sampled all of the batches of greengage jam, the children had returned to the cottage and Mrs. Prentice seemed completely recovered from her outburst. Then a look of concern flitted across her face once more.

"I promised Simpkins that after we had tasted all of these, I would send some sample jars to Minnie Mumford at the Silver Spoon so that she could try them out on her customers. Simpkins is eager to get a wider range of feedback before he brings the recipes to Colonel Kimberly's. By the time I get them into the village I don't know what I'll do about getting dinner on the table for my husband," Mrs. Prentice said.

"I've got the motorcar. I can run them into the village and drop them off with Minnie myself," Beryl said.

"Are you sure it's no trouble?" Mrs. Prentice asked, looking relieved.

"It is no trouble at all. I am always looking for an excuse to get behind the wheel."

Even though the typewriter seemed to call to her to put in a bit of time on her novel, especially since both Beryl and Simpkins were away from the house, Edwina had agreed to meet with Charles at his office to go over some upcoming cases for the Magistrate's Court. It had proven a fine morning for a walk and Crumpet had been eager to head out the door with his mistress not long after breakfast. While she wished to get back to the further adventures of Bart Dalton and the gang of cattle rustlers he was pursuing, she knew she would not be able to settle down and lose herself in her creative pursuits while her obligations required attention.

Charles greeted her with his usual quiet enthusiasm and offered to make coffee before they settled down to work. Edwina declined and wondered why Charles might have taken up drinking such a noxious beverage. He had become noticeably more worldly in his views and pursuits in the last several months and she suspected Beryl had been exerting some influence upon him. Beryl was a confirmed coffee drinker and exhibited an inexplicably reluctant attitude towards the drinking of tea.

Crumpet stretched out in front of the doorway as if to block Edwina from leaving without his notice and promptly fell asleep. She and Charles spent the next hour going over the upcoming cases and how legal precedent might affect them. But before long they had concluded their responsibilities and Edwina thought it time for her to head home. She might just be able to write a few pages before Beryl burst back onto the scene. As she pushed back her chair Charles cleared his throat.

"I wondered if you had heard about Cornelia Burroughs?" he asked.

"What about her?" Edwina asked.

"She's dead," Charles said.

Edwina's heart sank in her chest. Could this be related to the poisoned pen letters? She had worried something like this might happen from the very moment Michael Blackburn had slid his letter across the magistrate's bench. The concern had only grown with each passing letter cropping up in the village, not to mention Margery's attempt on her own life. Her distress must have shown on her face because Charles pushed back his chair and came around the side of the desk and took her hand. He gave it a gentle squeeze.

"I didn't realize the two of you were close. I am sorry to have shocked you," Charles said. "Are you quite all right?"

"We weren't at all close, but I do confess I am deeply distressed. Do you know the cause of her death?" Edwina asked.

Charles shook his head. "I have no idea. Why do you ask?"

"It's just that she seemed to be in robust good health when I last saw her on the day of the Magistrate's Court. She was leaving the garden club meeting at the Women's Institute. Like usual, she was pestering her husband and ordering him about. Then she took off in her motorcar with as much verve as Beryl. She looked not the least bit ill."

"Sometimes these things happen quite suddenly. You don't think there's anything more to it than a heart attack or something of that sort, do you?" he asked.

"As an officer of the court I'm sure that you can be discreet, can you not?" Edwina asked.

"You know that I will," Charles said. He squeezed her hand again. "Whatever is the matter?"

"You remember the letter Michael Blackburn received anonymously?" she asked.

"Of course I do," Charles said.

"Unfortunately, he's not the only one to have received such a letter. There's been quite a rash of them going about the village. They've caused a great deal of mischief and I have felt very concerned that they might lead to someone's death," Edwina said.

"Surely you can't be serious," Charles said.

"I'm afraid that I am."

"Don't you think you might be overreacting just a smidge?" Charles asked. "You have no idea what happened to Cornelia any more than I do."

"That may be the case, but I won't be able to put it from my mind until I find out. We've finished here, haven't we?" she asked.

"We certainly have. But from the look of you, I don't think you'd be able to concentrate even if we hadn't," he said.

"Then I shall be going," Edwina said. She stood and Crumpet immediately jumped to his feet.

"You look like you're off on a mission," Charles said. "Would you like for me to accompany you?"

"I will be perfectly safe, thank you. But I am going to stop in and speak with Constable Gibbs," she said.

Chapter 12

Beryl pulled the motorcar to a stop at the curb in front of the Silver Spoon Tearoom. She gathered up the crate of greengage jam samples from the boot and bustled into the shop with a bubbling sense of enthusiasm. Generally speaking, Beryl had always thought of food as little more than fuel and hadn't spent enough time preparing any of it to give much thought to how the overall process even occurred. But between Simpkins's involvement in his company and her recent experience of harvesting fruit, she found it had sparked a level of interest in the viability of the product that she would not previously have considered possible.

Humming under her breath, she pushed open the plate glass door of the shop and stepped inside. Generally, Minnie Mumford's shop bustled with activity. Hers was one of the only places in the village to stop in for a bite to eat, and although Minnie gave Prudence Rathbone a run for her money in the gossip department, one could not fault her for the quality of her baked goods or, should one's interests run to such things, her pots of strongly brewed tea.

But this afternoon Beryl was surprised to see only one customer in the shop when she entered. And it had to be said, the atmosphere was a strange departure from the normally cheerful and welcoming one the shop generally exuded. In place of the gentle chatter of satisfied patrons and the clinking of cutlery against fine china cups, the noise of a heated argument filled the space.

Beryl wondered if by any chance the air of hostility had driven off other patrons. She stood in front of the door with the crate of jam jars poised on her hip, considering how best to proceed. Unlike Edwina, who certainly would have known exactly what to do to smooth the waters while simultaneously feeling agonized at the discomfort the circumstance produced, Beryl simply took in the scene unfolding in front of her.

Mrs. Scott, the wife of Mr. Scott, the village greengrocer, stood red faced and shouting at the far end of the room. Within arm's reach and prudently cowering behind the counter used to hold the ornately wrought brass till, was Minnie Mumford. Although Beryl could not drum up a great deal of enthusiasm for Minnie based on her tendency towards gossip, she generally found her to be a benign and gentle sort of a woman. She generally seemed eager to please and as though her highest goals in life were putting her customers at ease and connecting with them in a friendly way.

Beryl had sometimes wondered if that was the reason for Minnie's tendency to gossip. Prudence always came across as someone who took on the role of gossip as a way to distinguish herself from her fellow villagers, but Beryl wondered if Minnie did it as a way to find common ground. By commiserating with them or chewing over the business of others, she could while away a few moments with them in a manner that made it seem as though they were all part of some connected circle.

But today, that circle did not seem to include Mrs. Scott. In fact, Mrs. Scott, who tended to be a fairly mild-mannered woman herself, had raised her gloved hand and was jabbing it in the direction of Minnie's chest. Beryl wondered if contact would have been made between the two women if the counter had not separated them. Neither of the women appeared to have taken any notice of the fact that Beryl had entered the shop, in itself a wonderment as the bell on the door still jangled. Beryl had never known Minnie not to attend immediately to arriving customers even if the most she could offer was a warm smile of greeting.

"I wanted you to hear it from me. My daughter will no longer be working at the Palais Cinema. I am absolutely appalled at your husband's behavior and if I had known about it sooner it never would have gotten to this point," Mrs. Scott said, her voice shrill with fury.

"But, Mrs. Scott, I have no idea what you're talking about," Minnie said, lifting her hands in supplication.

"If you don't know about the way your husband runs his hands over everything in a skirt here in Walmsley Parva, then it is high time you found out," Mrs. Scott said. "I am advising you to reel him in before he ends up hauled up before the court over his behavior. If he lays his hands on my daughter again, I promise you that it will come to that."

"Are you telling me you think that my husband has behaved in an improper manner towards Eva?" Mrs. Mumford said.

"That's exactly what I'm saying. The man is an octopus, but I had thought that he at least confined himself to women closer to his own age. Apparently, he is perfectly willing to rob the local cradles to appease his unbridled lust," Mrs. Scott said. "You'd best reign him in or you haven't heard the last of this. I don't want to have to speak to my husband about this, but if I hear any more about your husband harassing my daughter, I will."

She leaned in even closer and shook her finger right in Minnie's face. Then she wheeled around on her sensibly low-heeled shoe and rushed out the door. In her haste she actually careened into Beryl, and it was with some effort she managed to hang on to the crate of jam. Mrs. Scott, usually a courteous woman, never even stopped to apologize for bumping into her. She just rushed on out the door setting the bell jangling wildly in her wake.

Beryl turned and watched as Mrs. Scott strode down the street at such a pace it could almost be considered a trot. In fact, she reminded Beryl distinctly of Crumpet as he tried to keep up with Edwina on one of their enthusiastic walks. Beryl turned back towards Mrs. Mumford, whose mouth hung open, speechless with shock. Beryl stepped further into the shop and placed the crate of jam upon the nearby table. She headed for the counter and Mrs. Mumford.

"Minnie, are you quite all right?" Beryl asked.

"I daresay, I am not. I don't know that I've ever been so humiliated in all my life," Minnie said, placing a hand over the base of her throat as if willing her heart to slow its frantic pace.

"Mrs. Scott did seem to be rather worked up, didn't she?" Beryl said, coming around the side of the counter and taking Minnie by the arm. She led the shopkeeper to one of her own tables, pulled out a chair, and pressed her down into it. Beryl took a seat across from her and gave Minnie her full attention.

"I've never seen anything like it. I'm afraid she must have had some sort of breakdown to come in here spouting such outrageous accusations. Whatever could have happened?" Minnie asked, her mild blue eyes still wide with shock.

"She seemed to me to be very much in control of her faculties, although her temper was certainly threatening to get out of hand," Beryl said. "I would not have said she seemed to have lost her wits."

"But she must have done. I've never heard anything so unbelievable about my husband in all my life," Mrs. Mumford said.

Now it was Beryl's turned to be shocked. Although she hoped that it did not show on her face, Beryl felt astonished that Mrs. Mumford had never before been apprised to her husband's unsavory reputation. Beryl had not been in the man's company for more than five minutes when he had done his best to put his hands where he ought not. He also was the sort of person who thought nothing of doing his very best to seduce any woman in his path.

Although, Beryl couldn't imagine anyone reciprocating his advances. She had thought him to be an odious sort of person and, unfortunately, found herself through much practice well equipped to fend him off. But if what Mrs. Scott had said about Eva had been true, Beryl's heart went out to the much younger woman. She doubted that Eva Scott had had a great deal of experience with the sort of unpleasantness that she knew Mr. Mumford capable of attempting. With a shudder she recalled his roaming hands groping at her in the back of a motorcar whilst returning to the village from the scene of a murder.

But how should such a topic be broached? It wasn't really her place to inform Mrs. Mumford of her husband's reputation, was it? She dearly wished that Edwina had been there in her place. Although, to be fair, Edwina had never experienced the sort of revolting attempts upon her person by Mr. Mumford that she and Eva Scott had endured. In fact, Edwina had been just as shocked as Minnie seemed to be that Mr. Mumford had any such tendencies. Still, Edwina was much more adept than she at soothing the ruffled feathers of her fellow villagers. Perhaps a change of topic was the best way to proceed.

"Do you have any idea what would have caused Mrs. Scott to say such a thing?" Beryl asked.

"None whatsoever. I was simply here cleaning up from the late morning rush when she appeared in the shop waving her arms about and shouting. The other customers left in a hurry, and I was lucky to have even been able to settle up their bills. You appeared very shortly afterwards. She never mentioned what could have given her cause to make such monstrous claims."

Beryl suspected Mrs. Scott had received a nasty letter. She thought that was a likely explanation but did not see any value in mentioning it to Mrs. Mumford. Beryl had not been particularly skilled at turning a blind eye to the foibles of errant husbands, which was one reason why she had gone through so many of them. Not that she was without a roaming eye on occasion herself. After all, what were eyes for if not to look about? If Mrs. Mumford had figured out a way to stay happily married for years to a man so disinclined to honor his marriage vows, Beryl was not the one to hand her a pair of correcting spectacles.

"Perhaps what you need is a distraction. I'm sure that things will work themselves out in the end," Beryl said.

Mrs. Mumford attempted a feeble smile. "I'm sure you're right. There must be some explanation, although for the life of me I can't imagine what it would be. But what brings you by this afternoon? I see you've brought a crate," she said.

Beryl nodded and reached into the box in front of her. She withdrew a sparkling jar and slid it across the table towards Minnie.

"Simpkins and Mrs. Prentice have been hard at work preserving the greengage harvest and trialing some new jam recipes. Mrs. Prentice thought that your tea shop would be the perfect place to test them out and to discover which of the recipes was most preferred by potential customers. I offered to bring some samples and to ask if you would be willing to serve them and to let Simpkins know the favorites," Beryl said.

"I'd be happy to. In fact, I'll make sure to put them into rotation this afternoon. It'll give me something to take my mind off those wicked lies about Clarence," Mrs. Mumford said.

Beryl thanked her for her willingness to help and said her good-byes. On her way out of the shop she congratulated herself at holding her tongue with Mrs. Mumford and decided that while the shopkeeper was content to simply wonder about the cause of Mrs. Scott's anger, she herself was not.

Not only did she feel as though it might be part of the case they were working on, but she also had a fondness for Eva Scott that would not allow her to simply turn a blind eye to what might have happened to the young woman. She left the motorcar parked at the curb and turned towards the street leading to the Scott residence. It sounded as though it was unlikely she would find Eva at the Palais Cinema.

Edwina couldn't shake her feelings of concern at the news of Cornelia Burroughs's death. The sense of dread that had been building in the pit of her stomach ever since Michael and Norman had appeared before the magistrate's bench had magnified into roiling nausea. Something was eating at the heart of her beloved village, and she couldn't help but wonder if the worst had come to pass. With a feeling of urgency, she left Charles's home and headed straight for the police station.

Constable Gibbs looked up from her usual spot behind the counter that separated the general public from the inner sanctum of the police station. She took one look at Edwina's face and waved her into her private sanctuary at the back of the building. Edwina sank heavily into one of the chairs ringing a small wooden table.

"You look as though you've seen a ghost," Constable Gibbs said. "I can't say I've seen you look quite like this even at a crime scene."

"I've just been told by Charles that Cornelia Burroughs has died," Edwina said. "Is there any possibility that the poisoned pen had anything to do with her death?"

Constable Gibbs leaned back in her own chair and drummed her fingers on the top of the table. "You know that's exactly what I wondered when I first got the call about her passing, but it seems as though she died of natural causes."

"But I saw her just the other day in the village ordering her husband about and appearing to be the very picture of rude good health. What on earth could have happened?" Edwina asked.

"Apparently it was an asthma attack," Constable Gibbs said.

"An asthma attack? Are you quite sure?" Edwina asked.

Constable Gibbs nodded slowly. "I had the same question you did about whether the poisoned pen letters could have had something to do with it, especially after what had happened with Margery Nelson. So I spoke with Dr. Wilcox about it. He assured me that Cornelia Burroughs had a long history of difficulties with asthma and that apparently, she suffered from a debilitating attack. Her husband came home and found her dead."

"A long-standing difficulty with asthma," Edwina said. "Dr. Wilcox is quite certain about that?"

"So it seems. He's treated her for it for years."

"Did he say what could have brought it on?"

"He indicated that perhaps it could have been caused by some sort of emotional distress but that sometimes these things just happened. Cornelia was not a young woman after all, and she had contacted influenza when it came through years before as well. He said it was possible that her lungs were further weakened as a result," Constable Gibbs said.

"Did Dr. Wilcox have any sense that Cornelia was distressed by something in particular that could have brought the attack on? Did he say whether or not he knew if she had received one of the poisoned pen letters?" Edwina asked.

"I didn't pry into it any further. I didn't want to appear to be questioning his medical judgment. After all, he's been a doctor for long enough to know when someone has succumbed to a preexisting condition, hasn't he?" Constable Gibbs asked.

Edwina thought it likely that Dr. Wilcox did know of what he spoke. If it had been Dr. Nelson who had written the death certificate, she would have had more questions. With his new-fangled ideas and dismissive behavior, she couldn't bring herself to simply accept his authority as a medical professional.

But Dr. Wilcox was an eminently sensible sort of man who neither over- nor under-reacted to the circumstances in which his patients found themselves. And she supposed if Cornelia had had a long-standing condition of asthma, it was more likely that she herself was imagining things on account of her concern over the poisoned pen letters. Although, if Cornelia had received one and the distress it caused brought on an asthma attack that led to her death, she wondered if the author of the letters could be considered culpable.

"Did you ask her husband any questions about whether or not she had received any of the letters?" Edwina asked.

"Godfrey wasn't in any fit state for me to question him about something like that at the time. In fact, I've been rather concerned about him."

"Has he taken her death especially hard?" Edwina asked.

"I should say he has. I found him driving Cornelia's motorcar most erratically," Constable Gibbs said. "In fact, he had run it off the road and into a ditch when I came upon him. I didn't think that adding to his distress by asking him if something other than natural causes brought on his wife's death seemed like the kind thing to do."

As much as Constable Gibbs had always had a firm hand on law and order in the village, she also was concerned about the overall well-being of her fellow villagers. Edwina could easily imagine her not wishing to make what was already a difficult situation any worse for another.

Edwina felt her heart begin to thump loudly in her chest. Every time she found herself in Beryl's motorcar, she imagined just such a scenario. Beryl was convinced she was invincible, but even with her eyes clamped tightly shut, Edwina couldn't help but imagine the pair of them in a crumpled heap at the bottom of an embankment each time Beryl took a curve at her preferred rate of speed.

"Was he injured?" Edwina asked.

"Fortunately, he wasn't. The motorcar had to be winched out by a tow truck, so I ordered it to be taken to Blackburn's Garage," she said.

"Was it badly damaged?" Edwina asked.

"It could have been worse. But that wasn't the reason I had it taken to the garage. It was more that I wanted it to be out of Godfrey's possession until he was more fully in command of his emotions. Watching him veer off down the embankment made me fear that he might hurt himself or someone else if he were allowed to remain in possession of it, at least for now."

"I suppose it would be the right thing to do to pay a call on him as a private citizen," Edwina said. "You won't feel offended if I put my mind at ease by asking him if his wife was in receipt of one of the letters, would you?" Edwina asked.

"I would consider it to be part of your investigation into the poisoned pen situation. I'm sure you'll proceed gently and will not manage to drive Godfrey to any ill-considered behavior."

"I'll be sure to handle him with kid gloves. But I don't think I will feel I have done my duty in pursuing the truth in this matter without speaking with him about it."

With that, Edwina pushed back the chair and exited the police station. She definitely wanted to speak with Godfrey Burroughs, but felt she ought to catch Beryl up on how the case stood and to inform her of Cornelia's death before she took any further action.

Chapter 13

Sure enough, Beryl found Eva Scott at home. The dejected-looking young woman opened the door and appeared surprised to find Beryl standing on her front step. She looked up and down the street as though worried someone might see her conversing with Beryl and quickly waved her inside. Eva had never shown any hesitation in being seen chatting with Beryl in the past and she had to wonder if the situation she had witnessed between Mrs. Scott and Minnie Mumford was the cause of the girl's trepidation.

Beryl waited until they were seated in the pleasant sitting room at the front of the house overlooking the street before she divulged the reason for her visit. Beryl couldn't help but notice that Eva glanced repeatedly out the window as though bracing herself for trouble.

"I stopped by because I wanted to ask how you were doing," Beryl said.

"Doing? Whatever do you mean?" Eva asked. Beryl thought she detected a faint blush rising to Eva's cheeks.

"I happened upon your mother giving Minnie Mumford a blistering scolding at the tearoom just now," Beryl said.

"Oh dear. I was afraid something like that might happen," Eva said. Beryl noticed tears shimmering in Eva's eyes.

"Are you quite all right?" Beryl asked. "If what your mother had to say is true, I imagine that you might not be."

The tears in Eva's eyes spilled down her cheeks. Once again that day Beryl found herself confronted with a sobbing woman. As much as Mrs. Prentice's tears had made Beryl feel uncomfortable, Eva's wrenched her heart. Although she did not dwell on it, Beryl well remembered the shame and humiliation she had felt as a very young girl being put into uncomfortable situations with her father's friends and business acquaintances. Until she had developed her own way of dissuading them, it had been excruciating. Even now she did not manage to navigate such situations without having it tarnish her mood for the day.

Eva fished a handkerchief from her pocket and wiped her eyes after a few minutes' time. She sagged back against the sofa cushions and stared down at the floor as though she could not meet Beryl's gaze.

"I don't know what my mother had to say to Mrs. Mumford, but I can tell you that she had good reason to be angry on my behalf."

"Mr. Mumford does have an extremely difficult time keeping his hands to himself. I am very sorry to hear that he roamed them over you," Beryl said.

Eva's eyes widened. "Did he try something similar with you?"

"Unfortunately, I experienced his unwanted attentions first-hand—no pun intended—almost immediately upon being introduced to him. I'm just very sorry that you have had to put up with it," Beryl said.

"I had no idea what I ought to do."

"Has it been going on for some time?" Beryl asked.

"He's been making uncomfortable comments for the past several months. At first, I thought I was simply imagining more than he intended, but when I tried to ignore it, he took it as encouragement. He's become far more insistent over the last few weeks," Eva said.

"How very miserable for you."

"It's been terrible. I loved my job at the cinema except for enduring the unwanted attention from Mr. Mumford. Now I shall have to find another job instead," Eva said. "I am not sure I will be able to with the economy being in such a slump."

"You are better off even if you don't find another job quickly. Did you tell your mother what he had been doing? Is that how she knew to go to Mrs. Mumford?" Beryl asked.

Eva shook her head. "No. I was still trying to figure out what I ought to do when my mother received a letter in the post telling her what he'd been up to," Eva said.

"Was the letter by any chance sent by an anonymous sender?" Beryl asked.

"How did you know that?" Eva asked.

"Your mother is not the only person in the village to have received an anonymous letter accusing someone of bad behavior," Beryl said. "It seemed that that was the most likely explanation for the sudden information coming her way."

"As much as I didn't want to quit my job and certainly didn't want to have an uncomfortable conversation with my mother, it was something of a relief for her to know what had been happening. I've been sick to my stomach with shame. I thought I must have been doing something to encourage him," Eva said. Her eyes shone again with tears.

"This wasn't your fault. You have nothing to be ashamed of and it is best that your mother found out."

"Do you really think so?" Eva asked.

"I most certainly do. And you're very fortunate to have a mother who would take your side in this appalling situation. I know you probably feel embarrassed that your mother spoke to Mrs. Mumford, but the fact remains that she only had your best interests at heart and was willing to make a breach in her relationship with a prominent person in the village in order to protect you. You're a very lucky young woman indeed," Beryl said.

She felt a small lump rising in her throat as she thought back to the way her own mother had responded when she had tried to tell her about a deeply distressing incident on the back stairs with one of their houseguests. Not only had her mother refused to believe her about the way the man had behaved, but she had also chastised Beryl for having such malignant and unnatural thoughts. At the time, Beryl had felt confused and abandoned to her fate. But it was not in her nature to remain a victim of circumstance. Her mother had never been a particularly involved or affectionate figure in Beryl's life, and it was just after that point that she decided she would seek her own best interests regardless of the opinion of her parents.

She concluded that if they were going to put her in harm's way with no sense of concern, she certainly could go about throwing herself into the sorts of risk-taking adventures she had always longed to pursue. If she were going to come to harm, she decided it would be through her own willingness to try something new, rather than at the grasping and dirty fingers of some predatory man. As she looked at Eva Scott, her heart squeezed a bit at that type of love that Mrs. Scott must have had for her daughter, a thing that Beryl did not feel that she had ever experienced. At least, not until she had pitched up in Edwina's driveway and had found a place to call home.

"I thought from the way she stormed out of here that she was just very angry at me," Eva said.

Beryl shook her head. "From what I witnessed at the Silver Spoon, I can assure you that your mother assigned no blame to you. You are a beloved daughter and I hope that you will remember that. Not everyone can say the same," she said. "If anything like that should happen again, I hope you will keep in mind how much your mother values your personal safety and that you are worthy of speaking up on your own behalf," Beryl said.

"You mean I should be expecting something like this to happen again?" Eva asked.

"I'm not saying you ought to expect it, because that would be a very discouraging way to go through life. What I am saying is that should it happen again, you should feel emboldened to speak up for yourself. You do not need to endure such sort of behavior. I have found throughout the course of my life that pushing back against unwanted advances becomes easier every time one does it. I'm sorry that this is part of the coming-of-age process for so many women. Maybe one day, it won't be."

There was no doubt about it, it had been a long and trying day. Edwina realized she was relieved to find herself alone in the company of Simpkins and Beryl. How strange it seemed that Simpkins had come to feel like family. If anyone had told her a year previously that she would be comforted by the sight of Simpkins and his hobnailed boots seated in her front parlor, she would have scoffed at the idea.

But as she took up the new ball of wool she had purchased earlier in the week and cast on stitches for a jaunty new beret, she found herself lulled into the first feeling of peacefulness she had experienced all day. Beryl joined them and busied herself concocting a batch of gin fizzes. As her friend took up her customary spot at the end of the sofa, Edwina lost count of the stitches she was casting on for her new project and laid the knitting in her lap. She took a sip of the drink Beryl had left next to her.

"Have you unmasked the poisoned pen while I was in London?" Simpkins asked.

"Not yet. To tell the truth, even with all of the information we've gathered, I don't know that we're any further along on this case than we were when we started out," Beryl said.

"I am feeling rather discouraged about it myself," Edwina

said. "It seems there's no end to this stream of letters or the havoc they're wreaking throughout the village."

"You're right about that. I've encountered two more of them today," Beryl said.

"Two more?" Simpkins said. "That's some kind of busy letter writer."

"Who received them?" Edwina asked, running her hands over a plump skein of wool once more in an attempt to soothe her frazzled nerves.

"Mrs. Prentice for one," Beryl said, raising a long finger towards the ceiling. "And Mrs. Scott."

"Mrs. Prentice received one of those nasty notes?" Simpkins asked, a protective tone creeping into his rough voice.

Beryl nodded. "I'm sorry to say, she did. She was really very distressed by the whole thing. In fact, it had to do with you." Beryl turned her gaze on Simpkins.

"Me? What does this anonymous writer seem to think I've been up to now?" Simpkins asked.

"The writer implied that you had only allowed the Prentice family to live on your property in exchange for certain favors from Mrs. Prentice. Favors her husband would find objectionable."

Edwina drew in her breath sharply and her and Simpkins's gazes met across the room. Certainly, such a topic was not one she wished to dwell upon. She knew herself to be rather prudish about illicit liaisons, or romantic entanglements of any sort, come to mention it. But it wasn't just the notion of Simpkins embroiled in something unsavory with a far younger woman that caused her to feel a wave of new concern wash over her. She knew at a glance that Simpkins was troubled by the same, far more worrisome, thing.

"Was she alone when she received the letter?" Simpkins asked.

"The children were all there. I came upon her just after she had received it. The poor woman simply burst into tears. Who knew you had such a strong effect on women?" Beryl said.

"It's not funny in the least," Edwina said.

"I would have to agree with Miss Edwina," Simpkins said.

"But surely it's just a silly stab in the dark that means very little," Beryl said. "Which is essentially what I said to Mrs. Prentice when I was trying to comfort her and make her see reason."

"I rather think the important thing here is that her husband might come to hear of it, and it could cause a great deal of grief," Edwina said.

Simpkins nodded. "As much as I'd have to say I'm flattered to hear that whoever is writing these letters seems to think that I have the youthful vigor necessary to attend to so many ladies in the village, I would hate for Mr. Prentice to catch wind of this. He's too unstable to take this sort of news with the kind of good humor necessary not to make trouble from it."

"And the Prentice family certainly doesn't need any more trouble coming their way," Edwina said.

Even the softness of the ball of wool in her lap did little to comfort her as she considered the possible damage this letter could cause. The Prentice family had worked so hard to get back on their feet and the idea that it could be ripped apart by such malicious gossip was unconscionable. If Mr. Prentice came to hear of it, he would be unlikely to continue to accept the much-needed assistance Simpkins provided since it was likely the village would wonder what had been at the root of his generosity.

"I'm sure that Mrs. Prentice has no intention of telling him about it herself, and the three of us would do no such thing, either," Beryl said. "With any luck he won't come to hear of it."

"Do you think the children knew that anything untoward had happened?" Edwina asked.

"No, as soon as I saw that Mrs. Prentice was upset, I sent them off looking for some sort of imaginary exotic toad in the far reaches of the property. She managed to collect herself before they returned," Beryl said.

Edwina was impressed. She had not given Beryl credit for being the sort of person who would understand how to urge a group of children away from any dramatic happenings through a clever suggestion about something they would find even more interesting. Perhaps her friend had grown through her time in Walmsley Parva just as Edwina herself had ever since Beryl had arrived.

"You said that you discovered that there were two letters. What about the one to Mrs. Scott?" Simpkins asked.

"That was dramatic, too. Everywhere I went this morning it seemed that there were women bursting into tears," Beryl said.

Edwina knew that her friend had just as little interest in interacting with crying women as she did with children. Perhaps Beryl would be wise to take up knitting herself in order to have a distraction from life's difficulties. But somehow Edwina could not imagine Beryl sitting still long enough with anything in her hand other than some sort of stiffening drink to produce any kind of handicrafts. The very notion of it made her stifle a giggle. Now was no time for lighthearted imaginings.

"What terrible and outrageous accusations did she receive in her letter?" Edwina asked.

"It informed her that Mr. Mumford was making unwanted advances towards young Eva," Beryl said.

"How did you manage to hear that?" Simpkins asked.

"When I took the jam samples to Minnie Mumford's tearoom, Mrs. Scott was at the shop yelling at Minnie about it. Mrs. Scott told her she had best take her husband in hand and announced that she had insisted Eva quit her job at the cinema," Beryl said.

"How appalling," Edwina said.

She had been shocked to the marrow when on their first case Beryl happened to mention that Mr. Mumford had made a nuisance of himself in just such a way. Edwina had never found him to be anything other than a perfect gentleman and it had been truly shocking for Beryl to make such an accusation. Not that she didn't believe her friend, but she had thought perhaps there was just something about Beryl's attractiveness that caused him to lose control of himself. She had not credited the notion that he might make a habit of plaguing the women around him. She doubted very much that Minnie knew anything about it, either. The poor woman must have been humiliated to hear such news right in her own shop.

"Minnie was completely stunned by the confrontation. After Mrs. Scott stormed out of the tearoom, I stayed and spoke with her for a few moments. Apparently, Minnie had no idea of the reputation her husband has throughout the village," Beryl said.

"Then she must be the only one," Simpkins said. He shook his head as though laying judgment at Mr. Mumford's feet. "As much as he puts on airs because he owns the cinema, he's no gentleman and everyone knows it. Although I have to say I am surprised that he would take the risk of foisting himself upon Eva considering how protective her father is."

"Do you think that the letter was telling the truth?" Edwina asked. "After all, none of the other letters have been in the least."

"Unfortunately, this one was," Beryl said. "I headed straight to the Scotts' home after I left the tearoom and asked Eva about it. She confirmed that he had been most inappropriate in his dealings with her over the past few weeks and that she had not known what to do about it. She said that as much as she loved her job at the cinema and hated to have to leave it, she was relieved when her mother found out what had been going on and insisted that she quit," Beryl said.

"The poor girl," Edwina said. "What a thing to endure."

"The man deserves a good hiding," Simpkins said. "If Eva's father decides to give it to him, I'll be happy to help," he said, gesticulating wildly with his half-drained glass.

Edwina did not quite like the glint in Simpkins's eye. She had worried about the sorts of riling up the letters might create, but she had not considered that Simpkins might turn vigilante on account of them. Generally, she thought of him as someone who was unlikely to get stirred up enough to take a great deal of action no matter the cause. But it had to be said, Eva Scott was a well-liked young woman in the village, and Edwina could well understand why he would feel angry to think that she had been made to suffer needlessly. The notion of suffering brought back her biggest news of the day to share with the others.

"Sadly, more letters were not the only surprising news today," Edwina said.

"What did you discover?" Beryl asked.

"Cornelia Burroughs is dead," Edwina said.

"On account of one of the poisoned pen letters?" Beryl asked.

Edwina shook her head. "I stopped to speak with Constable Gibbs, and she assured me that the death was a natural one. It seems she suffered from asthma and had an attack that claimed her life. I did wonder if her attack was brought on by one of the letters, however. I believe that asthma can be triggered by emotional distress."

"If that's the case, I wonder if the poisoned pen writer could be considered responsible for killing her," Simpkins said. "That only seems right, doesn't it?"

"I should think so. What did the death certificate say?" Beryl asked.

"According to Constable Gibbs, Dr. Wilcox signed off on it as purely natural causes. There was no mention of emotional distress," Edwina said. "I expect that if anyone should know about a thing like that, it would be Dr. Wilcox. He treated her for years before Dr. Nelson came to town and would have been likely to have spotted if something was amiss."

"How is Godfrey taking it all?" Simpkins asked.

Edwina looked up at him sharply. Simpkins had not been a widower for so very long himself as to have forgotten what it was like to feel the sting of recent loss. His wife Bessie had been his loving partner for decades, and Edwina had been quite concerned about him when he had found himself without her not so very long before Beryl arrived on the scene.

"Constable Gibbs mentioned that the shock of it had been difficult for him. As a matter of fact, he was out driving Cornelia's motorcar and ended up running it off the road and down into a ravine," Edwina said.

"Do you think he ran it off the road on purpose?" Beryl asked. "You don't think he was trying to do away with himself, do you?"

"A man might get up to all sorts of desperate measures when left on his own after the loss of a good woman," Simpkins said. "Although I'm not entirely sure Cornelia would have qualified as a good woman."

"I think the least we could do would be to stop by and check on him. Paying a condolence call is the neighborly thing to do and it might give us the opportunity to ask him if his wife had received any poisoned pen letters that he knew of," Edwina said.

"I propose we head over there tomorrow. The only thing on our diary is the session with the photographer for the Colonel Kimberly's advertising campaign," Beryl said.

Edwina looked down at the knitting in her lap. She had completely forgotten that she had agreed to be photographed. With all that had been going on, she had not even made time to shop for a new hat. It seemed she was a busy working woman after all.

Chapter 14

Beryl had wanted to take the motorcar, but Edwina insisted a walk would do them good, so Beryl found herself trudging along on foot despite the warmth of the day weighed down by a cake tin filled with one of Edwina's home-baked delicacies. She had spent two hours in the kitchen the evening before concocting it. Beryl had never understood the finer points of condolence calls, but she had made a point of keeping Edwina company by sitting at the table and chatting with her while she turned out a lemon drizzle cake without consulting a recipe.

The Burroughses' home sat near the center of the village, and from the street it appeared larger than seemed necessary to house only two people. They stepped up to the glossy black front door with its gleaming brass knocker and Edwina rapped upon it firmly. Beryl stood just behind her holding the tin of cake, which she thrust into Edwina's hands just as the door creaked open.

The man standing on the other side of the threshold appeared nothing like the man who so often had been seen hurrying at his wife's beck and call throughout the village. Beryl had not felt any particular interest in getting to know either of the Burroughses beyond a simple nod in passing if they encountered one another on the street, but even with her cursory knowledge of him, she could tell he was incredibly altered. Whenever she had spotted him trailing in Cornelia's wake, he had appeared henpecked but irreproachably neat and tidy. She had never seen him with a hair out of place or without his tie neatly knotted and cinched tightly to the base of his throat. But the man standing before them was another creature entirely.

Unless her eyes deceived her, Godfrey Burroughs was standing in his doorway for all the village to see wearing a mismatched pair of pajamas. The pajama top was buttoned incorrectly, and his hair stood up on end like a baby chimpanzee. She had never seen anyone go to pieces as quickly as Godfrey seemed to have done.

"Hello, Godfrey. We thought we ought to come to see how you were managing. We heard about poor Cornelia yesterday and we just wanted to drop by to ask if we could be of any assistance," Edwina said, thrusting the tin of cake towards him and stepping up into the hallway.

Godfrey's eyes widened in surprise, and he took a step backwards. While Beryl never thought of Edwina as a pushy sort of an individual, she was known to take matters into her own hands when she felt it necessary and for the greater good. Evidently, she thought that Godfrey Burroughs needed a firm hand, and from the looks of him, Beryl would have to agree. Edwina turned him round and gave him a gentle nudge towards the interior of his house. Beryl followed them and shut the door behind her.

The interior of the house was nothing like Beryl would have imagined from having seen the Burroughses about in the village. Or perhaps, the house had fallen to pieces in the short time since Cornelia's death. The post lay unopened on a hall table and discarded shoes and a hat lay on the floor near the door to the sitting room. Edwina steered Godfrey towards the sofa and pressed his shoulder down into it, silently indicating he ought to take a seat. He obeyed wordlessly, like a traumatized child.

Beryl looked around the room, taking in the disarray. Mugs of tea and half-eaten pieces of toast littered the side tables. Unread newspapers lay discarded on a table in front of the sofa. The draperies were still closed and what little light penetrated the room only served to make it look all the more despondent.

"I still can't believe she's gone," Godfrey said, finally managing to find his voice. He squeezed at something he held clutched to his chest.

"It did seem very sudden. I had no idea that Cornelia's asthma was quite so serious," Edwina said.

"Oh yes, it was of constant plague for her. I begged her to give these up, but she wouldn't and now look what's happened," Godfrey said, extending his hand and waggling a partial packet of cigarettes at Beryl.

"I had no idea that your wife smoked cigarettes," Edwina said.

"She was secretive about it. She didn't think it was entirely ladylike to do so and never smoked in public. In fact, I think she thought I was the only one who actually knew. That is until Dr. Nelson warned her that she ought to stop," he said, a sob rising up in his throat.

"I can't imagine she enjoyed being told what to do by the doctor or anyone else," Edwina said.

Beryl thought she heard a note of understanding in Edwina's voice. She had never liked Dr. Nelson and, even though Beryl knew that her friend was not all that enamored of Cornelia Burroughs, it seemed that she could empathize with her feelings about the doctor.

"She was outraged by his advice. He told her that a recent study had indicated that it looked as though cigarettes might be detrimental to everyone's health, not just asthmatics, and that he was encouraging all of his patients to refrain from their use. My wife was never one to take any suggestions that implied she might be in the wrong. She told him she would no longer require his services and sent him away with a flea in his ear," he said.

"Did this happen long before she died?" Edwina asked. "I hadn't heard anything about an argument between them."

"I suppose it must have been a week ago or so. She told me she thought that he was a quack, and she would be better off with no doctor at all. I can't help but think that if she had heeded his advice, she might still be with me," Godfrey said.

"It's possible that the smoking had nothing to do with her asthma attack. I had heard that any kind of emotional strain could cause such an attack as well. You don't know if your wife had received any sudden shocks lately, do you?" Edwina asked.

"What kind of a shock?" Godfrey asked.

Beryl and Edwina exchanged a glance and Edwina bobbed her head.

"Someone in the village has been sending poisoned pen letters and we thought it was possible that your wife had received one and that it could have triggered her difficulty with breathing," Beryl said. "Do you happen to know if she received any such letter?"

"Not to my knowledge. Although, to be fair, I'm not sure she would have shared such a thing with me. Cornelia was always inclined to follow her own counsel and I don't know that she would have thought a letter of that sort would be worth discussing with another. She might have thought it a sign of weakness. Do you have any idea who has been sending the letters?" he asked.

"No, we don't. You haven't received one of your own, have you?" Beryl asked.

Godfrey's eyes widened. "I certainly have not. What sort of

hateful person would send a poisoned pen letter to a recently bereaved man?" he asked, looking from Edwina to Beryl.

"It seems that whoever has been writing these letters is not particularly concerned with how hurtful they might be. I doubt bereavement would make a difference to the sender. If you receive one, will you let us know?" Edwina asked.

"Are you investigating the letters as a part of a case?" he asked.

"Yes. We are working on behalf of several clients on the matter and would be grateful for any assistance," Edwina said.

"Then I will certainly let you know if I receive one," Godfrey said.

Edwina stood and smoothed the wrinkles from her skirt.

"Thank you. Be sure to eat some of that cake, won't you? And do call upon us if you need some assistance even if you don't receive a nasty letter. It's not easy to be on your own as I well remember after my mother passed," Edwina said.

By the time they reached the pavement outside the house, Edwina appeared lost in thought.

"He certainly seems to be a changed man, doesn't he?" Beryl asked.

"Grief can do that, don't you think?" Edwina asked. "I'm sure that I looked quite a fright when my mother passed on and I'm not sure that her death was as much of a loss to me as Cornelia's is to Godfrey."

"I should think that the removal of such an imperious and irritating woman from his life would do him a world of good," Beryl said.

"That's the strange thing about marriages though, isn't it? From the outside it's impossible to know what they provide. Godfrey appeared to be henpecked and harassed, but maybe he valued the direction that his wife provided in his life and without it he feels completely adrift," Edwina said.

"Or maybe his wife's death isn't the thing that's really weighing on him," Beryl said.

"What do you mean?" Edwina said, coming to a halt right in the middle of the pavement.

"Someone is sending the poisoned pen letters. Perhaps that someone is Godfrey. Maybe he realizes the damage he's caused, and he's tipped over the edge about it," Beryl said.

"I believe you'll find that most often poisoned pen letters are written by a woman," Edwina said.

"Surely you're a bit more open-minded than that," Beryl said. "Most private enquiry agencies are run by men. That hasn't stopped us from opening one."

"I'm not sure it's entirely the same thing," Edwina said.

"I think you ought to stash your antiquated notions in a back closet somewhere and not look at them again. We need to be the sort of women who believe in modern ideas if we're going to help Simpkins sell his new products. That old-fashioned attitude won't help one bit," Beryl said.

"The world may be changing at a rapid pace, but I'm not entirely sure that human nature keeps up with it. Say what you will, I think it's far more likely that we are looking for a woman letter writer."

Beryl suggested it might be a good idea to check on Cornelia's damaged motorcar. If there was any chance that Godfrey had attempted to do away with himself in his distress over his wife's death, of the pair of them Beryl would be far more qualified to detect that evidence in the damage the vehicle had suffered. Besides, Edwina desperately wished to shop for a new hat before their appointment with Bernard Stevens. She and Edwina parted ways soon after leaving the Burroughses' residence and within a few moments time Beryl found herself standing on the pavement in front of Blackburn's Garage.

The pleasant and industrious sounds of clanking wrenches

and sputtering motors drifted towards her from within. Beryl knew just how irksome it could be when slid underneath a vehicle if a passerby stopped to ask questions. A quick glance at the interior of the garage revealed that Cornelia's motorcar was not the one Michael Blackburn seemed to be so diligently fixing. She recalled that Edwina mentioned that Constable Gibbs had requested they delay fixing it in order for Godfrey to have a few days of recovery from his bereavement before having access to it once more.

It was that sort of kindness that was a new experience for Beryl. While she was someone who tended to see the best in humanity and had often been the recipient of incredible acts of generosity throughout her travels across the globe, she did not have much familiarity with the sort of kindnesses that were associated with long acquaintance. The fact that the constable would surreptitiously look after the best interests of a grieving neighbor was outside Beryl's general experience of the world.

Until she had landed in Walmsley Parva months earlier, she had no awareness that such intimate knowledge between neighbors even existed. If someone had asked her if she thought it was possible, she likely would have assented that in some places it might happen. But she would not have dreamed it up from the depths of herself. While she had found her life of travel exciting and satisfying, there was something utterly beguiling about setting down some roots in a place where people might one day know her as well as they appeared to know Godfrey Burroughs.

Rather than disrupt the Blackburns, she made her way along the narrow alleyway dividing the garage from the coal merchant. She came to a stop in an open space behind the garage where the Blackburn siblings stored equipment not in use, as well as vehicles awaiting attention. There, parked directly behind the building, sat Cornelia's elegant vehicle.

Beryl approached it and ran a long finger across the shiny

black finish. While she would not say that the motorcar in front of her set her heart racing in the way her own beloved vehicle did, she would have declared it a sound investment. It had obviously been incredibly well maintained according to the deep tread she could see on the tires, a complete lack of rust anywhere in its frame, and the shiny luster of the paint. Someone had lovingly lavished attention on the cleaning and upkeep of the vehicle, and she could well imagine that Godfrey was the one who had been expected to perform such duties.

As Beryl noticed the sparkle of the wax protecting the black paint, her hands practically itched to get busy washing her own beloved motorcar. Even if she had a willing partner like Godfrey, she would not have asked someone else to attend to that particular duty. Beryl adored rolling up her sleeves and ministering to her own red Silver Ghost with a bucket of soapy water and an oversized sponge. Buffing the spots from the finish at the end of the job was her favorite part. Standing back and seeing a sparklingly clean vehicle gleaming under the sun was always guaranteed to fill her with a sense of satisfaction and time well spent.

As she made her way around to the other side of the vehicle her breath caught in her throat sharply. On an otherwise pristine motorcar a crumpled dent damaged the front right fender. Godfrey Burroughs must have been traveling at a fairly high rate of speed to have inflicted so much damage on something as sturdy as a metal fender. Going down over an embankment certainly could do quite a bit of damage as Beryl had found on more than one occasion. But this still startled her.

She thought of the highways and byways of Walmsley Parva as not particularly dangerous. Unlike her birthplace in New England, where the roads were treacherously encrusted in ice many months of the year, Walmsley Parva's location, not so very far from the southern coast of old England, rarely found itself pressed under any such severe weather. As such, wintertime motor vehicle accidents were practically nonexistent, at least not those caused by ice and snow.

And it wasn't simply the weather conditions that made Beryl feel surprised at what she saw before her. It was also that there were not so very many cars traveling the roads. One was far more likely to be trapped behind a doddering donkey pulling a milk cart than to be overtaken from behind by an urgent motor vehicle. With the exception of Cornelia Burroughs's vehicle and her own, Beryl could only think of a handful of other residents of the village who owned a motorcar or delivery van or lorry of their own. Norman Davies used a vehicle to make deliveries of produce and there were a few others that came to mind, but Godfrey Burroughs would not have likely encountered another vehicle that could explain his accident.

No, this was the result of some sort of absentmindedness or lack of focus, unless it had been a deliberate attempt to harm himself. She wondered if Godfrey had lied to them about not receiving a poisoned pen letter himself. Could Godfrey have felt guilty about something? Could he have received a letter accusing him of some sort of behavior that provoked an unpleasantness between himself and his wife not long before she died? Would that have been enough to cause him to attempt to take his own life or to be so distracted that he ran off the road?

She wondered if the car would start or if it had been so badly damaged that it would not. She had never driven this particular model and could see no reason why she should not slip behind the wheel and imagine herself owning one. It was one of her chief delights to explore the advantages and weigh the disadvantages of different models of motorcars.

Cornelia was certainly in no position to forbid her from doing so and Godfrey was unlikely to appear behind Blackburn's Garage to question her actions. Without any thought to the propriety of it, she reached for the door handle and yanked it open. She would not hold its arthritic lack of ease in opening against the car manufacturer. Not only had the fender received damage during the accident, but the driver's side door also had a dent near the hinge. She hopped up onto the seat and slid behind the wheel.

When she was a child, her mother had often accused her of being the sort who looked at everything with her hands rather than her eyes and this had not changed as Beryl had grown into adulthood. She wrapped her hands around the steering wheel and then reached out and fiddled with each and every knob and dial within sight. She bounced gently up and down on the springs of the bench seat and stretched her legs out to feel for the pedals.

Satisfied that she had explored every mechanical item within sight, she turned her attention towards the door. Considering she was someone who did not let a little thing like personal safety affect the way that she piloted any vehicle herself, she had some interest in how well a vehicle could withstand a crash. She ran her hand over the side of the door to ascertain whether or not the dent had penetrated the fabric lining on the cabin side. Only the barest bulge could be felt beneath the stretched brocade providing an elegant finish to the interior compartment.

As she ran her hand along the door, she felt an edge that gave her pause. Looking down carefully, she noticed that a pocket had been created for the driver's convenience. Beryl thought it rather a clever addition to the vehicle and made a note to look for such things in future should she ever be in a position to purchase an additional motorcar. Perish the thought that something might happen to remove her own most valued possession from the roads. The pocket appeared deep enough to hold a roadway map or even a small book if one was inclined towards reading. Beryl slipped her hand inside and felt a bit of paper.

She pulled it out and lifted it into view. There in her hands was an envelope just like the one she had received from the poisoned pen. Block letters spelled out Cornelia's name and address. The envelope had been opened, and when Beryl gently tugged the contents from it, it was clear to see that the writer had indeed sent an ugly missive to Cornelia. Was it possible that Godfrey had seen it, too? Was that what caused him to drive so erratically and to have an accident? She folded the letter back up and placed it into the envelope once more before slipping it into her pocket. She exited the vehicle, and with a bit more speed than was her preference on such a warm day, she made off for the Beeches.

Edwina had just put the final touches on the latest chapter of her novel when Beryl burst through the door of the morning room holding an envelope above her head and waving it about wildly.

"You won't believe what I found when checking over Cornelia's vehicle," Beryl said, rushing to the desk and slapping an envelope down in front of Edwina.

She plopped herself into the chair on the opposite side of the desk and leaned back. Her face was flushed, and a line of perspiration had appeared on her forehead. Edwina did not generally think of Beryl as someone who engaged in vigorous exercise without purpose. While her friend was a determined athlete when the occasion called for it, such as trekking through dense jungles or climbing up mountains, she seemed to reserve such fits of physicality for places far from Walmsley Parva.

Despite the fact that Beryl was considerably taller than herself, Edwina found she needed to slow her pace whenever the two of them went out walking somewhere together. And it was difficult to persuade her friend to abandon her preference for driving the motorcar rather than walking even when the distances were too short to truly justify using the petrol. Whatever had lit such a fire beneath her friend would surely be of some account.

She lifted the envelope up and inspected it. It looked very much like all of the others, with a block style of printing displayed on the front of it. She withdrew its contents and unfolded the bulky letter it had contained. Sure enough, like all of the other letters this one was comprised of letters and words snipped from magazines and newspapers. As she quickly read through the letter, she felt her heart begin to thump wildly. The tone of this one was slightly different than the others, and rather than simply containing malicious gossip, it seemed somehow more purposeful.

Rather than obliquely reporting imagined gossip, this letter pointed a finger solidly at the recipient. The sender accused Cornelia of abusing her position as the president of the garden club and said that if she did not return the funds that she had skimmed from the club's account at the local bank, she would be publicly disgraced.

Edwina placed the letter back on the desk in front of her and looked over at Beryl. Her friend's eyebrows were twitched up towards the ceiling and a look of triumph crossed her face.

"I should think something like that might bring on an asthma attack, don't you?" Beryl asked.

"I expect that it very well could have done," Edwina said.

She drummed her fingers on the desk and looked at the letter once more. What she didn't know was whether or not such a thing, or its writer, could be considered responsible for causing Cornelia's death.

"The alternate possibility is that Godfrey found the letter and it caused him to swerve off the road because he was so agitated. Or, it might even have convinced him to attempt to take his own life if he thought the shame of such a thing was too great to bear," Beryl said.

"Where did you find this?" Edwina asked.

"It was tucked into a pocket in the driver's side of Cornelia's motorcar."

"Was it opened when you found it?" Edwina asked.

Beryl nodded vigorously. "If I had wanted to open up a letter not addressed to me, I would have brought it back here unopened and insisted the two of us steam the flap over the teakettle. As much as I think we have gotten on a far better footing with Constable Gibbs, I am not sure she would approve of tampering with the Royal Mail," Beryl said.

Edwina thought that Beryl was learning far more about the ins and outs of village life than she would have credited her for. It was one thing to remove the letter from the motorcar. It would have been an entirely different matter to open it.

Edwina wondered, not for the first time, how her new role as magistrate might be affected by her position as a private enquiry agent. It had seemed as though those two things might not be at odds when she first had accepted Charles's suggestion that she take the position. But now, listening to Beryl announce how she would circumvent the law, she had to wonder if there were new lines in the sand she might have to choose whether or not to cross. She felt an enormous sense of relief that the letter had already been opened.

But other than the simple fact that it kept her from needing to consider moral quandaries, it also indicated that someone who had been in possession of the car was aware of the contents of the letter. As she thought about what she knew of Cornelia's character, she could well imagine such a paragon of village life being deeply distressed by that sort of false accusation. One's reputation in such a small community was an incredibly important possession and Cornelia had always seemed to pride herself on hers. It was also the sort of accusation that was difficult to disprove. There would likely be a hint of suspicion surrounding her for the rest of her life if such a thing had gotten out

"Do you think that someone deliberately tried to bring on such an attack?" Edwina asked.

"I really have no idea. I suppose, from a practical standpoint, it would depend on how aware others were of Cornelia's condition. Did you know that she suffered from asthma?" Beryl asked.

"As a matter of fact, I did. It was a topic that came up in conjunction with her position as the president of the garden club. Some plants caused her a bit of breathing difficulty when they were flowering or had gone to seed in the autumn. Leaf mold in the rainy times seemed to bother her as well. In fact, I witnessed one of her asthma attacks during a meeting where members had decided to bring floral arrangements from their gardens to share with the others."

"So, it would have been a matter of common knowledge that she could be affected by outside, yet somewhat predictable forces," Beryl said.

"I think there's a great deal of difference between exposing someone to large quantities of pollen or leaf mold and providing them with an emotional shock," Edwina said.

"I'm sure you're right, but it does still drive home the point that there were any number of people in the village who could have known about her condition. That does indicate that there is at least the possibility someone was trying to do her in," Beryl said.

"I hate to countenance it, but we must consider that possibility. We could ask Charles if he thought the legal case could be made that someone had set out to do away with Cornelia or even that they were culpable for her death simply by causing such a level of distress. I suggest that we ask him at the next possible opportunity," Edwina said.

"I agree. But the fact remains that there's an entirely different question we have yet to ask," Beryl said.

"And what might that be?" Edwina asked.

"Is there any possibility that this letter is making an accusation that is actually the truth?"

Edwina leaned back in her chair. She felt shocked to the marrow. Of course, as an outsider Beryl had a very different sense of the residents of Walmsley Parva. But because of that she often had an insight into the possibilities that Edwina failed to possess. Edwina was much better at making connections between current events and past history or the type of subtle undercurrents that flowed between residents of the village that Beryl often missed. But she would have to admit that her ability to judge what someone might do could often be hampered by what she believed them to be capable of based on what she knew of them from the past. Beryl was coming to the situation from a blank slate and could ask troubling questions like the one she had just posed.

"I should not have thought her to be capable of such an abuse of her position, but to be fair, I cannot say for sure."

"Would there have been enough money in the garden club account to tempt someone to filch a bit of it?" Beryl asked.

"I think that it would depend on how you define *tempting*," Edwina said. "It certainly would not have amounted to thousands of pounds, but the club has had a fairly healthy history of fund-raising and dues collection."

"How is the money raised?"

"We hold a plant sale every spring and we sell bulbs in the autumn. The members all pay dues for their membership, and we also generally host booths at some of the local events like the summertime church fete and any others that pop up throughout the year," Edwina said.

"What's the money used for?" Beryl asked.

"Mostly we've been setting aside money for beautification purposes. The garden club purchased one of the benches that was placed overlooking the duck pond in the center of the village green. We've also been setting aside funds to help with any unexpected repairs the Women's Institute building might require. As it is the location where we hold our meetings it only seems right to contribute to the upkeep of the building itself," Edwina said.

"Is there any way that Cornelia could have been skimming some of that money for herself? It sounds as though there is not a lot of fixed expense that the garden club is beholden to and that might make it easier to help oneself to some of the takings without anyone noticing."

Edwina considered this possibility. Cornelia always read the president's report at the beginning of any of the garden club meetings. She would read from a prepared statement rather than hauling the ledger for the club's accounts to the meetings. Edwina had never given any thought to the fact that she had never seen any of the bookkeeping with her own eyes. No one would have thought to have mentioned it.

So many things were lugged in and out of the Women's Institute at each and every meeting that to encumber oneself with something like a financial ledger with no good reason for doing so would have seemed unnecessary. The garden club members were much more concerned with things like trays of cuttings and packets of seed as well as a hearty offering of refreshments. Edwina had often wondered whether or not the array of pastries and tiny sandwiches were the main draws to the meetings of some of the membership.

"I suppose that if Cornelia had wanted to help herself to some of the club funds it might have been remarkably easy for her to do so. Even if she were taking money out and then replacing it as soon as she was able to return it, no one would be any the wiser. She was in a position of trust and there was no reason why anyone would have questioned her integrity," Edwina said.

"It makes one think, doesn't it?"

"Yes, I suppose it does, which is likely what the sender wanted. If what the writer claims is true, we were lucky to be able to pay for the park bench at the duck pond or much else," Edwina said.

"Speaking of duck ponds, isn't the photographer supposed to be here to take our photo shortly? I know he's made great use of the bench the garden club paid for, what with taking so many photographs of the local duck population," Beryl said.

As if on cue Crumpet leapt from the basket beneath the morning room desk and began to furiously bark as he raced towards the front door. A moment later Beddoes appeared with Bernard Stevens in tow. He was weighed down by a great quantity of photographic equipment. Beddoes gave the visitor's encumbrances a look of trepidation, as though she were afraid she might be required to attack them with her trusty feather duster. But Beryl seemed completely at ease with all of the contraptions.

As an amateur photographer herself, Edwina felt curious about all of the devices available to a professional. After they had greeted one another, she carefully observed him setting up a tripod and attaching his camera to it. He adjusted the draperies in the morning room to control the amount of light and directed Beryl and Edwina into positions in the best spots in the room to produce quality photographs for the campaign.

As he snapped their photos and stepped forward to slightly adjust their positions, Edwina could not help but feel a shudder slither up her spine. She had never taken particular notice of Bernard Stevens as he made his way throughout the village taking photographs of waterfowl and other natural features.

As much as she did not believe the rumors the letter writer generally put forth, she couldn't help but wonder if it was possible that Bernard Stevens was involved with taking sordid photographs. She tried to convince herself that such musings were simply nonsense and were the very reason why such anonymous letters were referred to as poisoned.

As she forced a smile to her face and tried to push the thought from her mind that he might be involved in something she would consider unseemly either with or without the knowledge of the women whose photographs he took, she could not shake the feeling that something had been fundamentally eroded in her sense of ease with her neighbors. The suspicion that Cornelia might have been skimming money from the garden club funds only made her all the more uncomfortable with Mr. Stevens. She felt herself in the unenviable position of having no idea what to believe.

She had not been eager to force herself out into the public spotlight by agreeing to be a spokeswoman for Colonel Kimberly's and now she regretted acquiescing all the more. While she did her best not to betray her inner turmoil to Beryl or even most importantly to Mr. Stevens, she couldn't help but feel an impending sense of dread. What else might be coming to the forefront with the spate of letters plaguing them all? Was there nothing sacred? What was happening to her beloved village?

Chapter 15

Edwina felt her nerves begin to fray by the time the photographer had completed his task. She was not accustomed to being ordered about in quite such a detached manner or in any manner at all for that matter. It was not an experience she wished to repeat. She could only hope that the photographs would prove to be worth the trouble when they were developed. It was with a deep sense of relief that she escorted Mr. Stevens, with his myriad of photographic equipment in tow, to the door.

She thought she had earned a bit of a reward for her patient acceptance at being prodded this way and that by a virtual stranger and a man at that. Not only was the situation disconcerting, but it had also been all the more irksome as Beryl seemed to take it all in stride. Of course, her friend had much more experience of such things than had she, but it still was somewhat galling to hear Mr. Stevens tell Beryl over and over how much the camera loved her.

Edwina was well aware that the camera loved Beryl. After all, did she not have a scrapbook she had made of her friend filled with clippings from newspapers and magazines showing

Beryl's many adventures and documenting her travels around the world? In every one of the photographs Edwina had so carefully clipped and pasted into the album, Beryl had looked utterly at ease and undeniably radiant. Even when she was dressed in clothing more often seen on a man or sported smudges of dirt on her face, she looked happy and thoroughly charming.

As Edwina sat in her favorite chair in the parlor and picked up her ball of celebratory wool and pair of knitting needles, she wondered if her attitude towards life itself was the reason the camera loved Beryl so much. Her friend had a knack for seeing the fun in every situation and that spirit seemed to come through the images of her that the camera captured. Edwina wondered suddenly if that was perhaps the reason Beryl seemed to be so often the recipient of good luck.

Could it be that simply by expecting the best in any and all situations and looking for what was fun about them, her friend had somehow drawn helpful people and events to herself? Could it be that the camera was not so magnanimous with Edwina because she felt tight and closed off? She thought back to her experience at the artists' colony recently and the painting her dear friend Charles had made of herself and Beryl. She remembered feeling lighthearted and relaxed as he sketched and painted her, and she wondered if her behavior and attitude had contributed to the success of the finished painting.

Truth be told, she had been very flattered by his rendering of her and did not think that she came off the worse of the pair of them in the way he had captured their essences. Not that it was a competition, mind you. It simply had pleased her to think that she could hold her own in their partnership and that it appeared that way to someone else, too.

She suddenly had an urge to call the photographer back and beg him to try again. Perhaps none of the photographs would turn out well enough for them to be used in the advertising campaign and they would have to set up a second session. She told herself if that turned out to be the case, she would try to recapture the feeling of adventurousness she had enjoyed while serving as a model for Charles. Again, her thoughts drifted to the notion that perhaps simply by putting out a welcoming attitude into the world, good things would come one's way.

As she sat moving her needles through the smooth red wool, she decided to indulge her notion and to give it a try. She softened her gaze as she looked across the sitting room and allowed a wide, warm smile to stretch across her lips. She imagined herself beaming with pleasure at something as yet unspecified. Her attention snapped back to the room before her as Crumpet leapt down from the ottoman positioned in front of her and ran down the hallway towards the front door.

He returned almost immediately, followed by Charles holding something hidden behind his back. On his face was a bit of a sheepish expression. Edwina wondered what could have brought him to visit in the middle of the workday. He was not generally given to leaving his office during normal business hours. Perhaps he was experiencing a lull in his own business at present. He rarely mentioned anything so sordid as finances other than to say that he was well aware that some people were currently feeling an enormous strain from the downturn in the economy. As Charles was the only solicitor in the village, she had always imagined that such things did not weigh too heavily on his own mind.

He took a few tentative steps in her direction and came to a halt. He cleared his throat and brought his hand from behind his back and stretched it out towards Edwina. She could not quite believe what she saw.

"Charles, is that an orchid?" Edwina asked, laying aside her knitting and rising to her feet.

Charles bobbed his head and pressed a small glass case holding a tiny potted plant into her hands. "Yes, at least I think it is," he said. "But to be honest, I wouldn't know one tropical plant from another. I am basing my knowledge on what the tag indicated."

Edwina blinked. She had longed for an orchid and had often looked wistfully at the collections of others as well as those advertised by leading plantsman off and on over the years. But generally speaking, the cost of them was outside her budget. They were not an item that grew rampantly in the open garden nor were they the sort of thing that one could easily root cuttings from in a pot of damp sand in a hothouse. Even that consummate plant enthusiast Dr. Wilcox did not have orchids to share. She swallowed a lump that had risen in her throat.

"It's absolutely enchanting," Edwina said.

And it was. It was even more beautiful than she had imagined when reading descriptions in plant catalogues or in books she borrowed from the Walmsley Parva reading room on the subject of houseplants and exotics. The glossy deep green leaves at the base glowed with health and vibrancy.

But the blossoms themselves were what made her heart race. They were of a rich purple with even darker splotches the color of aubergine and they dangled gracefully from the sweeping stem. Not only were there many blossoms fully unfurled, but as she inspected the plant more carefully, she counted at least half a dozen buds beginning to swell along the length of the stem. There would be weeks and weeks of pleasurable viewing to come.

Edwina had been raised with sufficient money not to give finances a great deal of consideration. But between the war years and the economic slump that followed, she'd been entirely unprepared for the dire financial straits in which she had found herself. At the time it had been surprisingly difficult to continue to keep a roof over her head and food in the larder for Crumpet and herself.

It wasn't just that her stocks and shares had taken a tumble in value. It was also the estate taxes that had accompanied the rapid succession of deaths in her family. On the surface of things, it appeared as though she had inherited a comfortable life from her father to her mother. Some people might even have assumed that the death of her brother would have left her with a small income as well. But the truth of the matter was that while to outward appearances she seemed to be considerably better off than many other villagers, her circumstances had left her decidedly reduced.

Even before her mother had died and had pushed things over the edge, Edwina had been concerned with making every shilling stretch as far as it might go. There had not been any leftover money for something as frivolous as an exotic plant. And although things had improved to a great extent since Beryl's arrival and commencement of their private enquiry agency, as well as the injection of funds into the running of the household by the generosity of Simpkins, Edwina still did not feel particularly flush in her bank account.

Beryl brought home extra money from time to time as a result of her winnings at various gambling sessions or when she had put money on a bet with Chester White at the pub. And although Beryl always made decisions with that money to purchase little luxuries like the typewriter or some sort of repair to the household, Edwina did not have more ready cash of her own with which to indulge something like a completely unnecessary plant purchase. Even the renovations to the gardens at the Beeches were down to Simpkins footing the bill. He had tactfully included Edwina in all of the discussions over what should be done with her property, but the fact remained that she had paid for none of it, nor could she have done so. She had almost forgotten what it would be like to have a large enough surplus to make such a purchase.

The garden club had invited a speaker some years prior who had arrived with a collection of Wardian cases, each filled with beautiful specimens including many rare orchids. Edwina had found the notion of a miniature greenhouse with only one jewel of a plant specimen encased within it to be absolutely enchanting. She had longed for such a thing just as soon as she had laid her eyes upon them. After the speaker had completed his presentation and the meeting had ended Edwina had rather embarrassed herself by spending more time than was strictly polite inspecting the collection the speaker had brought with him. She had had to take herself firmly in hand in order to allow the poor man to load his possessions back up into his motorcar and drive off. Edwina had never been one inclined towards thievery, but she had for the briefest of moments considered absconding with the smallest of the cases, which had held the tiniest and most delicate orchid she had ever seen.

And now, thanks to Charles's generosity, here was one of her own. As she leaned over the case once more and peered down at the plant, she felt a swell of affection for Charles. It wasn't just that he had brought her this exact gift. It was more that he had bothered to know what it was that she might truly desire. Beryl had cajoled and urged her towards paying more attention to the fact that Charles thought of her as more than a dear friend. Edwina had never wanted to consider such a thing. After all, her notions of romance always tended towards mysterious strangers from far-off lands.

But perhaps there was something to be said for being known by another on quite such a profound level. Was it possible that someone so staid and familiar could also be the most romantic? She didn't even know what to say.

"I do hope you like it," Charles said.

"I absolutely adore it. How on earth did you know I wanted any such thing?" Edwina said.

She carried the orchid to the table next to her favorite chair and sat down where she could look at it in comfort and at her leisure. She would have to determine where it might most enjoy being placed in order to remain in such rude good health. But for now, she wished to keep it nearby to her.

Charles sat opposite on the sofa and leaned back with a relaxed posture as though he were well pleased with himself.

"I would have had to have deliberately ignored your preferences over the years not to have been able to guess such a gift would please you," Charles said. "But if I had known how much you would seem to enjoy it, I would have chosen one for you long ago," he said.

"I could not have picked out a more perfect choice myself," Edwina said. "I've had my eye on one like it for simply ages."

"I know just what you mean," Charles said, looking at her with an unusual intensity. "I've had my eye on something I admire for ages, too."

Beryl regretted interrupting the scene she encountered in the parlor. She wasn't exactly sure what had preceded her arrival, but there was a certain something in the atmosphere that felt as though it had shifted. She had been hoping to spark something more between Charles and Edwina than had existed up until that point, but had feared her hints and suggestions had fallen upon deaf ears, at least on Edwina's part. But as she stepped into the parlor without giving it any sort of consideration, she had the decided impression that an important change might just be afoot.

She could not recriminate herself for stepping into the room for long, however. She had no reason to expect Charles would be there and the two of them were not engaged in conversation as she had approached the doorway. In fact, nothing in an outward appearance gave away the fact that she had come upon them at a time that was inopportune. But one thing that Beryl knew was when there was a current running between people, especially those who might be interested in each other romantically. To all outward appearances Charles was seated on the sofa much as he always would have been. Edwina occupied her usual place in her favorite chair and Crumpet sat like an old lady chaperone between the pair of them, keeping guard on his mistress's feet. The only thing that could account for the shift that Beryl could see was an unfamiliar item on the table next to Edwina. While Beryl was not an avid plants woman herself, she had intimate familiarity with what she saw before her.

Beryl had spent considerable time deep in lush jungles of South America accompanied by plant hunters. The sort of case that sat on the table at Edwina's side was something she had come to find exceedingly tedious. Although it was true that the cases made it possible to transport exotic plants from their natural habitat to far flung collectors across the globe, they proved to be almost as fragile as their contents. Nothing slowed down a trek through dense forest like the need to gingerly transport a precious glass-and-wooden-framed object.

Not only that, but she had also not particularly enjoyed the frenzied and fevered behavior of the collectors she had served as a guide. They were often terrible conversationalists with only one thing on their minds. She could not fault them for their adventurous spirits or their willingness to relentlessly pursue their aims, but she did find them to be so focused on their goals that they had little else to discuss, and as she was not someone who shared their passion, their company had proven more irksome than entertaining.

But from the look on Edwina's face, it was clear she did not share Beryl's view. Charles had a very satisfied look on his own visage, and she had to assume he was responsible for the appearance of the item in the parlor.

"Unless I'm very much mistaken, that is a rather spectacular orchid," Beryl said. She took a step further into the room and gestured towards the Wardian case.

"Charles has brought it to me as a completely unexpected gift," Edwina said. "Isn't it marvelous?"

"It's very handsome indeed. And how thoroughly unexpected," Beryl said, giving Charles a significant look. He simply nodded and turned his attention back to Edwina's beaming face.

"What's also unexpected is the fact that you knew it to be an orchid. Beryl, you never seem to know the names of plants. If you were to declare something to be a rose and turn out to be correct, I would be startled. How did you happen to know what it was?" Edwina asked.

"I spent considerable time in the company of plant hunters over the years and have more familiarity with orchids than any other type of greenery. It happens we were able to complete our time together more quickly if I assisted with the scouting and so I made a point to school myself in their appearance," Beryl said with a shrug. "It was much like other times when I accompanied people looking for animals on safari."

"You're a woman of such a broad range of experiences you never fail to surprise me," Charles said. He got to his feet. "I have a client coming this afternoon, so I must take my leave of you. I do hope you will enjoy my little offering." He sketched a small bow and headed out the door without another word.

"How extraordinarily thoughtful of Charles. I have no idea how he knew I would like such a thing. You didn't tell him, did you?"

Beryl shrugged. "Why don't you just allow it to be a mystery? Speaking of, I think we ought to go and speak with the Blackburns and ask if they remember seeing the letter in Cornelia's vehicle when they took it back to the garage."

Edwina got to her feet and gave the Wardian case one last glance. She whistled for Crumpet and in very little time the two sleuths and their faithful canine companion stood in the Blackburns' garage. Nora Blackburn stood behind the counter where customers settled up their accounts. Although her brother Michael was the one who was bent over the engine of a motorcar with a spanner in his one good hand, it could not be said that Nora did not do her part in the actual repair of vehicles.

All during the war years when Michael had been gone, and then when he had returned so terribly affected by the horrors of the battlefield, Nora had kept the garage open. She had learned a great deal about the business from her brother before he enlisted and had done a credible job at servicing any number of vehicles that needed her attention in his absence. In fact, she wore an overall covered in grease stains that gave proof that she had been just as busy tinkering with the machinery as her brother that day.

"What brings the two of you in?" Nora asked. "Surely you haven't gone and damaged that beautiful machine of yours."

"We're here about a damaged vehicle, but thankfully it isn't my own," Beryl said. "I wanted to ask you about Cornelia Burroughs's motorcar."

"Now, that one really was damaged. Such a shame considering the way Cornelia always took care of it," Nora said.

Michael Blackburn straightened from his task and crossed the room to return the spanner to a toolbox sitting on a nearby workbench.

"It was a tragedy," he said. "Godfrey Burroughs shouldn't be allowed to operate a bicycle let alone a motorcar if that's the way he's going to go about it."

"Was it as bad as all that?" Edwina asked.

"The front fender is crumpled something awful, and the driver side door may have to be replaced. Isn't that right, Michael?" Nora asked.

Michael nodded. "I'm going to see if I can pull the dent out of it, but the hinges may be irreparably damaged. It might be far more sensible to simply purchase a new door."

"That would be a terrible shame considering the rest of the vehicle is in such incredible condition. Cornelia treated it like a prized thoroughbred," Nora said.

Beryl knew how Cornelia must have felt. While she loved the exhilaration created by excess speed, she was an excellent driver and would not have considered putting her vehicle in harm's way unless life and limb demanded it. Cornelia must have been looking down from the afterlife with a heavy heart. That is, if such a thing really existed. Beryl was not particularly convinced that it did.

"Did you happen to take a good look at the vehicle when it first came in?" Edwina asked.

"Of course we did. We always give any damaged vehicles a once-over, especially if it's been in an accident like this one rather than simply some sort of mechanical trouble reported by the owner," Michael said.

"Did you spot anything unusual anywhere in the vehicle itself?" Beryl asked.

"What kind of something unusual?" Nora asked.

Beryl and Edwina exchanged a glance and Edwina gave the slightest of nods. Beryl continued.

"Was there a letter in the vehicle that was very similar to the one Michael received?" Beryl asked.

"A poisoned pen letter? No. I would have been sure to remember a thing like that," Michael said. "After all, one of them got me hauled up before your court, Miss Edwina," Michael said with a shrug.

"I don't remember seeing anything like that, either," Nora said. "Should I have?"

"Not necessarily. I found it when I took a look inside the vehicle earlier since it was parked behind the garage. I hope you don't mind, but I was trying to get to the bottom of what's been happening with these poisoned pen letters, and we did wonder if Godfrey's erratic driving could have been connected to receiving one."

"I suppose it might have done. Look at how badly it affected Michael when he received his," Nora said.

"What else would you have had me do when somebody was besmirching my name so thoroughly?" Michael asked.

"I didn't mean you should not have reacted that way. I just meant that these letters were capable of causing extreme distress. Do you think Godfrey received one?"

Edwina shook her head. "No. The letter was addressed to Cornelia."

"I can't imagine why I didn't see it. Where did you find it exactly?" Michael asked.

"It was in the pocket in the lining of the driver's side door. Unless you were looking in there, I don't suppose you would have seen it."

"That explains it. I was more interested in the mechanics of it rather than frills like a pocket. I suppose if the door needed replacing, I would have checked the pocket before discarding it. You never know what people will leave in their vehicles," Michael said.

"So, you have no way of knowing for sure if it was in the vehicle when you brought it to the garage?" Edwin said.

"I'm afraid not. Is it important?" Nora asked.

"Not necessarily, but we did want to ask. It would help to nail down a time frame for the way these letters have been circulating throughout the village," Beryl said.

"Do you think it's possible that this accident with Cornelia's motorcar was no accident at all?" Edwina said. "What I mean to say is can you tell from the condition of the vehicle if it had been deliberately run off the road?"

"We would be able to tell you if someone had run into it from behind and shoved it off the road, but there was no such damage to the rear fender. And even if there had been you would need to see multiple points of contact between Cornelia's vehicle and the one that had crashed into it to ascertain whether or not it was deliberate. If there were multiple dents in different locations it would appear that the vehicle had been repeatedly rammed, which couldn't be considered an accident," Michael said.

"Or you could take a look at the road itself and notice any markings on the surface of the pavement. Sometimes they can indicate the truth of what happened. But I can tell you in this case no such evidence exists. The dent in the fender and in the driver's side door are consistent with the vehicle going over an embankment and striking the trees that we found it crumpled against when we arrived at the accident scene," Nora said.

"Did you see Godfrey at the site of the accident when you arrived to collect the motorcar?" Edwina asked.

Michael shook his head. "It was Constable Gibbs who telephoned to ask us to retrieve it. When I come to think of it, there was no one at the accident site when we arrived. The motorcar was off the road and wasn't troubling anyone, so there was no reason why anyone would have needed to stay to direct traffic or anything like that," he said.

"I don't suppose there's anything else that you can tell us, is there?" Beryl asked.

"The only thing I can tell you is that I hope you catch whoever is going around doing this. It's one thing to get hauled up before the bench. It's entirely another to need to be hauled out of your motorcar and into a pine box."

"That's exactly what we're hoping to do. If you remember anything, please get in touch with us. But for now, we don't have any more questions," Edwina said.

"I suppose the only one who can really answer your questions at all is Godfrey Burroughs. I don't know if he would be willing to admit it or not, but he's the one person who could tell you for sure how the accident came to take place," Nora said.

Chapter 16

They had barely taken three steps from Blackburn's Garage when Godfrey Burroughs appeared on the pavement near them. He still looked to be a man who had lost his way in life. His face was ashen, and his clothing was not in a particularly better state than it had been when they had visited him in his home. The only real difference was that he was no longer sporting pajamas but had changed into street wear. Street wear, Edwina had noted, that looked as though it could have done with a wash.

She knew how he felt in terms of how exhausting the general niceties of life like brushing one's hair or tucking in one's shirt could be when mowed down by grief. Still, it was a commentary on the sort of ballast Cornelia must have provided for Godfrey's life that he would appear out in public looking so bereft. Cornelia never would have allowed such a thing from her husband during her lifetime. Edwina had to wonder if someone ought to take him in hand before he did himself a real mischief.

She had always thought of Godfrey as one of the most henpecked men she had ever met. Cornelia had been so relentless in her chiding that the relationship between the two of them had been regular fodder for the local gossip mill over the years. It was common to hear someone clucking away about what sort of a man would allow himself to be so terribly browbeaten by his wife. No one ever thought it seemly that Godfrey would permit her to direct his every decision and action throughout the course of the day. What no one had ever remarked upon was what was to become of such a person when the dictator of their life was suddenly unavailable to orchestrate every little thing.

Perhaps the truth of the matter was that Godfrey Burroughs had appreciated his wife's heavy- handedness and authoritative demeanor. Maybe he had not wanted to be bothered to make decisions for himself and had felt that there was real value to being treated like a child in his own home.

No one could say that he did not appear to have felt the loss of Cornelia intensely. But as Edwina discreetly looked him over, she did wonder if perhaps it was all an act. Could Godfrey Burroughs have found it easy enough to appear completely un- raveled by his wife's demise?

He was used to being the subject of quiet ridicule. Why not simply endure it for a bit longer by appearing in public com- pletely disheveled and out of his mind with grief? The villagers would likely accept that he was an unusual man based on his history of putting up with so much from Cornelia. Was there more to Godfrey Burroughs than had ever met the eye? Whether he had a hand in hastening his wife's death or not, she wondered if there was far more to Godfrey Burroughs than she had ever given him credit for.

He came to a stop in front of them and even in his grief- stricken fog came to his senses enough to greet them. Edwina felt a bit like she was taking advantage of him by her question- ing, but it simply could not be helped. Godfrey would have to be questioned regardless of his apparent fitness for enduring such an intrusion.

But at least they could try to be discreet about it. Edwina took a step forward and took Godfrey by the arm. She nodded to Beryl and began walking towards the village green. While she could not keep the other passersby from noting that she and Beryl were in Godfrey's company, she could ensure that no one overheard them. People were likely to speculate as to the reasons they were chatting with him regardless of what it was that they were actually up to. She had learned long ago that she could not stop people from thinking whatever they chose. But she could control the flow of real information to the best of her ability.

If Godfrey seemed surprised at being piloted away from wherever he had been inclined to wander, he gave no sign of it. Perhaps that was one of the legacies left by a lifetime spent with his wife. He thought nothing whatsoever of being derailed and detained from his own purposes by someone else's whims. Edwina meandered towards the village green until she reached a bench, in fact the very one funded by the garden club. It seemed fitting to discuss what had happened to Cornelia on a bench that was provided by the organization she had led.

She lowered herself onto its sun-warmed seat and tugged at Godfrey's arm for him to join her. Beryl took a seat at his other side and sat with uncharacteristic quietness gazing out at the pond. Edwina's thoughts jumped briefly to Mr. Stevens and his love of photographing the local duck population as well as the possibility he was taking other sorts of photographs. She took herself firmly in hand and returned her attention completely to Godfrey.

"It's good to see you out and about," Edwina said. "I always think there's nothing like a nice long walk to lift one's mood."

Godfrey turned towards her with a look of incomprehension on his pale face. "I can't imagine my mood ever will be lifted no matter what it is that I do," he said.

Edwina felt her heart squeeze. How truly amazing it was that there seemed to be someone who mourned Cornelia's passing so deeply. It was funny how some people, despite not appearing to merit it, inspired such love and devotion. She felt all the more regret at the need to ask him if his wife had been involved in something nefarious. She wasn't exactly sure how much more burden he could take if he had not been the person involved in sending the letter to Cornelia. Perhaps Edwina would not need to come out and share the contents of the letter so long as she simply ascertained whether or not he knew Cornelia had received one. Hoping that Beryl would follow her lead and not come out with the contents of the letter either, Edwina launched into her questioning.

"Where were you headed if you weren't simply out taking a walk to take your mind off things?" Edwina asked.

"I was planning to stop in at Blackburn's Garage to ask if Cornelia's motorcar was repaired yet. I can't stop thinking of how much she would be disappointed in me at having damaged it," Godfrey said.

"I'm sure that Cornelia would understand that such things can easily happen to a motorcar no matter how much one prizes it. I know I feel that way about my own," Beryl said.

Godfrey turned towards her as if he had forgotten she was seated on his opposite side.

"I assure you, Cornelia would not have felt that there was any call for what happened. She was a most particular driver herself and would not have made excuses for my lack of ability," he said.

"What did cause your accident, Godfrey?" Edwina asked. "I know that you have understandably been very upset by your wife's passing, but I wondered if something had distracted you or distressed you even more intensely just prior to your running off the road."

"There was a rabbit. It simply hopped out in front of me from a hedgerow at the side of the road. I swerved without thinking and sent Cornelia's prized possession tumbling over the embankment," he said, shaking his head slowly.

"A rabbit?" Edwina said. "I completely understand. I did something similar myself when I was first learning to drive."

She looked over at Beryl, who raised an eyebrow. Edwina wasn't sure if that was in reaction to Godfrey's story or to the memory of an incident involving Beryl's motorcar, Edwina, and a squirrel some weeks earlier. Either way she felt it best she continue to lead the questioning.

"That was one of the reasons Cornelia was the one who always did the driving. She was much more likely to make a sensible decision when confronted by surprises than am I. I never could quite get the hang of it," he said.

"So nothing else upset you?" Edwina said.

"What sort of something else?" Godfrey asked.

"So many people in Walmsley Parva have received poisoned pen letters recently, and I did wonder if an upset like that could have made it difficult to keep your mind on the road," Edwina said.

Godfrey's eyes widened. "I've received nothing of the sort. I know that Cornelia had mentioned that there had been a few people in the village who had received some nasty shocks from such letters, but I have not been one of them."

"Do you know if Cornelia had received one herself?" Edwina asked. Continuing to take a high-handed approach with him seemed to be working and in fact almost seemed to give the poor man comfort.

"Not that I know of. I'm sure that if Cornelia had received such a letter, she would have spoken to me about it right away. She would have been terribly affronted by such a thing and I'm sure would have had a great deal to say on the matter. My wife was never one to keep her opinions to herself as I'm sure you well know," he said.

Edwina thought his voice was tinged with pride. Perhaps Godfrey had admired that side of Cornelia because he was not someone who felt empowered to express his own opinions. *What curious things partnerships are*, she thought. She and Beryl each brought such different skills and strengths to their business partnership, and she could well imagine how a marriage might work the same way. Perhaps the inner workings of any team could not truly be evaluated by those on the outside.

"So, you were not the one who placed an envelope addressed to Cornelia in the pocket of the driver side of her motorcar?" Beryl asked.

Godfrey turned his attention towards Beryl once again. "I certainly did not. Are you saying there was a letter in the vehicle at the time of my accident?" he asked.

"That's right," Beryl said. "And it appears to have been of the same sort as all of the other poisoned pen letters."

"Why in the world would anyone wish to harass Cornelia?" he asked. "She would have given no one cause to abuse her in such a way."

His tone had become strident, and he appeared livelier than Edwina had seen him since Cornelia's death. Outrage had a strengthening effect on most people, she had often noted, but in Godfrey's case it seemed especially magnified. She also found it interesting to consider how unaware Godfrey seemed to be of others' impressions of his wife's character. It wasn't as though no one ever had a good thing to say about Cornelia, but the fact remained that most people were just as ready with complaints about her high-handedness as they were compliments about her sheer force of will.

"I'm sure that whatever the letter had to say made no difference whatsoever. So far most of the poisoned pen letters have spouted the most outrageous lies," Edwina said. "If you haven't seen it, I wouldn't give it another thought."

"I'm sure I shouldn't want to see anything that had something offensive to say about my wife," he said.

"That's the spirit. There was one other thing that we wanted to ask you about," Edwina said, hoping Godfrey would not make a connection between the contents of the letter and her line of questioning. "Would you know if your wife kept the garden club ledgers in her possession? I'm sure that it would be best if a member of the club was to keep ahold of them."

"Mrs. Dunbarton said the same thing. She had come by to pay her condolences and asked if she might take possession of them. As the vice chair of the garden club, it was only right that she step up and fill in in Cornelia's absence. There will have to be new elections, of course, but for now it seemed best that she be the one to have them."

"I am glad to hear that is well in hand," Edwina said. "We mustn't keep you from your errands any longer."

"If it saves you a trip, your motorcar will probably not be ready for a few days yet. We were just in speaking with the Blackburns and they mentioned that they need to have a bit more time to get it back to its original condition," Beryl said.

They left Godfrey sitting on the bench staring at the duck pond. Edwina turned to Beryl as soon as they were out of earshot.

"We need to speak with Mrs. Dunbarton and get ahold of those ledgers."

"I completely agree. Who knows, we may finally be getting somewhere," Beryl said.

Chapter 17

On the high street Beryl parted ways with Edwina, who was determined to stop in at the stationer's to purchase another ream of typewriting paper for her novel before getting on with the far less pleasant task of the investigation. Beryl had no interest in shopping regardless of how many attempts Edwina had made to convince her otherwise. So, she struck off towards the center of the village on her own.

As she walked along, she wondered if the poisoned pen letters sprang from any particular neurosis. What sort of person would be driven to create such havoc? Why would anyone waste their time imagining such baseless claims and stirring up trouble unnecessarily? As much as she had chided Edwina for assuming that the sender was a woman, she would have to admit, if only in the privacy of her own mind, that the odds were better that a woman had done so. For one thing, there were more women than men in the village at present as the war years had reduced the male population so noticeably.

There was also the sense of impotent rage the letters seemed to exude. While Beryl had not bothered to take note of any such strictures herself, she understood that most of her female peers lived lives very different from her own. So many of the women of her acquaintance were bound by conventions that slowly, but surely, eroded their souls. The appropriate outlets for women were so tightly scribed, and if one did not fit neatly into one of the roles that were acceptable, Beryl could well imagine that such constraints might cause a level of frustration that had to seek an outlet somewhere.

And while the recent lifting of bans on professions for women had been a start at making it possible for the gentler sex to pursue any careers that interested them, the reality was that such things were still not easily accomplished. The fact that a woman could no longer legally be excluded from becoming a doctor or a lawyer or anything else for that matter did not mean that she was not thwarted at every turn in her attempt to do so. Just because women were allowed to hang out their shingle as solicitor did not mean that universities were eager to allow them to pursue an education in law or that the examiners at the bar would be eager to admit them.

And what about women like Mrs. Dunstable or Nurse Crenshaw, who were old enough that years of university education were far behind them and the responsibilities of the lives they had already embarked upon weighed heavily on their shoulders? Beryl could easily imagine a scenario in which the poisoned pen letters were written by someone who felt that her life had atrophied. She couldn't say she felt sorry for whoever vented their spleen on their neighbors in such a way, but she thought she could easily understand how being kept from pursuing one's passions could lead to nasty consequences.

She was surprised to find that she was thinking in this sort of way. Before she had moved to Walmsley Parva, she doubted she would have been so understanding of what could have led to this sort of behavior. She likely would have simply blamed the person for being weak or having bad character. Her patience with those who were not as inclined to grab life by the horns as she was had never been one of her strengths.

But having watched Edwina blossom under the subtle encouragement she tried to provide had given her a better understanding of different ways of being in the world. Living in the village and observing others and the impact of decisions that they each made on others had also had an effect on her perspective. As much as she liked to think she had had an influence on Edwina, and to a lesser extent other members of the village, when she stopped and thought about it, she had to admit they had had at least as much of an impact on her.

She had always thought of herself as someone who was bold and decisive and willing to take risks. But as she paused on the pavement outside the plate glass window of the greengrocery and peered in at Mrs. Scott, she thought that this generally mild-mannered shopkeeper had a boldness and bravery all her own. What sort of fiery spirit was needed to confront a neighbor about misbehavior in order to protect her child? With so many of the interactions in the village being unavoidable, one risked a great deal to upset the applecart with the neighbors. Confronting the possibility that a daughter was being interfered with had consequences. Every decision made would impact relationships for a long time to come.

Mrs. Scott looked up from a bushel basket of peaches she was sorting and raised her hand in greeting to Beryl.

"What brings you in this afternoon?" Mrs. Scott asked. "Edwina was just in doing the shopping yesterday. You must be in here looking for something special."

"I am here for something special, but it isn't any produce," Beryl said. "I wanted to ask you about a sensitive subject."

Mrs. Scott abruptly halted her sorting of the fruits and wheeled around to face Beryl. She crossed her arms over her chest and lifted her chin defiantly.

"What is it you want to talk about?" she asked.

"I overheard your conversation with Minnie Mumford, and I took it upon myself to speak with Eva about what had happened," Beryl said.

"Why ever would you do a thing like that?" Mrs. Scott said.

"There are two reasons. One of them is that I have found myself in a similar situation to Eva's on more than one occasion and I wanted to assure her that she was not at fault for what had happened. Such unwanted overtures have a tendency to make the recipient feel as though she were the one to blame, and I did not think Eva should be left questioning her own behavior," Beryl said.

Mrs. Scott unfolded her arms and her shoulders sagged as though she had put down a heavy burden.

"That was very thoughtful of you. I know that Eva looks up to you and I am sure it meant a great deal to her to hear that she was not the only one to have experienced such a thing. I tried to talk to her about it myself, but you know how girls are with their mothers. I don't think she quite believed me. What she sees is an old married woman who would not be likely to experience such a thing. I don't think she really realizes I was once a young girl like herself," Mrs. Scott said.

"While that may be, I would say that there doesn't seem to be any age limit on this sort of nonsense being attempted. I expect that there are quite elderly ladies who are put in positions they don't care to find themselves as well," Beryl said.

"I suppose you're right about that. As much as it surprises me when it happens, I still occasionally find myself fending off unwanted overtures from delivery men or customers. It seems to be just a part of life. But I didn't want it to be something that happened to Eva. At least not without comment and certainly not from someone who might be able to pressure her far more than a delivery man could pressure me," Mrs. Scott said.

Beryl nodded. "It does change things considerably when one's employer or someone in a position of authority is doing the suggesting. I applaud you for doing whatever was necessary to help your daughter," Beryl said.

"If she were your child, I am sure you would have done the same," Mrs. Scott said.

Beryl felt an odd squeeze in her chest. What on earth was becoming of her? First, she had found herself capable of deftly handling the gaggle of Prentice children, and now she had been imagined as a mother by a woman experienced in the role. She wondered, for the briefest flicker, if that odd squeeze had been a whiff of regret. Surely not. She squared her shoulders and smiled.

"That is very kind of you to say," she said, relieved that her voice sounded entirely normal to her ears.

"You said there were two reasons for your visit. What was the second one?" Mrs. Scott said.

"When I spoke with Eva, she said that you became aware of her difficulties through a poisoned pen letter you had received. Would you be willing to show it to me?" Beryl said.

"Why would you want to see it?" Mrs. Scott asked. "Don't you believe me about what it said?"

"Of course I believe you. It's just that there has been a rash of poisoned pen letters in the village. I received one myself. Edwina and I would like to put a stop to it as it's been causing a great deal of trouble. I had hoped your letter might offer a clue to the writer's identity."

"I see. I would show it to you, but I destroyed it right after I read it. I threw it into the cooker and burnt it up. I didn't want my husband to see it," Mrs. Scott said. "You won't tell him about it, will you?"

"I see no reason for your husband to be involved. You seem to have taken care of matters yourself and I very much doubt Minnie Mumford is going to say anything," Beryl said.

"I'm sure she won't," Mrs. Scott said.

"Since you burnt it could you describe it's appearance to me instead?"

"It was just an ordinary sort of envelope like any other you might get in the post. My name and address were carefully printed all in uppercase."

"What about the letter itself? Anything unusual about that?" Beryl asked.

"The words and letters were cut from magazines and newspapers and pasted down. Someone had gone to a lot of trouble to write it," Mrs. Scott said. "Can you imagine taking all that time to find just the right words to deliver your message? It would take a lot of dedication."

"You're right about that. Someone must have been very determined to spread that information," Beryl said.

Before she could say anything else, however, Mr. Scott appeared in the doorway to the back room. Mrs. Scott clamped her lips together and Beryl understood their interview was over. She purchased a pound of peaches in order not to give Mr. Scott any reason to question her reason for being in the store, and without another word of the events that had taken place, took her leave.

As she waited for Edwina to appear she stood on the cobbles just outside the shop and bit into a peach. She was beginning to despair of ever turning up any sign of who could have been responsible for the rash of unpleasantness. It occurred to her that it had been easier to ferret out government secrets during the war than it was proving to run down this particular miscreant.

It seemed to her a terrible waste that such a person had turned his or her talents to harassing their neighbors rather than to collecting information from enemy camps or heading up a wartime misinformation campaign. Beryl thought the government could have made good use of such a person during the war years.

* * *

Edwina emerged from the stationer tucking her ream of typewriting paper surreptitiously into her shopping bag. The errand had given her a moment's pause as the owner of the shop had commented in passing at how much paper she seemed to require for a venture like a private enquiry agency. While Edwina was not one to spread untruths without a twinge of guilt, she had no intention of publicly announcing her venture into the sphere of novelist.

Instead, she had simply smiled and allowed the comment to pass without responding, feeling the slightest twinge of guilt as she knew that the shopkeeper would interpret her lack of correction as confirmation. And although she had to admit that a large part of running an investigation involved poking one's nose into other people's business, she found that she had no qualms about not sharing her own.

Perhaps it was unfair, but she knew there was absolutely no way she could complete her novel if anyone besides her most intimate circle was aware of her activities. She felt incredibly unsure as to whether or not she would be capable of finishing an entire first draft, and the notion of anyone asking her how it was proceeding produced a spasm of discomfort through her entire being.

So it was with a sense of relief she looked up the high street towards the greengrocery and spotted Beryl standing in front of the shop. She quickened her pace to join her friend and to propose another angle for the investigation.

"I just confirmed that Mrs. Scott was another victim of the poison pen," Beryl said.

She caught Mrs. Scott's eye through the plate glass window. She raised a hand in greeting and urged Beryl to step away from the front of the shop. She could have sworn that Mrs. Scott looked relieved to see them moving away from her doorstep. She waited until they were well away from the front of the Scotts' store before replying.

"How absolutely dreadful for her. While we are in the village there is another line of enquiry you were right to suggest we pursue," Edwina said. She inclined her head towards the post office. "Although I cannot convince myself that Prudence is the poisoned pen, perhaps she has some information as to the sender. After all, she handles all the post in the village."

"There's no time like the present," Beryl said, taking her by the arm and heading towards Prudence's shop.

Prudence eyed them as they crossed the street and headed for her establishment. If there was one person in the village who ought to be in the know about who sent the poisoned pen letters, it really ought to be Prudence. Between her absolute devotion to being at the forefront of any rumormongering and her immediate contact with all of the letters sent to and fro in the village, Prudence was perfectly positioned to have some special insight into the goings on. The trick would be whether or not they would be able to pry it from her.

Although Prudence loved to share any juicy gossip that she felt first to know, she was remarkably stubborn about opening up should she have the slightest inkling that some scrap of information she had might be of benefit to someone else. Of long habit and experience, Edwina had come to realize that the best way to handle Prudence was to act as though one did not care one bit about what she had to say. It was far better to allow her to believe she was the one leading the conversation and whenever possible to cast aspersions on the reliability of her claims. Over the last few months, she and Beryl had come up with a fairly reliable system of prying anything they wished to know from Prudence's brain. It simply took a bit of finagling.

As they stepped through the door Beryl made a beeline for a small display of diaries. Edwina headed towards the candy counter and made a great show of admiring a charming display of marzipan fruits and flowers. Whatever Prudence's other faults, one could not cast aspersions on the quality of her confectionery offerings. Edwina had a decidedly sweet tooth and found that even though she did not enjoy having to put up with Prudence, she could endure almost anything the shopkeeper got up to if it meant taking home a few pieces of choice sweets. As she bent over the glass case to more closely inspect a tiny marzipan pineapple, she heard Beryl call out to her.

"Edwina, I think this is exactly the sort of diary you were looking for to keep all of your appointments for court straight in your mind, isn't it?" Beryl said, holding up a linen-bound book. Edwina had not given a great deal of consideration to the notion she might require a diary for such activities, but Beryl had certainly found a sneaky way to introduce a topic Prudence would surely find irresistible. Besides, she would feel a bit more like the professional woman she felt she was becoming if she had such a handsome diary in which to write down her schedule and plans for the weeks ahead. Perhaps she might even note down the pages she managed to complete in her novel. And it would prevent her from overlooking important events such as the garden club's plant swap meetings. She left off viewing the confectionery and crossed the shop to join Beryl. But before she could manage to get there Prudence had come from behind the counter and sidled up to Beryl's side.

"You must need something to help you keep so many different activities in your life straight," Prudence said, stretching her thin lips wide and exposing her small sharp teeth in what Edwina could only imagine she thought of as a welcoming smile. "After all, between your work as a magistrate and any investigations you must be undertaking, I'm sure you're run right off your feet. You are working on a new investigation, aren't you?"

Edwina glanced at Beryl as if to confirm whether or not they could share such information with anyone else. Beryl made a show of looking carefully around the shop and then even looked out the window onto the pavement. She lowered her voice dramatically.

"We are actively pursuing a new case right now, but I'm sure it's of no interest to someone as busy as you," Beryl said, gesturing around the store.

"We certainly wouldn't want to waste any of your time talking your ear off about our problems, no matter how baffling they might be," Edwina said. "Let me take a closer look at that diary." Edwina stretched out her hand to take the book from Beryl.

"It seems to be quite a nice one. With the hours marked off you could certainly manage to fill it with the times you are expected at court as well as the different hours in which you would be pursuing investigations. You can see that there is even room for you to jot down any findings from our interviews with suspects or clients," Beryl said.

Edwina had the peculiar impression that she could see Prudence's ears elongating at Beryl's words. Her slim figure seemed almost to vibrate with curiosity, as if it were a harp string plucked by an unseen giant's hand. All they needed was to ignore her interest a moment or two longer.

"If it's a diary for writing down notes, you might want to consider this model," Prudence said, pushing past Beryl and plucking a slightly larger volume from the rack behind her shoulder. She handed it to Edwina triumphantly, having opened it to an example page and tapped one of her long, clawlike fingernails on a weekly spread.

"This might be just the thing," Edwina said, taking it from the shopkeeper's outstretched hands.

"Do you end up needing a lot of room for writing down the information you've gleaned?" Prudence asked.

"That depends on the quality of the interviewee. Not everyone is as observant as they might be. I can't tell you how many times we've spoken with someone about some aspect of the case, and they've taken no notice whatsoever about the details. It's really quite a shame," Edwina said.

"Someone such as yourself would have a good excuse for not

having noticed the things happening around her what with all the busyness running a shop would involve. But as to others, who seemed to have an abundance of leisure time, I find it inexplicable," Beryl said, shaking her head sadly.

Prudence seemed to have grown approximately three inches in height as she drew herself up, looking as though she might explode from the incredibly offensive suggestion that she might not have noticed those things that occurred around her.

"As the good book says, to those who much has been given much will be expected. I do have a tremendous responsibility in running this shop, but I pride myself in being attentive to details no matter what else I may have on my to-do list. In fact, unless I miss my guess, the investigation you're currently undertaking has to do with some rather nasty letters that have been making the rounds. I heard that you even had one of them entered into evidence at the Magistrate's Court," Prudence said.

She loomed over Edwina as though she might pluck her up and open her head to pry out the knowledge hidden away in her brain. Edwina forced herself not to take a step backwards.

"If you can believe it, I received one of those letters myself. And I can tell you, I was not best pleased by it, was I?" Beryl said, turning towards Edwina.

"No, not in the least. Although I suppose with your reputation as a world class adventuress you would certainly be the target for that sort of thing. It's not as though you haven't received unusual letters in the past. There is absolutely nothing remarkable about it," Edwina said.

Prudence huffed. "Nothing remarkable about poisoned pen letters spattering the village with vile gossip? You can't be serious," she said, crossing her arms across her chest and glowering at Edwina.

"I wouldn't say that one letter received by Beryl and one by Michael Blackburn is enough to make ever so much fuss about,"

Edwina said. "Besides, there's nothing to say that the two things are related, is there?"

"I should say that there was. Who ever heard of two different people in such a small village receiving that sort of mail in so short a span of time?" Prudence asked. "In any case, I happen to know that there were more letters than just the two you mentioned."

"But even if there were dozens, is there really anything to tie all the letters together? How can we be certain?" Edwina asked.

She allowed her eyes to widen slightly and shrugged. She watched as Beryl tapped her gloved finger against her lips as she kept her gaze pinned on the ceiling above her.

"I know," Beryl said, snapping her fingers. She pointed at Prudence. "You haven't taken note of any sort of suspicious letters coming through the post office, have you?"

Prudence cocked one eyebrow. "Perhaps I have and perhaps I haven't. What are you implying?"

"I was merely suggesting that as the local postmistress you would be in a position to have handled all the mail that passes through the village. Perhaps there was something strange about these letters that could help lead to the unmasking of whoever is sending them," Beryl said.

Edwina held her breath as she wondered if her friend was laying it on just a little too thick. Prudence seemed less eager to discuss the matter further than she generally was when a juicy bit of gossip was dangled in front of her.

"I hope you're not suggesting I had anything to do with the sending of these letters," Prudence said.

Edwina knew she needed to intervene. "Certainly not. But Beryl's right. The letters have come through the post, which means you would have been in contact with them. I would have thought you, as a conscientious civil servant, might be in a position to remark upon anything that caught your attention."

"Just so. Now that you come to mention it, I understand

that the letters were addressed using black pen and capital letters," Prudence said.

"The ones we have seen or heard about match that description," Edwina said.

"I can confirm that I have seen several letters come through the post office that fit that description. But there has been nothing else remarkable about them. The handwriting is distinctive only in the fact that it is so very neat," Prudence said.

Not surprisingly Prudence seemed to know more about the letters than the average resident. Still, Edwina was more sure than ever that sending nasty letters was not Prudence's style. Still, it was interesting that someone as dedicated to ferreting out secrets as was Prudence had not been able to ascertain anything noteworthy.

"That's just what I would have said about the one I received," Beryl said. "I do wonder if perhaps we could track down the sender by figuring out who might have used that sort of envelope."

"I doubt very much that that would be of use to you as the envelopes are the most popular brand that I sell," Prudence said. "The quality is decent enough for everyday use and the price is very reasonable."

"If they are that common, I expect you couldn't possibly remember who might have purchased them from you," Edwina said.

Prudence bristled. "I've recently sold boxes of them to Nora Blackburn, Godfrey, Minnie, and even Nurse Crenshaw. I bought a box of them myself only last week," she said. "It wouldn't surprise me if every household in the village had a box of them tucked away for regular use."

"What about the dates? Could there have been any funny business with the postmarks? Is it absolutely certain they were sent from this village?" Beryl asked.

"Are you suggesting that I have been lax with keeping ahold

of my cancellation stamp?" Prudence asked, drawing herself up even taller.

"Certainly not. But this shop does become rather busy from time to time, and I suppose it's possible that someone might even have broken in. You haven't noticed any irregularities with your cancellation equipment, have you?" Edwina asked.

Prudence seemed to soften slightly. "No, I haven't. The letters have come through in different postboxes throughout the village and I have canceled them just as I have everything else. I hope you are not intending to accuse me of anything. I'm as much a victim here as anyone else in the village," Prudence said.

"A victim? I'm sure that no one will blame you for the post office being used to send such egregious abuses of the Royal Mail," Edwina said.

"Not that sort of victim. I received one of the letters myself, so certainly I couldn't be the one to be performing any funny business about them, now, could I?" Prudence said.

Beryl and Edwina exchanged a glance. Whether or not they had intended for it to appear to be a look of disbelief, that seemed to be what Prudence interpreted.

"I most certainly did receive one of those letters. Right nasty it was. If you can believe it, it accused me of being a gossip and told me that if I didn't stop, a complaint would be lodged with the postmaster general."

Prudence stomped around to the back side of the counter again and withdrew a piece of paper from beneath it. She held it out fluttering it over her head. She crossed back around to the front of the counter and shoved it towards Edwina, who took it from her hands and looked it over. Indeed, the letter writer had lambasted Prudence for her unrelenting inclination to gossip. It stated in no uncertain terms that she could be considered in breach of her duties to subject postal customers to the onslaught of nastiness she served up every time anyone stepped across her threshold.

The tone of the letter was forthright, and Edwina wondered if it was part of the reason that it had taken extra effort to prompt Prudence to divulge what she knew. Although Edwina could not say she had been pleased with an outbreak of poisoned pen letters in the village, she felt rather cheered by the notion that someone had finally given Prudence a well-deserved scolding. Edwina could not think of a thing to say that would not betray her agreement with the letter writer. She simply shook her head with what she hoped looked like shock and handed the letter back to Prudence.

Beryl threw herself into the conversational breech and asked Prudence to put the cost of the diary on their account. Without waiting for a reply, Beryl steered Edwina and the new diary out the door.

Chapter 18

Beryl had rather enjoyed their trip to Prudence's shop. There was little she liked more than to see someone unpleasant on the receiving end of their comeuppance. And the idea that the poisoned pen writer had targeted Prudence warmed the cockles of her heart. She waited until they were well away from Prudence's doorstep before allowing a look of pleasure to spread across her face. She turned towards Edwina with a beaming smile.

"Well, at least some good has come of this nasty campaign," she said.

"I was thinking much the same thing," Edwina said. "That's the thing about this sort of letter, isn't it? People say things in them that they might not say in person."

"It seems to me someone should have spoken to Prudence about her behavior ages ago."

"Still, I am glad we weren't the ones to do it. She is staring at us like she has more to say. Let's head to the Woolery for the ledgers before Prudence comes out to discuss it further. I am not sure you will be able to hold your tongue if she does."

"You aren't planning to do a little shopping while we are there, are you?" Beryl asked.

There was never going to be a time that she was interested in poking around in a yarn shop, or any shop so wholly devoted to domesticity. Beryl did not fancy a protracted session spent watching Edwina fuss about, deciding on colors and weights of skeins of yarn or even worse, sifting through baskets filled with knitting patterns.

"I assure you I have plenty of knitting wool on hand. I stopped in only the other day, as you well know, and I have not used up what I purchased earlier in the week. Perhaps I could set aside a time to do so in my new diary," Edwina said with a smile.

"Let's just hope Mrs. Dunbarton has the ledgers with her. I have a feeling the case may finally be unraveling."

They walked to the Woolery and let themselves in. Mrs. Dunbarton was busy helping another customer when they arrived, and Beryl braced herself for the inevitable sifting and sorting Edwina would embark upon when in the presence of heaping baskets of wool. Sure enough, Edwina spotted something that forced a gasp of delight from her the moment they stepped across the threshold. Beryl couldn't understand what about a pale pink ball of fluff could elicit such an enthusiastic response, but apparently, it could.

It took all of Beryl's patience to sit quietly at the table in the center of the room and wait for Edwina, Mrs. Dunbarton, and the other patron to conclude their comparison of the relative benefits of mohair versus angora. But eventually, Mrs. Dunbarton wrapped up her first customer's purchases in a brown paper parcel and wished her a good day. Beryl was relieved to see Edwina immediately replaced the balls of wool into their baskets and turned her attention to the matter at hand.

"Are you not interested in those skeins after all?" Mrs. Dunbarton asked, pointing towards the basket behind Edwina.

"I shall make a return visit for them another day, but I'm afraid my attention is needed for the case we are working on at present and I should find them entirely too distracting to have on hand," Edwina said. "We stopped in to ask if you happen to have the garden club ledgers that belonged to Cornelia Burroughs."

"I have them right in the back room. Godfrey asked me to collect them after Cornelia died," Mrs. Dunbarton said. "I have the club minutes, too."

"Do you think we could borrow all of it for a few days?" Beryl asked.

Mrs. Dunbarton widened her eyes in surprise, then shrugged.

"I suppose you must have a good reason for asking." She turned her gaze to Edwina and waited for reassurance.

"I just wanted to take a look at them as part of the investigation we've been going into. There was some unpleasantness suggested in one of those poisoned pen letters and I thought it best for us to check it out," Edwina said.

"You mean there's some question as to whether or not there have been shenanigans with garden club funds?" Mrs. Dunbarton asked.

"I'm afraid that Cornelia received a letter that alleged that there were some irregularities in her handling of the monies," Edwina said.

"I certainly hope that isn't the case," Mrs. Dunbarton said. "I am not happy to have to step into the role of club chairwoman under any circumstances, but certainly not if it will involve a scandal."

"If the letter ends up being like most of the rest of them, there won't be any truth in it, and you'll have nothing to worry about. Why don't you just leave it with us, and we'll get to the bottom of it one way or another," Edwina said in the same tone she used with Crumpet when attempting to remove a burr from his fur.

Mrs. Dunbarton nodded and hurried towards the back room. She reemerged a moment later holding a well-worn leather ledger. As she handed it to Edwina, she let out a deep sigh.

"You don't suppose that the letter Cornelia received had anything to do with her sudden death, do you?" she asked. "The very thought of it sends a goose over my grave."

"We have no way of knowing if she even saw the letter. Perhaps such a nasty accusation never even reached her," Beryl said.

"I certainly hope it didn't, especially if it was not true. Godfrey needn't know about it, I hope," Mrs. Dunbarton said.

"If it's possible to keep him ignorant of it we most certainly will do so." Edwina reached out for the ledger. "I can see no reason to trouble him if it comes to nothing."

"The poor man has been through enough of a shock with Cornelia's sudden death. The idea that her name might be dragged through the mud on top of it is not something a recent widower should have to endure," Mrs. Dunbarton said. "I hope you catch who's ever doing this. I found my letter upsetting, but it couldn't hold a candle to something as outrageous as this."

"We're doing everything we can to get to the bottom of it as discreetly and quickly as possible. I'll be sure to get these back to you just as fast as I can and to let you know if we discover any problems with the books."

"I'd appreciate that. I'll hold those balls of wool to the side for you, Edwina. It looked as though they might be popular with another customer," Mrs. Dunbarton said with a tap to the side of her nose.

Beryl still couldn't understand the appeal of yarn, but as they made their way out onto the sidewalk, she noted a decided spring in her friend's step. She made a mental note to go back and pick up the purchase for Edwina just as soon as she possibly could.

Edwina had had a sinking feeling from the moment she reached out and relieved Mrs. Dunbarton of the garden club's ledger. Even though there had been no hint of scandal attached to Cornelia's name during her lifetime, Edwina felt as though little bells were going off in the back of her brain. One of course did not like to speak ill of the dead and Cornelia was no exception. But there was something about the accusation that she had been skimming money that made Edwina run through her memories of experiences she had had with the former garden club president. The more she thought about the ways that the poisoned pen letters had affected the village, the more disturbed she became.

Was it really the case that a reputation could be called into question so very easily? Hadn't years of devoted service to an organization without thought of acknowledgment or compensation earned someone the right to be trusted? Was it such a fragile thing, the fabric of society?

Edwina thought about the way that so many things she had been raised to believe were true had been called into question over the last few years. Certainly, the war had taken its toll on the connection between neighbors as well as the expectations villagers had about their lives. She couldn't say she blamed anyone who wished to radically alter the trajectory of their lives. She had benefited herself in meaningful ways from expanding her notion of what might be possible both for herself and for others. No, it wasn't the idea of change or even the underpinnings of social structure that bothered her. It was the idea that relationships could come apart at the seams with the stroke of a pen.

As she trudged along next to Beryl, lost in thought, she considered a far more cheerful use of the written word. In the years since they had left Miss DuPont's Finishing School for Young Ladies, hadn't she managed to stay connected to her dear friend through letters? Hadn't she enjoyed reading about Beryl's exploits as reported in newspapers and magazines? Surely not everything could be unraveled quite so easily.

By the time they had reached the front door of the Beeches

her heart felt lighter. So far, the majority of the letters had proven to be nothing more than nonsense. And even the ones that had struck upon the truth were calling into account things that were widely already acknowledged. Minnie Mumford seemed to be the only person in Walmsley Parva who was unaware of her husband's roving eye and grasping hands.

Although truth be told, Edwina had not long been one of the people in the know concerning his true character. It had taken Beryl's insistence that he was a man with whom she would not like to find herself in the back seat of a motorcar without a chaperone for Edwina to credit the extent of his misbehavior. But it seemed common knowledge, according to Beryl, that he behaved in such an egregious way. The letter writer could easily have known that he might be inclined to harass young Eva Scott.

As for Prudence, even the most oblivious of villagers was surely aware of her tendency towards gossip. After all, she ran the only post office in the village, and it would be impossible to avoid her completely. If one needed postage stamps, wished to appease a sweet tooth, Prudence's shop was the place to procure such items. Edwina had never darkened Prudence's doorstep without having her ears filled with generous helpings of gossip. No, there was nothing about Prudence's letter that was not easily attributed to common knowledge. There was absolutely no reason to suspect that the letter accusing Cornelia of misdeeds was any more likely to prove to be accurate than all of the others that were filled with outrageous falsehoods.

With a hopeful feeling she entered the house and greeted Beddoes, who was occupied with applying her considerable domestic attention to the baseboards in the front hallway. Crumpet appeared at her feet and happily hurried ahead of her towards the morning room. Beryl brought up the rear and closed the door behind her as they entered the sunny, cheerful space.

Edwina pulled the ledger from her satchel and laid it on the table placed in front of a long set of windows overlooking the garden. She smiled to see the stooped figure of Simpkins in the border curved next to the goldfish pond tossing what appeared to be crumbs of bread into the still water. A sleek golden flash crested the surface of the water right near Simpkins's outstretched hand.

Beryl stepped up next to her and tapped on the ledger, returning her thoughts to the task at hand.

"All right then, let's take a look," Beryl said.

Edwina nodded and opened the leather-bound volume. She ran her eyes along the columns starting at the very beginning. As she sifted through the figures and took note of the expenditures a cold clammy feeling began to spread through her stomach. She stepped away from the table and located a pad of paper and a pencil. Pulling a chair up to the table, she began sorting out some of the jumble of numbers by making some calculations on her paper. Beryl stood over her shoulder peering down at her work.

"Who is the Amalgamated Amendments Company? Do you know why the garden club would be spending quite so much with them?" Beryl asked. She tapped on an entry on the page in front of her. Edwina flipped back several pages and noted that a payment seemed to have been made to that company repeatedly. She shook her head, the clammy feeling growing ever stronger.

"As far as I know there's no such reason for any payments to be made for soil amendments. The garden club took pride in civic projects and beautification in the village, but all of the materials were donated. We used the same donors for such things year after year, and in all the years I've been involved with the garden club I cannot recall the membership ever voting to pay for soil amendments. There was simply never any need. Lots of local merchants and establishments are happy to contribute to beautifying the village."

"Did you vote as a group on other sorts of expenditures?" Beryl asked.

"Yes. That was one of the first orders of business in any of our meetings. If there was something to be paid for, it was proposed and voted upon. There were minutes of those meetings kept as well, and so it would be easy enough to prove that such expenditures were not something the membership had knowledge of," Edwina said.

"It looks pretty grim then, doesn't it?" Beryl asked.

"I think it would be best to check the bank balance. I know that there was quite a hullabaloo about how much money we had managed to raise at the most recent plant sale. Let me double check it against the minutes," Edwina said.

She pulled out a sheaf of papers containing minutes of the meetings and flipped to the most recent page.

"Here it is. We raised a total of nineteen pounds and forty-three pence in our plant and jumble sale in the spring. It was our most successful year ever and the entire membership was surprised by the success. We had tabled a discussion of how to use the money as we wanted there to be sufficient time to consider how it might best be used. In fact, there were several people who were supposed to be bringing potential project ideas for the next meeting," Edwina said.

"What does the ledger have to say about that money?" Beryl said.

"The amount raised at the plant sale is duly noted here in the ledger, but once again a payment for soil amendments to Amalgamated Amendments comes up," Edwina said. "It has dropped the total in the account by a considerable amount."

"Perhaps we ought to enquire at the bank as to the balance," Beryl said.

"I'm afraid it has come to that."

"Are you authorized to enquire about the account? In my experience banks can be quite touchy about privacy," Beryl said.

"I'm not, but I do happen to have more than nodding acquaintance with one of the cashiers there. I expect it's quite possible I can find out what we need to know," Edwina said.

With a heavy heart she returned to the front hallway with Beryl following behind her. She lifted the telephone receiver from its cradle and asked to be connected with the Walmsley Parva Savings and Trust.

In only a moment she found herself being warmly greeted by a young woman she had overseen in the Women's Land Army during the war years. Beatrice Walker was eager to be of assistance to Edwina and was just as inclined as she had been during her time in the Women's Land Army to simply acquiesce to whatever she was asked to do by someone she perceived to be her superior.

Edwina felt ever so slightly ashamed of herself for taking advantage of Beatrice's trusting nature, but there would be no value in making things more difficult. The greater good was to get to the bottom of the poisoned pen before anyone else was stung. By the time she returned the receiver to its cradle the uncomfortable feeling in her stomach had swelled to a tidal wave.

"According to Beatrice there were no checks written out to any amendments company. The account rarely had checks drawn upon it, but there were numerous withdrawals," Edwina said.

"Let me guess, cash withdrawals?" Beryl asked.

"Unfortunately, yes. It seems that her cash withdrawals corresponded with the dates of the supposed checks to the amendments company. All of the money from the plant sale has been removed from the account. In fact, if the garden club were asked to pay rent to the Women's Institute for use of the building, it would be hard pressed to do so," Edwina said.

"So, it seems as though the poisoned pen writer had knowledge of the embezzlement," Beryl said. "Do you think that if Cornelia had read a letter accusing her of theft, it would have brought on a fatal asthma attack?"

"I really don't know how Cornelia could have lived such a thing down. And the letter did not seem to indicate that the writer was looking to blackmail her in any way. It seemed as though the letter was simply stating knowledge of her activities. It didn't sound as though any opportunity was being offered for her to hush the person up and make the problem go away. If she saw no way to get out of her present difficulty, it might have brought on an asthma attack," Edwina said.

"I think the next thing we ought to do is to take Godfrey Burroughs up on his offer to look through the rest of Cornelia's papers," Beryl said. "Do you think that Godfrey knew what his wife was up to?"

"I have no idea whatsoever. For his sake, I hope he did not. After all, unlike Cornelia, he will still need to live with what he has done if that's the case," Edwina said.

"If he's involved, I think the sooner we take a look at Cornelia's papers, the better."

"Do you think that there's any chance he's involved if he offered to let us take a look at them?" Edwina asked.

"He hasn't been thinking all that clearly ever since Cornelia died. I'm not sure his willingness for us to take a look at her things is any indication of his complicity one way or another. But somehow he doesn't seem like the sort of person she would include in a thing like that, does he?" Beryl said.

"If you had asked me that before I saw these ledgers, I would have completely agreed. That said, before I had seen them, I would have said that Cornelia was a somewhat difficult but extremely straitlaced sort of woman. Now I have no idea what to think."

"Then I guess we'd best go to see for ourselves," Beryl said.

Chapter 19

Beryl knew that Edwina must have been agonizing about the matter at hand when she had suggested they take the motorcar to Godfrey's home in order to arrive as quickly as possible. Beryl told herself to drive as sedately as she could in order not to fray Edwina's nerves any further. They arrived in only a few moments' time and she noticed Edwina seemed to steel herself for the event in front of them by drawing in a few deep breaths before reaching for the motorcar door latch and heading for the front step of the Burroughses' residence. Beryl hurried to join her and took it upon herself to take the lead. She knocked on the front door and beamed at Godfrey when he creaked it open.

"Hello, Godfrey. I do hope you won't feel that we are imposing, but we decided to take you up on your kind offer to have a look at Cornelia's papers. We were not able to find all that we needed in the ledger that Mrs. Dunbarton had in her possession," Beryl said, flashing him one of her famous smiles.

She deliberately toned down the wattage enough to be respectful of his bereavement but allowed it to work its magic even in a dimmed state. She was gratified to see that no matter how recently bereaved the man might be, he responded to the softening effect of her attention. He pulled the door open wider and stepped back to allow them to pass into the hallway.

"It's no problem at all. But if you don't mind, would you show yourselves to the sitting room? I have a terrible headache and would like to lie back down," he said.

Edwina made a soothing sound and assured him they would be perfectly capable of taking care of things on their own. Beryl watched as he took himself off to the far end of the corridor and out of sight. Edwina strode purposely towards the opposite side of the house and Beryl followed in her wake. She did not realize that Edwina had been on terms of such intimacy with the Burroughs family to be able to find her way throughout the building without any assistance. But sure enough, Edwina struck off for the sitting room without further guidance. Beryl closed the door to the room behind her and looked around.

"How did you know your way around?" Beryl asked.

"Occasionally members of the garden club meet in the homes of members and Cornelia had held such meetings here on more than one occasion. Besides, over the years of paying calls and serving on various committees, I have probably been in and out of most houses in the village," Edwina said, heading straight for a desk at the far corner of the room. Beryl followed her and the two of them looked it over in silence.

It was a large, old-fashioned sort of a desk and not the type of thing Beryl could imagine wanting to own. It would simply weigh one down should one wish to ramble off somewhere. Not only was it wider than she thought strictly necessary, but it was also quite tall and featured a rolltop front.

Edwina slid the door up and out of the way, exposing a myriad of overstuffed pigeonholes crammed with papers and detritus of all sorts. Just looking at it gave Beryl a feeling of claustrophobia. Even though she had been cooling her heels in one location for several months, she had not felt inclined to acquire additional possessions. She found it astonishing that anyone would allow themselves to be so weighted down by so much flotsam and jetsam.

Edwina was made of far different stuff. Although Beryl did not criticize her for it, she knew that Edwina's tolerance for such things was far greater than her own. After all, her family had lived at the Beeches for several generations and in such time a great quantity of possessions had accumulated. Beryl thought it likely that Edwina had never needed to purchase a single household item of her own and yet the house remained completely furnished. Even though Edwina had been unfortunately forced to sell off many of the items of value in order to stay afloat during the lean years after so many death duties had to be paid, Beryl still sometimes felt the oppressive nature of bric-a-brac in the form of occasional tables and paintings covering the walls of the house.

Even so, Edwina was of far too tidy a mind to ever allow paperwork clutter to spring up around her as Cornelia had done. Edwina pulled a chair in front of the desk and seated herself. She leaned forward and peered carefully into the pigeonholes as if trying to decide which ones would prove fruitful to explore. Edwina reached her hand into a lower compartment and withdrew a jumble of papers and envelopes. A cloud of dust rose up and set her to sneezing. Edwina handed Beryl the stack of items and pulled another out towards herself. Slowly but surely the two of them worked their way through a third of the pigeonholes before Edwina let out a gasp.

"What is it? What have you found?" Beryl asked, leaning towards her.

"Look at this," Edwina said, sliding an oversized envelope towards Beryl. She opened it and shook out the contents. A scattering of letters and words clipped from newspapers and magazines spilled out onto the leather desk blotter. A pair of tweezers clunked down onto the desk in front of them with a thud. Edwina reached into another cubbyhole and withdrew a pot of paste. Further inspection produced a box of envelopes, two thirds of which had been used, and appeared to be of the same sort as the poisoned pen letters.

"I'd say we found the anonymous writer, without a doubt," Beryl said.

"It certainly appears that way," Edwina said, drumming her fingers on the desk.

"Are you not entirely convinced?" Beryl asked.

"I shouldn't like to assume anything in this case. After all, Cornelia was not the only person who lived here or who had access to this desk," she said. She stood and moved about the room, her slim arms crossed in front of her chest as she looked over what else the room contained. "There is equal evidence of Godfrey and Cornelia in this room. It's not as though it was her private space."

Edwina pointed towards an end table placed next to the sofa. Upon it sat an overflowing ashtray and a half-filled mug. Edwina lifted the cup and took a delicate sniff. "Coffee. Cornelia never drank coffee, but Godfrey did."

"Are you suggesting that Godfrey might be the poisoned pen?" Beryl said, lowering her voice to barely above a whisper.

"I'm suggesting that it's just as possible that he was the one to send the letters as for Cornelia to send them. After all, why would she send such a letter to herself?"

Edwina makes a good point, Beryl thought as she considered it further. Why would Cornelia send any such letter to herself? Was it possible that Godfrey was so tired of being ordered about that he found an outlet for his suppressed rage? After finding it possible to get away with sending such poisonous missives to people who most likely had done him no wrong, had he felt emboldened to send one to his wife in a fit of spite?

Could his involvement explain why he had taken her death so very much to heart?

"I suppose it's possible that he could have sent her a letter. I know I would have been tempted to do so if I had been him," Beryl said.

"Not only that, but the letters have continued after Cornelia's death. If she were the letter writer, they wouldn't have done so, would they?" Edwina said.

"You're right. They've continued uninterrupted both before and after her death. But do you think that Godfrey would have allowed us to look into the desk if he thought there was any chance we would discover what he was up to?"

"I really can't say for sure. These things were stuffed well into the back behind a bunch more clutter. Perhaps he didn't think we would be so nosy as to snoop down into the backs of the cubbyholes."

"Or maybe he simply wanted to be caught. Sometimes someone needs an outside force to stop them from doing those things they ought not do," Beryl said. "Godfrey has, by all appearances, spent his adulthood being kept on the straight and narrow by the firm control of his spouse. Maybe he's looking for someone else to take him in hand," Beryl said with a shrug.

"Either way, I think it's time to make ourselves scarce before he sees what we have discovered. Let's go back to the Beeches and decide our next move."

They headed straight for the sitting room, and without consulting Edwina, Beryl got to work concocting a batch of gin fizzes. Before she had finished cracking the ice Edwina heard the sound of heavy footfalls coming along the corridor and Simpkins appeared in the doorway. He had almost a preternatural ability to appear just as any form of refreshment was in the offing. He crossed the room and settled on the far end of the sofa across from Edwina.

Although it had surprised her when she had first noticed that it was the case, Edwina had come to understand that Simpkins had a similarly uncanny ability to put in an appearance just as she most needed some cheering. Something had shifted ever since he had moved into the back bedroom at the Beeches, and she thought that something was likely her own attitude. Perhaps Simpkins had always looked out for her best interests, but she had not been able to see it or to give him credit for having done so until he was such a constant presence underfoot. She lifted her beret from her knitting basket and felt her shoulders relax down from around her ears as she moved her needles through the stitches and felt the wool slipping comfortingly through her fingers.

"You've had some bad news, haven't you?" Simpkins asked, keeping her under close observation as she wrapped the yarn round the tip of the needle and slipped a tight stitch from the left to the right.

Her knitting always took on a mirror image of her own emotional state, and when she encountered stitches that proved difficult to move from one needle to the next, she knew she had been under some degree of strain when she had added that row to the project. How like Simpkins to have noticed such a small detail as that. Perhaps what she had always perceived as indolence on his part was merely a contemplative nature that she had not given him credit for. She lowered her knitting back into her lap and gave him her full attention.

Beryl appeared beside her and placed a glass on the table at her elbow. She handed one to Simpkins, who thanked her with a toothy smile. Edwina waited for Beryl to settle herself into her own favorite spot on the sofa at the opposite end to Simpkins and launched into the status of the enquiry.

"As much as I hate to say so, this case has proven thoroughly discouraging," she said.

"Why is that?" Simpkins said, leaning slightly forward.

"I haven't at all liked the sorts of thoughts I've been having about my neighbors ever since these letters have appeared."

"But why should you be so badly affected by what's turned out to be a whole lot of malarkey?" he said. He sent a glance over towards Beryl as if to gather some support for his point of view.

"But that's just it, you see. Not all of them have turned out to be malarkey," Beryl said.

"You mean some of them have ended up telling the truth?" Simpkins asked.

"Sadly, yes. We've had some very disturbing news about Cornelia," Edwina said.

"More disturbing than that she's dead?" Simpkins asked.

"I found a letter in Cornelia's motorcar accusing her of skimming money from the garden club funds," Beryl said.

"That doesn't surprise me none," Simpson said with a slow nod. He took a maddeningly long sip of his drink before continuing. "I always thought she acted a little too eager to handle all the details of the garden club goings on for my taste."

Edwina felt taken aback. Had Simpkins spotted some chink in Cornelia's façade that she had missed? Perhaps he really had always been far more observant than she had given him credit for.

"I just thought that she was a very enthusiastic gardener," Edwina said.

"Begging your pardon, miss, but she's never been any such thing. Have you ever taken a close look at her gardens?" he asked.

Edwina thought about the question for a moment. Her own gardens at the Beeches had gotten away from her somewhat over the years as they had needed to let one gardener after another go until they were finally reduced to the inadequate and infrequent ministrations of Simpkins, who, to be fair, had grown a bit long in the tooth for some of the heavier aspects of the job. Nevertheless, Edwina's gardens were overflowing with

every manner of blooming bulb, flowering shrub, and unique tree she could get her hands on.

Nothing had delighted her more than perusing plant catalogs and dreaming of the day she could afford to purchase new specimens to tuck into every square inch of the space. She had enthusiastically divided plants and traded with others and never failed to clip out articles on plant care from newspapers and magazines. Dr. Wilcox had behaved in the equally enthusiastic manner as had the majority of the other members of the garden club.

In fact, they always offered to have the group around to see various specimens of their gardens during peak seasons in order to show them off. All except, that was, for Cornelia Burroughs. Come to think of it, Cornelia had never been one to haggle with another garden club member over a prize cutting or to show up at a meeting breathless with the news that a certain shrub she had nurtured for the last few years had finally deigned to bloom for the first time.

No, Cornelia was extremely active in the garden club activities, but they were always more administrative than horticultural. As Edwina cast her mind back over her memories of Cornelia, she could only picture her standing at the front of the room announcing fund-raising efforts or congratulating members on public projects they had completed. Her offers to allow others to have their pick of the choicest plants that had come in for swap meetings took on a different hue as she thought about them with Simpkins's point of view in mind.

Edwina had assumed that as garden club president Cornelia would allow others their first choice as a way of being a good leader. But perhaps what it really boiled down to was that she had very little interest in the plants themselves. Had she simply seen the enthusiastic gardeners of Walmsley Parva as easy prey?

"I see what you mean," Edwina said. "But that's even more distressing, isn't it?"

Simpkins shrugged. "People are going to behave the way that suits them and there's not much the rest of us can do about it. The only thing you can do is to ask yourself if something is too good to be true, why that might be. In the course of my lifetime I have come to understand that there's always a reason."

"There was some other shocking news involving the Burroughses' household as well," Beryl said. "Let's not forget that."

"More bad news?" Simpkins asked, rattling his glass as if to encourage Beryl to refill it. She ignored him and Edwina rushed in to fill a void in the conversation. It would be best to keep Simpkins's mind keen if he was contributing so much value to the conversation about the case.

"It appears that someone in their household was sending the poisoned pen letters. We found newspaper and magazine cuttings just like the ones the letters have been constructed from, a pot of paste, and a partial box of the same sort of envelopes in which the letters were sent."

Simpkins whistled long and low. "Do you think that Cornelia was the one sending them?" he asked.

"We're fairly certain that someone in her household was the one to send them, but whether or not it was Cornelia or Godfrey, we're not sure," Beryl said.

"Aren't poisoned pen letters usually something that women send?" Simpkins asked.

Edwina had expressed the same sentiment herself to Beryl earlier, but somehow hearing Simpkins say it put her back up.

"I think it would do us a great deal of good to be more open-minded about the possibilities. For one thing, the letters have continued after Cornelia's death. Even if she was the one who had originally sent them, someone else has taken over."

"Or Godfrey is the one who's been sending them the whole time," Beryl said.

"Or there's a third possibility," Simpkins said.

"Which is?" Beryl asked.

"Maybe Cornelia had written a whole passel of letters before she died and there was a delay in sending them out for some reason," Simpkins said.

Edwina felt her jaw slacken. She quickly snapped it shut and looked over at Beryl. Her friend had an eyebrow cocked high up on her forehead as though she too were quite surprised at the suggestion. But how could such a thing be accomplished? Could there have been some sort of postal delay? Could Godfrey have sent the letters into the post after his wife had unexpectedly died? Had someone else helped him with some tidying up and sent them? Had Cornelia merely not had the postage before her sudden attack?

"That still wouldn't explain why Cornelia received one herself," Beryl said. "My money is still on Godfrey."

"Maybe she sent herself a letter to make sure she was not among the suspects," Edwina said.

"Didn't you say that you found her letter in Cornelia's motorcar?" Simpkins asked.

Beryl nodded. "It was shoved well down in the pocket of the driver's side door."

"That's not a particularly good place to leave it if you wanted to make sure others knew you had received one, is it?" he asked.

"Perhaps she died before she was able to display it somewhere for her husband to see as if by chance," Beryl said.

"But if she sent the letter to herself, she would not have managed to give herself an asthma attack about it. Besides, I doubt she would have sent herself a letter accusing herself of a crime she had actually committed," Edwina said, looking from Beryl to Simpkins and back again.

The three of them sat in silence for a moment and then Beryl got to her feet to mix up a fresh round of drinks.

"You know, it strikes me that these letters have had a mixed effect on the village. As much as some of them have just proved disruptive, at least one of them has done some real good," he said.

"What do you mean?" Beryl asked.

Simpkins looked over at Edwina and she felt she knew exactly what he meant. While so many of the letters had caused dissension and disagreement between neighbors, there had been one or two that urged the recipient to take action on something that needed correcting.

"It just seems to me that in amongst all of the rumors, there have been a few useful things mentioned."

"Useful or not, I don't know as we've gotten any further ahead than where we were when this all started," Beryl said.

"Come now, that can't be the case," Simpkins said. "At the very least you have a lead to follow and a plan of action you could take," he said.

"What might that be?" Edwina asked.

"It seems to me that you could keep an eye on Godfrey Burroughs and his nearest postbox. If he's the one sending the letters instead of Cornelia, you should be able to catch him at it fairly quickly," he said.

"I suppose you're right," Beryl said. "We could surreptitiously keep an eye on both Godfrey and his postbox, over the next few days, couldn't we?" she said.

Simpkins nodded. "Now that the greengage harvest is in, I could even take a turn keeping an eye out myself. We could start in the morning before the first post," he said.

Chapter 20

As Simpkins and Beryl continued to natter on about the logistics of keeping a watchful eye on any post Godfrey Burroughs might choose to send, Edwina's mind turned elsewhere. She couldn't get over something that Simpkins had said. People always had a reason for doing the things they did. He also was right about his observation about the letters. There were some that attempted to do some good and those had been very different than the ones that simply seemed designed to stir up trouble between neighbors. She reached for a pad of paper and a pencil she kept in her knitting basket for counting rows and sketching out potential patterns and began to empty her mind of all she knew about the case.

She listed each of the letters that she knew to have been received and the order in which she had heard reports of them. First there had been Michael's letter and then the one to Beddoes. Beryl had received one and so had Mrs. Prentice. She mustn't forget Mrs. Dunbarton or the photographer Mr. Stevens or Margery Nelson. Dr. Wilcox had received a letter and so had Prudence. Mrs. Scott, Nurse Crenshaw, and Cornelia had all been on the receiving end of the missives.

As she looked at the list she had written, it occurred to her that not only did there seem to be two different sorts of purposes intended by the letters, but it also appeared that the sort of letter fell on either side of Cornelia's death. All of the letters before she had died seemed to be aimed at stirring up trouble and causing as much harm as was possible without any basis for their contents. But the letters Edwina had become aware of after Cornelia's death seemed to be much more bent on advising members of the community to correct their behavior or to take action where someone else was being harmed.

Mrs. Scott's letter advising her about Mr. Mumford harassing her daughter had appeared after Cornelia's death. Prudence's letter admonishing her to stop her gossiping unless she wished to be reported to the postmaster general was also from the time after Cornelia died.

But what about Cornelia's own letter? How could that be explained? Edwina felt certain she had been onto something important, but the puzzle piece of Cornelia's own letter simply did not fit. But it must have been sent before Cornelia died because it had been opened and found in her own car at the driver side door. Surely that wrinkle in the argument must matter.

Edwina placed the notebook on the table beside her and leaned back in her chair, allowing her gaze to settle on the wall opposite. As she gave the problem further thought, she could not simply assume she knew about every letter that had been received. After all, one of the hallmarks of a poisoned pen letter was that it contained the sorts of things that one did not prefer to show to others, especially others not connected to oneself with any degree of intimacy.

Edwina had to admit to herself that there was every possibility that most of the village had received such letters. In fact, hadn't Prudence indicated that there had been a steady stream of them coming through the post office? So, in reality, she was only able to make a case for those few that she knew about having landed on either side of Cornelia's death and how that might be a clue as to their sender.

She felt even more adrift than she had been on their very first case. In some ways, a dead body that had clearly been the victim of foul play was so much more concrete than this sort of crime. And looking at it another way, it was almost as though there was a serial murderer of reputations working in the village. As much as she would not have thought so before this had all begun, Edwina had to admit to herself that she was more personally affected by the damage that these rumors and letters had done than she ever had been by an actual murder.

She just couldn't shake Simpkins's assertion that there had to be a reason behind it. If Cornelia and the way that she behaved in the world was clear to Simpkins but not to her, what did that say about her powers of observation? Was she really cut out to be a detective at all? She had rather prided herself on her ability to ferret out lies and deceit behind the actions of fellow villagers. She didn't think of herself as someone over whose eyes the wool was easily pulled. In fact, she thought of herself as someone rather more inclined to be suspicious and skeptical.

Nevertheless, it had done her very little good when it came to this case. She had to admit, she was well and truly discouraged. She didn't even know for sure if Cornelia had been driven to her death by the contents of the letter she received or if it was all simply a coincidence. She didn't know if Cornelia was the letter sender and if she had simply received a dose of her own medicine.

She felt so unsure of it all that the thought crossed her mind that perhaps someone had planted that evidence in Cornelia's study. After all, it had been easy enough for Beryl to convince Godfrey to allow them in to take a look through his wife's belongings. Was it possible that someone else had done the same and had simply left the incriminating evidence where it could be found by Godfrey or someone else at a later date?

As her thoughts tumbled and jostled, she wondered if perhaps she had been wise to accept a second gin fizz. Usually, they had rather a bracing quality about them, but nothing felt particularly invigorating to her at that moment. She found herself suddenly longing for the peace and quiet a more private life had always offered her. An evening of listening to the wireless while working on a knitting project or perhaps indulging in a few rubbers of bridge with friends seemed like a particularly appealing notion as the sound of Simpkins and Beryl discussing the logistics of the investigation floated towards her.

With a start she remembered that she had extended a real invitation to Charles to come round for a few rubbers of bridge. She glanced at the clock on the mantelpiece and realized he was due any moment. Driving off the effects of her cocktail with a few deep breaths and a shake of her head, she got to her feet.

"I had completely forgotten with all of the excitement of the day that Charles is on his way for bridge. If the two of you will set up the card table, I will go and see about some refreshments."

Before she could reach the kitchen, she heard Crumpet barking and rushing for the front door.

Beryl had been rather pleased with Charles concerning the gift he had brought to Edwina. When she had first arrived in Walmsley Parva the previous autumn, she had immediately sussed out the fact that shy solicitor Charles carried a great, blazing torch for her friend. But he had done little more than to pay her the sort of gentlemanly attention that was polite and safe.

His one exceptional behavior was to include a figure of a woman who looked remarkably like Edwina in all of his watercolor paintings. In fact, in Beryl's mind that had been the thing that had clinched his interest. He had shoehorned figures into landscapes where no improvement to the overall composition could be attributed to such inclusions.

During a recent case that had taken them to an artists' col-

ony, Charles had had the opportunity to paint Edwina less surreptitiously. In fact, his skills had improved considerably during
his time at the artists' colony and Beryl had to wonder if some
of it stemmed from the fact that he was able to be more open
about his subject matter. The fact that Edwina knew he was
painting her and that he was allowed to study her with intensity and to include details from life rather than from memory
had rendered work that showed off his commitment to his art.
Beryl had thought it rather showed off his commitment to Edwina as well.

Yes, something had decidedly shifted in his willingness to
make more direct overtures since their last case. Beryl thought
things were moving along quite nicely. But she had to admit,
even with her encouragement, she had been surprised at the di-
rectness Charles had shown in coming over with such an ex-
travagant and cherished gift. She waited until Edwina was out
of the room with Simpkins in tow before bringing up the subject. She could hear Edwina and Simpkins squabbling about the
merit of different sorts of chutneys and spreads to offer with
the nibbles tray. It was safe to assume they would be busy for
sufficient time for her to get to the bottom of Charles's sudden
fit of boldness.

She looked him over for signs of change in his appearance.
There, too, she spotted adjustments that might have gone un-
noticed to the average passerby but not to one as used to track-
ing down quarry as was Beryl. Unless she had missed her guess,
he was sporting a new suit and had pinned a flower to his button-
hole in a rather rakish manner. Instead of his usual plain white
dress shirt, the one he wore included a subtle blue stripe. Perhaps
it was not a particularly daring style choice, but for Charles it
represented quite a dashing change of pace. No, something had
decidedly prompted him to take greater and greater steps in the
direction of his domestic dreams.

"So, Charles, you made quite a success with your unexpected gift," Beryl said, gesturing at the Wardian case that had taken pride of place on the mantelpiece. It could be viewed to perfection from Edwina's favorite chair and Beryl had noticed her friend taking long looks at it from time to time ever since it had arrived so unexpectedly.

"I'm so very glad she's enjoyed it," Charles said, a slight flush appearing on the side of his neck.

It was something he had in common with Edwina. They both had a charming tendency to blush when complimented. Edwina had demonstrated this trait far more obviously since she had spontaneously gone to Alma Poole's House of Beauty and asked to have her hair bobbed. But for poor Charles, his neck had always been on display and inclined to give away his emotions.

"She's enjoyed it immensely as I'm sure you can tell from the location in which she placed it. Not an evening goes by that she doesn't spend her time gazing lovingly up at it," Beryl said.

Sure enough, Charles's neck grew even more fiery in appearance. He cleared his throat nervously.

"Then I'm very glad to have taken the chance on offering it to her," Charles said.

"It's been a roaring success. But I must say, I was rather surprised by it. I don't think of you as a particularly more avid plants person than am I. Or do you have hidden depths that are still awaiting discovery?"

Charles cleared his throat again. "I should very much like to think that I had hidden depths, but you are correct about the fact that I am not a particularly devoted gardener. I leave such things to those with greener thumbs than my own," he said, glancing over at the plant wistfully.

"You're not a member of the garden club then?" Beryl asked.

"I'm not actually. In fact, it's one of the few organizations in the village I have managed to still stay well clear of," Charles said. "Even though there is a great deal of enthusiasm for roping bachelors such as myself into every social activity on offer, the members of the garden club seem reconciled to the fact that they're better off without me in their midst."

"Then how is it that you knew to choose such a perfect plant for Edwina? After all, it's not as though you could have picked this up at a roadside stand or even the local florist, could you?" Beryl asked.

"I thought you said you knew very little about plants," Charles said, shifting into solicitor mode with a piercing follow-up question.

"I don't, but Edwina was so effusive in her praise of its unique qualities that I was quite certain it was not easily available locally. You did rather bowl her over with the novelty of it," Beryl said.

"I was hoping that a gesture of this kind would prove popular with Edwina. She is not always the easiest person to shop for when it comes to gift giving," he said.

"Exactly. I'm often stumped myself when it comes to thinking of ways to treat her to something wonderful from time to time. You must tell me how you managed it," Beryl said. "After all, it won't be so very long before it is her birthday, and I shall be wanting to think of something equally remarkable myself."

"Surely her birthday is still a few months off yet," Charles said, swallowing dryly. Beryl had not wished to throw him into a panic.

"Not until September, but if it takes some doing to gather the necessary, I'd like to be prepared ahead of time. Or are you feeling like guarding your source of inspiration?"

"I wish that I could admit to having any such source to guard, but the fact of the matter is I cannot really take the credit for it," Charles said, glancing at the doorway as if to assure himself that they were still alone.

"Can't take credit for it? But you've provided her with such a splendid gift. How can you not be someone who is inspired?" Beryl asked.

"It wasn't my idea," Charles said.

He looked over at the door again.

"If it wasn't your idea, then whose, pray tell, was it?" Beryl asked.

Charles shrugged helplessly. "I've no idea. You see, I received a poisoned pen letter and that's what put the thought in my head," he said.

Beryl was astonished. Was there anyone left in all of Walmsley Parva who had not received one of those letters? And how had this one managed to be turned for good rather than ill?

"A poisoned pen letter enabled you to make such a perfect purchase for Edwina?" she asked.

"It did indeed. I wish I could thank the sender for the suggestion. Honestly, I think it was just what I needed to force me to take a little action," he said.

"What exactly did this letter say?" Beryl asked.

"It began by excoriating me for being so self-centered. It was really rather humiliating," he said.

"You? Self-centered? About what?" Beryl asked. Self-centeredness was not an attribute she would ever use to describe Charles.

"The writer suggested that it was no more than my duty as one of the few unmarried men in the village to pursue a lady of my choice with more deliberateness. It went on to report that the sender understood that that lady was Edwina. It scolded me for being so reserved in my attentions and that with so many women finding themselves relegated to being surplus women, it was most self-centered of me not to be more robust in pursuit of her affections," he said.

The red flush on the back of his neck had crept ever higher and had suffused his face with color as well. If Beryl had not been so entirely astonished at this news, she might have changed the subject. But as it was, she simply could not quell her curiosity.

"But how did that end up leading you to purchasing exactly the right gift for Edwina?" she asked.

"The letter told me exactly what to purchase. It even told me where. All I had to do was to telephone the plant purveyor and place an order. It arrived the next day special delivery," he said.

"Are you sure that you received the same sort of poisoned pen letter that has been plaguing the village?" Beryl said.

"I should think it was the same sender. But I guess I couldn't know for sure, could I?" he said.

"Describe it to me, this letter of yours," Beryl said.

"It looked quite like the one entered into evidence by Michael Blackburn. I suppose that's why I was quite certain it was from the same sender."

"It was constructed of letters and words cut from newspapers and magazines and pasted onto a sheet of paper?" Beryl asked.

Charles nodded. "Precisely. It was addressed in block lettering just like the envelope Michael had received. I simply assumed it was the same person. Do you have any reason to believe that it was not?" he asked.

"Edwina and I were discussing that earlier. We found the supplies for making such letters in the pigeonholes of Cornelia Burroughs's desk," Beryl said.

"But that doesn't make any sense," Charles said. "I received my letter after she died."

"We did wonder if perhaps Godfrey was the one who had been sending the letters instead of Cornelia," Beryl said. "After all, he had access to her desk. But Cornelia had received one of her own that was not the sort of thing we would have expected a loving husband to send to his wife."

"It sounds like quite a conundrum," Charles said.

"Quite. But I think the fact that this letter was so specific may be an important piece of the puzzle. Could Godfrey possibly have known that Edwina would have prized that particular plant?" Beryl asked, gesturing towards the mantelpiece once more.

"I have no idea. As I said, I'm not a member of the garden club, but Godfrey is. Perhaps he could have known," he said.

"Charles, I hate to put you in an awkward position, especially when your gift has proven to be such a hit, but I think we're going to have to ask Edwina who could possibly have known that she admired that plant," Beryl said.

Charles shrugged and nodded sadly.

"I suppose it really was too much to hope for that I could appear to be so well versed in her preferences. After all this time she certainly would be surprised to think that I had taken such an interest in plant material. As an officer of the court, it's my duty to aid an investigation in any way I possibly can," he said.

Just then Beryl heard the rattle of teacups on saucers and Simpkins appeared in the doorway holding a tea tray aloft in his gnarled hands. It was heaped high with cakes and buns and pots of jam. It seemed as though rather than coming to a compromise on what to serve they both simply added their own choices to the mix and there was an abundance of offerings as a result. Edwina appeared just behind him, and Beryl gave Charles's arm a reassuring pat. She leaned towards him and dropped her voice low.

"You will still get the credit for having followed through even if the idea was not yours in the first place, you know," she said. Then she turned to Edwina.

"Edwina, we have some additional information about the case. It's about Charles's gift," she said.

Edwina glanced over at the plant on the mantelpiece, and a warm smile spread across her face.

"It's absolutely perfect. It's one of the reasons I was taking so long fussing with the tea tray. I wanted to offer my thanks in a tangible way. I think these are all of your favorites," she said, gesturing towards the overflowing tray.

"About that, Edwina," Charles said. "I have a confession to make."

Edwina's fluttering and gesturing came to a screeching halt. She peered up at Charles as though she were afraid he was going to ask for her to return the gift.

"Yes, Charles, what is it?" she asked.

"As much as I wish to take credit for having the wonderful idea of gifting this to you, I'm afraid that I cannot," he said.

"What are you saying? That you didn't select this gift yourself?" Edwina asked.

"I did purchase the gift. It is just that it was not my idea to do so," he said.

"Then whose idea was it?" Edwina asked.

"I received one of the poisoned pen letters and it suggested that you would like this particular species of plant," he said.

Beryl thought he had edited his admission carefully not to include the writer's admonition not to remain in his bachelor state. But perhaps Edwina had intuited what had also been part of the poisoned pen's message. The color drained from her face, and she let out a small gasp.

"It's the thought that counts, Edwina," Beryl said, trying to smooth things over. She could feel Charles deflating as he stood next to her.

"It's not that," Edwina said. "I think I know who's been writing these letters."

Chapter 21

Edwina was so rattled by the knowledge of the letter writer's identity that she barely noticed the reckless nature of Beryl's driving as they flew through the village leaving Charles and Simpkins to make justice to the tea tray. With a heavy heart she pushed open the passenger side door as the motorcar screeched to a halt and slid out into the pleasant early evening air. She stepped around the side of the house and rapped upon the door, not sure she would find the owner within doors on such a beautiful evening. But as chance would have it the door opened and there stood Dr. Wilcox.

"Edwina, my dear, what brings you by this evening? Did you wish to have another chance to view my beautiful gardens? The rudbeckias are looking rather grand if I do say so myself," he said, stepping backwards and waving them inside.

"I'm rather afraid that we're here on a far more serious matter than that," Edwina said.

She was beyond grateful to feel Beryl standing directly behind her like a sturdy mountain of support. Truth be told, as much as Edwina was absolutely incensed at the way the letters had been tearing the village apart, she was hesitant to confront Dr. Wilcox about his part in spreading such misery. She never would have believed he could be involved in any such thing, and she felt as though she could not trust her own judgment about the character of even those people she had known for so very long. If she had been able to forget about the whole thing and shirk her duty, she would gladly have done so.

But if the war years had taught her anything it was that shirking one's duty or burying one's head in the sand was not ever the route to take. Things in life were sometimes extraordinarily unpleasant and not facing that fact would not make them go away. She slowly drew in a deep breath and squared her small shoulders. The doctor looked her up and down as though evaluating her for symptoms of illness.

"That sounds very serious indeed. You'd best come into the sitting room then," he said, turning and leading the way down a dark corridor to his familiar inner sanctum. Edwina had spent so many happy hours in his company, oftentimes in that very room, that it seemed all the more surreal to be confronting him with such behavior in a space so associated with happy memories.

Edwina looked over at Beryl as if to steel her nerves and the two of them sat next to each other on a small sofa. Dr. Wilcox took up a spot in his shabby and well-worn leather armchair and leaned back holding his hands together and placing them in his lap. Edwina looked around the room as if to tether her to the site, preserving those last few moments before everything about the man before her suddenly became a lie.

"Do you remember the plant catalogue that I lent to you some days ago?" Edwina asked.

"Of course I do. As a matter of fact, I have it right here," the doctor said. "Is all this seriousness about you wanting to have it back? All you needed to do was ask," he said, reaching out and sorting through a stack of similar catalogues on a side table. He leaned forward and extended it to Edwina.

She thumbed through it and opened to the page that she was sure she would find but had desperately hoped she would not. There in her own neat handwriting she saw the asterisk and the words *this one!!!* printed neatly beside the description of the orchid Charles had brought to her as a gift.

"I was surprised to be the recipient of this very plant earlier this week. It was purchased for me by Charles," Edwina said.

"How very fortunate for you, my dear. I always thought that Charles Jarvis held you in very high esteem," the doctor said, a smile of satisfaction spreading across his face.

"Charles said that he had received a letter from the poisoned pen writer essentially saying that very thing and directing him to purchase this plant for me," Edwina said, tapping on the entry.

"What does that have to do with me?" the doctor said, peering at her from beneath his shaggy white eyebrows.

"The only way someone could have known I wanted this specific plant was if they had seen the way I marked up this catalogue," Edwina said.

"I see," the doctor said.

"That's all you have to say about it? 'I see?'" Edwina asked.

"What else would you have me say?" the doctor said. "I don't know to whom you have shown this catalogue."

"Well, I do. You are the only one besides me who has seen it," Edwina said. Her sadness about the doctor's possible involvement in the poison pen letters was fading and being replaced by righteous anger. "How could you have sent such awful letters around the village? I never would have credited you with behaving in such a way."

"Are you accusing me of something?" he asked.

"I'm accusing you of being the person sending such hateful letters all around the village. After all your years of caring for the residents and ensuring the health of Walmsley Parva, how could you possibly have done a thing like this?" Edwina asked, hearing a shrill note creeping into her voice.

She suddenly felt a wave of relief that her mother was not alive to see what had become of the doctor.

"It's precisely because I love the residents of this village so much that I did send the letters I sent," Dr. Wilcox said, his voice tinged with sadness.

"I can't imagine how you would think that such nasty letters would be a way of showing your concern for the village," Beryl said, speaking up for the first time.

Edwina watched as a flicker of pain crossed the doctor's face. Suddenly another thought occurred to her.

"Perhaps you were not responsible for all of the letters," Edwina said.

"I was only responsible for some of them. And I'll admit I was rather pleased with myself as to how effective the letters I sent happened to be," he said.

"You're the one who sent the letter to Mrs. Scott, aren't you?" Beryl said.

The doctor nodded. "That was the very first letter I sent. It seemed to me that something ought to be done about the disgraceful way Clarence Mumford was pestering young Eva Scott."

"How did you happen to know about that?" Beryl asked.

"I saw it with my own two eyes. I had stopped in to ask Eva to tell her mother that I had managed to produce enough grapes on my vines that I had extras available if she wanted to sell them in the shop. I happened upon Eva trying to fend Mr. Mumford off and I was very grateful I arrived just when I did. If I hadn't, I'm not quite sure what would have happened."

Edwina thought about the other letters that had been so different than the malicious ones.

"Did you send the one to Prudence advising her to stop being such a gossip as well?" she asked.

"Indeed, I did. That woman has been needing to be taken to task for making the post office an incredibly unpleasant place for years. Once I saw how effectively the letter to Mrs. Scott had set something right, it occurred to me that it might be a good way to resolve all sorts of ills in the village," he said.

"Then were you the one who also sent the letter to Cornelia about her embezzlement?" Beryl said.

"You got me there, too," Dr. Wilcox said. "Guilty as charged."

Edwina couldn't help but notice he did not seem quite as pleased with himself about that letter as he had the others.

"Did you know that Cornelia was the sender of the earlier letters? The really nasty ones?" she asked.

"I'm afraid I made that remarkably unpleasant discovery when I was calling upon her while I was filling in for Dr. Nelson. She was aggravated with him for having suggested that she was endangering her health by her habit of smoking cigarettes and wished to unburden herself to me about it." he said.

"How did you discover she was the letter writer?" Beryl asked.

"She was one of those women who prided herself on being a good hostess and had bustled off into the kitchen to harangue her husband about how best to prepare a pot of tea. She thought he was doing it too slowly or some such a thing. While she was out of the room, I wandered about looking at some of the artwork hanging on the walls and the books on the shelves. I find that such things can oftentimes give some insight into the inner workings of a patient. She had left her rolltop desk open and a few scraps of magazine cuttings were scattered on the surface of it. They caught my eye, and I must admit, I rather high-handedly decided to have a bit of a snoop round in her desk," he said.

"And that's where you saw the evidence that she was the letter writer?" Beryl asked.

The doctor nodded. "Scissors, a pot of paste, and a partially completed letter were shoved into one of the pigeonholes of the desk. After what Edwina had to say about the letter Margery had received, I knew that Cornelia needed a dose of her own medicine," he said with a smile.

"As a medical man weren't you concerned that sending Cornelia a letter accusing her of embezzlement might cause her to have a dangerous attack of asthma?" Beryl asked.

"As a medical man I am of a practical bent and would never have relied upon guesses and wishful thinking," he said. "A letter causing an asthma attack would be far too unpredictable. Besides, someone with the sort of character to send out such hateful letters was unlikely to be the sort to reliably become distressed at the same sorts of things that would bother people with a normal psyche," he said.

The doctor reached over towards his side table again and picked up a silver cigarette case. He opened the lid and drew out a cigarette of his own. As Edwina watched him holding it lightly in between his fingers, a new question formed.

"Did you discover the evidence that she was the letter writer after I told you that Margery had tried to take her own life?" Edwina asked.

"Yes. It was that very afternoon that I received a call from Cornelia asking me to come round. She was all worked up about the admonition from Dr. Nelson not to smoke, and as a fellow smoker she thought I would understand why it was such an outrageous claim. After all, she said, if a doctor is a smoker, how bad for one's health could it possibly be?"

He rolled the cigarette back and forth between his fingers and gazed down at it. Some memory tickled the back of Edwina's mind, and she closed her eyes trying to remember what it was that was floating around in the back of her skull. It was something about a room, one not very different from the one in which they now sat. Forcing a memory never seemed to be the easiest way to access one, and she tried to convince herself to just allow the images to float around freely. Frustrated, she opened her eyes once more, and as her gaze landed on an overflowing ashtray on the coffee table in front of her, the final piece of the puzzle clicked into place.

"No, you would not have relied on something as unpredictable as an emotional reaction to a letter. You're far too sensible for something like that," Edwina said.

"I'll take that as a compliment, my dear," the doctor said.

"Did you by any chance offer one of your own hand-rolled cigarettes to Cornelia on your last visit to her?" Edwina asked.

The doctor looked at the cigarette in his hand once more and sighed. "As a matter of fact, I did. It was a sort of conspiratorial offer, one designed to reassure her that I was just as dismissive as she was about Dr. Nelson's claims on the subject of the perils of smoking."

Beryl looked over at Edwina as though she had lost the thread of the conversation. But she remained silent. Though unsure of Edwina's line of questioning, she knew from experience it would be in the best interest of the case to allow her friend to continue uninterrupted.

"I can't help but think perhaps there was something quite perilous about the cigarette though, wasn't there?" she asked.

"Now, whatever gave that away?" the doctor asked.

"I saw the cigarette stubs in the ashtray overflowing in Cornelia's parlor, quite near to the desk where she would have been sitting and smoking as she wrote up such nasty letters," Edwina said. "At the time it seemed as though one of them was not quite the same as the others. I don't claim to be an expert on the subject of tobacco, not being a smoker myself, but something about it just struck me as unusual. Now that I see yours, I realize it was a hand-rolled cigarette stub."

"You have always been a clever person, Edwina. I've admired you greatly for it. And may I say, I'm not your only admirer," he said.

"I suppose that when you sent that note to Charles giving him a hint about a plant I had circled in the catalogue I lent you, perhaps you gave him some encouragement to be bolder in his overtures towards me?" Edwina said.

"Right again. I do hope you will consider the possibility of encouraging his attentions. I would like to think of you as having a happy and fulfilling life in every way possible," the doctor said. "You know I've always had rather a soft spot for you. I would like to think that you thought well of me, too." He toyed with the cigarette in his hand once more.

"You've always been a good friend to me, and I'd like to think that for the most part we have seen eye to eye on important matters like the health of the village."

"Then you understand my reasons for my actions?" he asked. "Those of my past and any I might wish to pursue in the future? We're in agreement that like any good gardener one must know what to prune and when, to be decisive about it and not allow rot and disease to spread?"

Edwina's heart began to thump loudly in her chest, and she felt a lump rising in her throat like a stone, hard and unforgiving. It was so intense she reached up and touched her neck.

"It was nerium, wasn't it?" Edwina asked. "You pruned her out with nerium."

The doctor leaned forward eagerly and pretended to doff his hat to Edwina.

"Correct again, my dear. It was guaranteed to be effective, and I was certain that it would not cause difficulties with Godfrey attempting to smoke it as well, since he isn't a smoker. Quite an elegant solution I thought," he said.

"Nerium?" Beryl asked finally, unable to keep quiet any longer.

"It's the flowering shrub that Dr. Wilcox invited me over to view a few days ago. It's so terribly poisonous that people have died from burning clippings of it in their brush piles," Edwina said.

"It's very lovely to look at, but one must be extremely careful with all parts of it," he said. "I suppose that if Cornelia had been a bit more interested in actually being a participant in the garden club rather than simply skimming money off the club funds, she might have been in a better position to recognize it than she was," he said.

"You added bits of the leaves to one of the cigarettes you gave her, didn't you?" Edwina asked.

"And a few twigs as well, don't forget that. I wanted to be sure that it would do the job in one go," he said. "She barely had time to finish the cigarette before it brought on a terrible attack," he said.

"Were you the one who sent her the letter about her embezzlement? How did that timing work out? It seems as though almost as soon as you discovered that she was the one who was involved with the poisoned pen letters, you determined to murder her," Beryl said.

"I did write the letter to Cornelia, but she never saw it."

"How did you manage that?" Beryl asked. "It was opened, and it was in her driver's side door compartment."

"How did you happen to find that letter?" the doctor asked.

"I went round the backside of Blackburn's Garage and opened the motorcar door," Beryl said.

"I did the same. Only instead of discovering the letter in the pocket of the door, I am the one who put it there. It disrupted the timeline of the letters rather well, don't you think?" he asked.

Edwina was not so sure she appreciated how pleased with himself the doctor seemed at his cleverness. While she had to admit he had done a thorough job of muddying the waters, it was somewhat disturbing to think that someone she thought she had known so well had been as capable of hiding such a terrible secret.

"It's my fault that you took this action, isn't it?" Edwina said. "If I had not confided in you about the reason for Margery's suicide attempt, you would not have been so inclined to take action against Cornelia when you discovered she was the letter writer, would you?" Edwina asked.

"Don't blame yourself. I would have come to know sooner or later what had happened with Margery and I certainly would not have been inclined to allow Cornelia to rip apart the fabric of society," the doctor said. "No, if you hadn't told me about Margery something else would have convinced me that she needed to be dealt with. If there's one thing I can't abide it's unnecessary misfortune. After all, we've all seen far too much of that in the last few years to allow someone to go about creating it on purpose."

"So, you're admitting that you murdered Cornelia with premeditation," Beryl said.

"I cannot see how I could possibly deny it. You have found me out, taxed me with it, and I'm assuming must have the evidence to prove it. After all, I didn't go back and collect the cigarette stubs from Cornelia's house, and Godfrey's in no condition to take care of the housekeeping, I shouldn't think," he said. "What good would it do for me to deny it now?"

"You don't even sound as though you regret it," Beryl said.

"I suppose that's because I don't. As I said, I'm a man of practical bent. When a thing needs doing, I take care of it. I saw it as my duty to care for the health of the village and that included the unnecessary heartache Cornelia was creating. No, I would say that this course of treatment was absolutely necessary."

"You know that we will have to turn this matter over to Constable Gibbs," Edwina said.

She felt the lump in her throat double in size as she heard the words in her own ears and watched a small smile play across the doctor's face.

"I would not expect you to do any less than your duty either, my dear," he said. "But as a fellow gardener I would ask if you might indulge me one last look around my beloved garden. It's so lovely at this time of day and I don't think I shall be having the chance to spend much more time in it in the future."

Edwina felt Beryl's eyes riveted to the side of her face. Perhaps as an officer of the court she should insist on telephoning for Constable Gibbs and keeping him where he sat right under close guard until she arrived. But if there was one thing Edwina had learned over the last few months of spending time with Beryl, there was often more than one way to do the right thing.

She was quite certain that her position as magistrate allowed for leniency. And she knew she would never forgive herself if she did not allow him that last chance to view his garden as a free man. She nodded and got to her feet. The doctor hoisted himself up from the depths of his leather chair and crossed the room to stand in front of her. He reached down and patted her on the cheek.

"Thank you. I'd like to be alone with my thoughts if you don't mind. I promise I won't go anywhere." With that he turned and strode out of the room with his head held high.

Edwina moved to the window where she could overlook the back garden and watched as he settled himself into his usual routine of moving along the garden borders bending forward to smell a fragrant blossom here or to pinch off a dead bud there. She felt Beryl step up behind her and peer over her shoulder. The doctor seemed to take one final look around and then he settled in a basket chair under the shade of a crabapple tree. He leaned back and fumbled in his pocket. Edwina watched as he drew out an ornate cigarette lighter and flicked a flame to life. The glow of his cigarette made a shudder run through Edwina's whole frame.

"You don't think there's something dangerous about that cigarette, too, do you?" Beryl asked.

"I'm quite certain there is," Edwina said.

The two of them stood and watched out the window as the

doctor drew in a few puffs of his cigarette and then leaned back in his chair with his hands folded across his lap. Beryl made to step towards the door, but Edwina held her back and waited until the smoke from the ashtray had stopped drifting skyward. When there was nothing left of the smoke, she crossed the room to the doctor's telephone and placed a call to Constable Gibbs.

Chapter 22

It had taken more than a fortnight since they had solved the case for Edwina to return to some semblance of her normal self. Beryl, Simpkins, and even Beddoes had quietly conferred as to what should be done for her. The discovery of the doctor's actions, towards himself as well as others, had left Edwina listless and apathetic for days on end. No number of walks in the countryside, diverting programs on the wireless, or feasts whipped up by Simpkins, amusingly sporting Edwina's own frilly pinny, seemed to cheer her.

Beryl had known there was very little that could be done for her dear friend. She had experienced her own dark days, more often than she cared to remember, during and after the Great War and knew that sometimes there was nothing to be done but to allow some time to pass. She advised the other members of the household to leave off their efforts to cheer Edwina, and that perhaps, if left to sort things out in her own time, she would return to herself before too much time had passed.

Late one morning on the third week, Beryl opened the door to her bedroom and heard a noise that lifted her spirits. She hurried down the hallway and rushed down the stairs. As she moved along the passageway towards the morning room, the distinctive sound of typewriter keys furiously clacking grew louder and louder. Beryl sagged against the hallway wall with relief. She did not realize how worried she had been until it seemed perhaps she needn't be any longer.

Simpkins must have heard the noise, too, as he appeared from the general direction of the front door, a magazine held in his gnarled hand. He crept towards her making an effort not to create any distracting noises of his own. A broad, snaggle-toothed smile spread across his face. He leaned in close and whispered in Beryl's ear.

"It sounds like Miss Edwina just might be on the mend," he said.

"I believe so. This is the first time I've heard her typing since we solved the case," Beryl said.

"Perhaps I shouldn't interrupt her with the post," he said, gesturing to the magazine.

Just then a knock landed on the door and Crumpet began barking from behind the morning room door. The sound of typing suddenly stopped and Beryl was quite sure she heard the sound of a drawer sliding open and then shutting. Beddoes appeared behind them with Charles following in her wake. In his hands he held another Wardian case. The door to the morning room popped open and Edwina looked them over with a smile on her face.

"I see my typing has drawn quite a crowd. Perhaps I should attempt to do so more quietly in future."

She turned away and headed back into the room. Crumpet sat down in a sunbeam in the middle of the room eagerly wagging his tail. As Beryl glanced over at the desk her startled gaze landed on a neat stack of typewritten pages. Edwina was making no effort to conceal them; in fact, she was calling attention to them by drumming her slim fingers on the stack.

"You have been far too quiet about most everything lately, miss," Simpkins said. "It does the heart good to hear you clattering away again."

Edwina gave a quick bob of her head. "I couldn't agree more. I feel much more like myself and decided that I should like to get back to writing my novel."

Edwina looked at them each in turn. Beryl's breath caught in her throat as she awaited the other's reaction to Edwina's news. As far as she knew, no one besides herself knew that Edwina was attempting to write a novel.

"I told your mother years ago that you'd write a book one day," Simpkins said. "I'd be willing to wager it has at least one cowboy in it."

Edwina's cheeks pinked. "Several, in fact."

"What made you decide to mention it?" Beryl asked, unable to contain her curiosity.

"There has been a great deal of trouble because of secrets. I suddenly felt disinclined for my novel to be another of them," Edwina said.

"What a marvelous undertaking," Charles said, stepping forward. "Perhaps you will find this an inspiring addition to your desk." He held out the Wardian case.

"Charles, you shouldn't have," Edwina said as she reached out to take the case from his outstretched hands.

"I cannot take the credit for this. I am acting as the executor of Dr. Wilcox's estate. He has left this, as well as the rest of his collection of hothouse plants, to you."

Edwina clutched the case to her chest and blinked rapidly, as if to stave off a spate of tears.

"I shall treasure them," she said with the slightest catch in her voice. "They will remind me of the memories of the doctor I wish to keep."

"Then you are sure to have plenty of reminders. There are dozens of plants all told," Charles said.

Edwina's eyes shone with tears once more and Beryl hurried to change the subject. She couldn't stand the notion of Edwina falling back into a maudlin state.

"It looks as though you have something to show us as well," she said, indicating the magazine Simpkins held behind his back.

"I do indeed." He opened the magazine and thrust it at Beryl. "It turned out beautifully, don't you think?"

Beryl carried the magazine to the table in the center of the room and spread it out for all to see. There, in black and white, Edwina's image and her own beamed up at her. A speech bubble appeared above Edwina's head endorsing Colonel Kimberly's Convenience Foods as a thing no modern woman's kitchen should be without.

"You know what this means, don't you?" Beryl asked, turning to Edwina.

"I'm not sure that I do," Edwina said.

"It means that I shall have to start a scrapbook of newspaper clippings of you," she said with her most dazzling smile yet.